Peter was born in London towards the end of 1960, the second son of an English father and Austrian mother. Following his retirement from a long career spent within the London insurance market, Peter moved to Frinton on Sea, a small town that sits on the north Essex coast overlooking the North Sea. This is Peter's second book and continues the adventures of Tom and Isabelle, which began in *The Last Wish*, published in 2022 but originally drafted many years earlier.

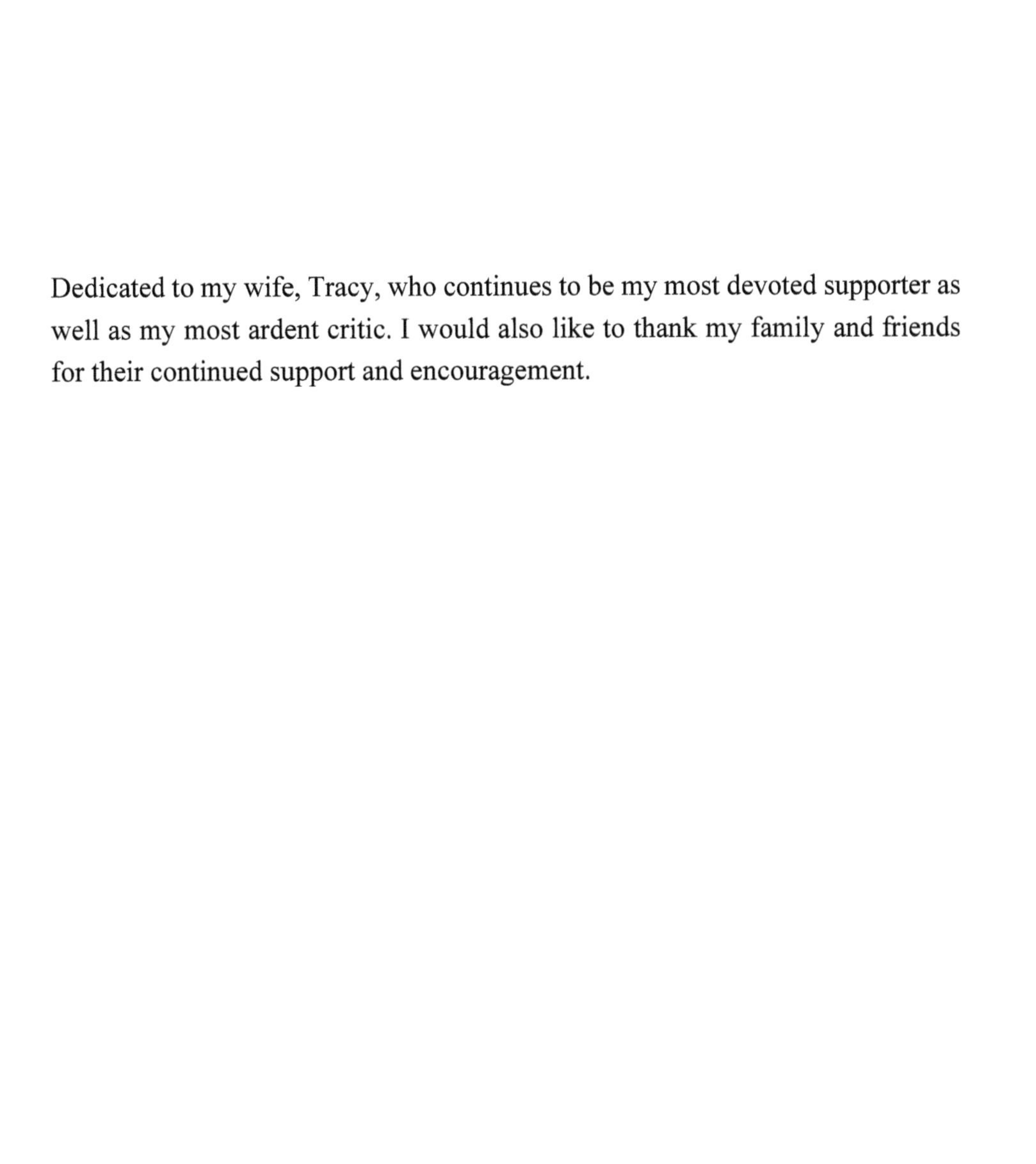

Dedicated to my wife, Tracy, who continues to be my most devoted supporter as well as my most ardent critic. I would also like to thank my family and friends for their continued support and encouragement.

Peter Parsons

The Last Wish 2—
Cursed Swag

Austin Macauley Publishers™
London • Cambridge • New York • Sharjah

A CIP catalogue record for this title is available from the British Library.

ISBN 9781035813193 (Paperback)
ISBN 9781035813209 (ePub e-book)

www.austinmacauley.com

First Published 2024
Austin Macauley Publishers Ltd®
1 Canada Square
Canary Wharf
London
E14 5AA

Table of Contents

1
Of Lust and the Fire Starter

Two years earlier

Horace Pasternak sat nervously within the air-cooled confines of his car. Outside, the Floridian night air was heavy, warm and oppressive. Horace's was the only car in the industrial estate's parking lot, which didn't see much traffic during the night time hours. Nonetheless, Horace had been careful to avoid those areas of the lot brightened by the yellow haloes of the surrounding street lamps. He had also taken care to dodge the security cameras that surrounded his target.

Suddenly, a police siren wailed in the distance, the sound making Horace gasp and hold his breath for several long seconds. He only exhaled once the night had again returned to its complete and deep silence. Ahead of him, about two hundred yards across the lot, a large illuminated sign on a corrugated warehouse building boldly identified *Pasternak's Original Home Furnishings.*

Horace had been so proud when he'd first acquired these premises for his then flourishing business. He had managed to secure several out of State and very lucrative contracts and these had not only provided him and his growing family with an enviable lifestyle but had also given Horace the confidence and ability to secure a number of large bank loans. The original and stated purpose of these loans was to further develop Horace's business.

However, now as he sat in his car, he wondered where, on his journey down the road to hell, he'd lost his good intentions. Deep within his heart, he knew the answer but stubbornly refused to acknowledge or accept it.

Life had been very good for Horace and outside of his long working hours; he had started to experience some of its finer aspects. Horace had taken up golf and also tennis and whilst he wasn't terrible at the former, his squat and barrel-like physique rendered him a comical figure as he stumbled with futile haplessness across the tennis court. But most of all, Horace enjoyed the post-game socialising, an aspect of Horace's life which soon became a preoccupation, much to the chagrin of the then Mrs Pasternak, who constantly found herself neglected and left at home to bring up their two young children.

It was at one of these post-game social events that Horace had met Roxy Laine, a young and vivacious blond, who exuded the kind of sexual magnetism that could transform an otherwise level-headed man into an inarticulate and gibbering wreck. Horace was lost from the moment Roxy stumbled into his arms. She had been quick to apologise for the accident and had insisted on buying Horace a drink to replace the one that she'd inadvertently knocked over him.

They seemed to hit it off from the very start. Roxy was seemingly awed by Horace's boasts of business acumen and openly impressed by the tales he told of the wealth he had managed to accumulate. She laughed at his jokes and pouted with sadness when the evening was finally drawing to a close. It was then that she had told Horace that she'd misplaced her handbag and asked whether Horace would be kind enough to call her a cab.

Initially, Roxy shyly declined Horace's chivalrous offer to drive her home but soon succumbed to his eager insistence. What then transpired, beginning within Horace's BMW X7 and concluding in Roxy's bed, forever afterwards caused Horace to blush at the recollection.

Soon, thoughts of Roxy overwhelmed and consumed Horace until every moment away from her, twisted and tore at his very soul. Horace soon became resentful and uncaring towards his previously adored family and in his frustration, blamed them for being the obstacle that prevented the life with Roxy that he dreamed of and desired with acute painfulness.

As for the business that had taken so many years to nurture and build, that was quickly and systematically dismantled in order to provide the finance required to sustain the lifestyle he had led Roxy to believe he could provide for her.

But now, the money was running out, as was the business's continued ability to provide enough income to survive whilst financing the demands of Horace's new found passion. Every credit line had been extended and exhausted and following his inability to continue the agreed repayments, the bank was now calling in its loans. However and despite his growing financial concerns, the knockout blow had come from his wife or rather, the divorce judgement her lawyers had acquired on her behalf.

Tired of his constant carousing and his overnight and poorly explained absences from the marital home, Mrs Pasternak had finally taken the advice of her family and friends and had sued for divorce. However and before doing so, she had tried to reason with Horace and had pleaded with him, for the sake of their marriage and the children it had produced, to stop, take a look at himself in the mirror and to return to the man she had loved and perhaps could, in time, love again.

Enthralled, deluded and still at that time, believing himself invulnerable, Horace had laughed in her face, gathered his belongings together and left for Roxy's apartment.

The loss of the marital home was not totally unexpected and neither was the payment of some level of alimony but really, twenty thousand dollars each month! What was the Court thinking? Through his own divorce lawyer, Horace had argued, begged and pleaded for the award to be reconsidered, telling the Court truthfully, that there was no way in which he could possibly afford to pay such a ridiculously high amount.

In response, the Court had referenced Horace's successful wholesale soft furnishings outlet, a business that he and the former Mrs Pasternak had created and developed during the period of their marriage. Unfortunately for Horace, it was the Court's considered opinion that the soft furnishings outlet generated sufficient income for Horace's personal needs and also, to enable him to make the prescribed alimony payments.

Perhaps, Horace should have disclosed the current fragile financial predicament of his business to the Court and the fact that it was struggling to stay afloat. He could have mentioned his failure to find new investors and the refusal of the bank to extend any further overdrafts or loans. Had he made these disclosures, Horace was relatively confident that the Court would have reconsidered and reduced the alimony payments to a more reasonable level. But that in itself would not have fitted in with Horace's future plans.

Horace was only too well aware that his new found lifestyle required a serious injection of cash and, it was during the litigious disentanglement of his marriage, that Horace devised a cunning but marvellously simplistic plan, which, if successful, would make him very rich indeed.

However, for this plan to succeed, it was important for his imminent financial collapse to remain as hidden as possible. It was for this reason that Horace had kept the Court and his erstwhile wife in the dark concerning his financial predicament.

It was a huge and daunting step for the previously law-abiding Horace Pasternak but so far as he was concerned, there was no other option. Of course, the driving force behind Horace's divorce and now illicit ambitions was Roxy.

Her birthname was actually Agnes Buff but Horace neither knew nor cared about these minor details for he loved Roxy. He loved walking into restaurants and bars with the stunningly sexy Roxy. He loved the way other men threw envious glances in his direction and most of all, he loved the new and previously unexplored sexual heights that Roxy would take him to, albeit far too rarely for Horace's complete contentment.

Taking a deep and shuddering breath, Horace exited the car and began his careful approach towards the corrugated building. Unobserved by the security cameras was a reinforced glass door leading directly into his office and this was fitted with a keypad, to which, only he knew the entrance code. His shaking fingers stumbled over the code a few times before he was finally able to enter the six digits in their correct order.

The warehouse was in total darkness but Horace had come prepared and the pencil torch he took from his pocket was sufficient for him to negotiate his way through the blackness. Horace cautiously made his way towards the neatly piled stacks of combustibles assembled the previous day, once the last of his employees had finally left for the weekend.

His heightened senses quickly detected the petrol fumes and not for the first time, he prayed the fire would be intense enough to obliterate all traces of the accelerants used to ensure the fire took hold. Holding the pencil torch between his teeth, Horace pulled two candles from his pocket. He lit both with a disposable lighter before tossing them onto the piles of assembled debris. The fire immediately took hold and so Horace turned and quickly retraced his steps.

Now, as Horace stood alone in the heat of the Floridian night, made more intense by the fire that raged some two hundred yards or so ahead of him and illuminated the tarmac surrounding the corrugated structure of the soft furnishing's outlet, he pulled out his cell phone and called his divorce lawyer. It was 2 AM and so Horace's call went straight through to answerphone.

"Hey George, this is Horace, Horace Pasternak. Just calling to tell you that you need to get back in contact with the Court. Tell them that I no longer have the means with which to support myself or to make the alimony payments. Just shit out of luck, the business is going up in smoke even as I speak. You'll probably see the fire crews on the morning news. I'm heartbroken."

Horace ended the call and then dialled 911.

"Yes, I'd like to report a fire."

Horace provided the emergency services with the details they required to respond and was about to put the cell phone back into his pocket when on a whim he called his ex-wife. After a couple of dozen rings the phone was finally answered by a sleepy-voiced Missus Pasternak.

"Hello?" slurred Missus Pasternak.

"Hello, sugar—ah sorry, Maureen. It's Horace. I have some really bad news."

"What's happened Horace, are you OK?"

Horace smiled as he heard the undisguised concern in his ex-wife's voice. He knew she still loved him deeply and would take him back in an instant should he want to return to her devoted and yet unexciting embrace.

"I don't know. I couldn't sleep and so decided to come to the warehouse and take a look at the books." His voice thick with feigned emotion Horace continued, "When I arrived, I found the whole place in flames. Everything we worked for just disappearing in fire and smoke. I have nothing left of us now, nothing—" Horace's voice trailed off with a manufactured sob.

"Oh, Horace! You just stay right where you are, I'm coming baby, I'm on my way."

Horace smiled as he ended the call and this time, he did return the cell phone to his pocket. *This will look good on camera and in the press*, he thought. Despite their irreconcilable differences, the estranged Pasternak's comfort each other as they witness the tragic destruction of a lifetime's sacrifice and labour. Horace almost sobbed himself when he considered the emotional impact such a story would have upon what he believed was the all too gullible public.

"It'll be like taking candy from a baby," he sniggered quietly. "I'll call the insurance company first thing in the morning."

He had never previously insured the business and Horace had been amazed at how eagerly the insurance agent had extended the limits of coverage he had requested. Limits which far exceeded the value of the business and which, once paid, would be the panacea to his financial malady as well as the launchpad for his new life with Roxy.

Horace chuckled as he suddenly remembered it was 4 July. His insurance had been arranged with none other than that Great British insurance institution, Lloyd's of London.

I'm not an arsonist, he thought happily. I'm a latter-day patriot!

2
Homecoming

Present day

Isabelle had hoped that her eventual return to France would be under happier circumstances. When she arrived by taxi at the family home situated within the small rural community of Aigurande, she was greeted by floods of tears from her mother and warm but solemn hugs from her younger brother and sister.

Isabelle strongly resembled her mother in looks, although her mother's dark blond hair was now generously mixed with grey. They both shared soft intelligent faces with blue catlike eyes. Conversely, the two younger children favoured their father's dark looks, with rich brown hair and dark blue eyes. Their physiques were also more strongly built than that of their mother's and Isabelle's who, in comparison, were both relatively tall and willowy.

Isabelle gazed up with apprehension at the house's large and foreboding facade. The house had been the Girardet family home for more than two hundred years and before she had left for Italy, it had been showing signs of neglect. So, she was surprised to see that some little effort had been made to rejuvenate the old lady, as the family liked to refer to their home. Isabelle was ushered inside by her mother and siblings, all of whom bombarded her with whispered comments and questions.

"Why are we whispering?" whispered Isabelle.

"Your father is asleep upstairs and we do not want to disturb him," replied Isabelle's mother.

"He's here at home?" Isabelle asked in surprise as she'd expected her father to be in the hospital. "How is papa?" she asked with misjudged optimism.

"There's no hope, Issi, it's just a matter of time. His lungs need oxygen and each day his pain gets worse. A nurse comes every day and she helps but there's no prospect of recovery. Sorry Angel but papa will not be with us much longer.

He is fading," her mother's voice began to crack and she suddenly put her hands to her face in an effort to stifle her sorrow.

The children quickly gathered closely around their mother in a protective and comforting circle until she regained her composure.

Drawing a deep breath her mother now looked towards her eldest daughter. "Now, Issi, where's your luggage?"

"That's a story for another day, mama," said Isabelle as she dried her own eyes on the cuffs of her blouse. "I would like to see papa now and then take a hot bath, I feel like I've been travelling forever. Oh, I notice, there has been some work done to the house?"

"It's the English," said her young brother Simone. "They are buying everything around here. They seem to have more money than sense. So, we thought we'd make the old lady look respectable and hopefully, we'll make a fortune when we sell her."

Isabelle gave her mother a hurt and questioning look. "Mama?"

"It's true, Issi," her mother replied. "Aigurande is dying. The locals are leaving and the English are buying up everything. There's nothing here for the young people and so, they move on like you moved on, Issi."

"Yes, I moved on," replied Isabelle who was a little vexed by the scarcely masked criticism within her mother's tone. "But it's easy to move on when you know there's something to return to. How can we do this to papa?"

"Issi," her mother whispered harshly. "Papa is dying and once he has passed, there is no longer anything to hold us here. We love you, Issi, but you need to know that you are not alone in wanting to stretch your wings and fly. Soon, Simone and Lilly will leave too and I don't want to be left alone here. One day, I would like to return to Paris."

Isabelle stared at her mother, first in disbelief and then in resignation. Without a further word, she turned and began to climb the stairs. When she reached the top, she could hear her father's laboured breathing from the hallway outside of the room that was her parent's bedroom. Quietly, she opened the door and peered inside.

The shuttered windows were open allowing the cool early evening air to freshen the room. Isabelle could see her father clearly through the shaded light of the late sun. He looked old, much older than he was. His cheeks were hollow and his pallor grey.

"Oh, Papa," she breathed as she slowly approached the bed. She sat on the chair that had been placed at the bedside and gently took her father's hand in her own. She sat with him like this for a long time until her mother entered the room.

"Come, Angel," she said as she set about closing the windows and drawing their long and embroidered curtains. "I have prepared some food and I think you will want to freshen up before we eat."

*

Later, the family sat around the large rustic table situated in the old lady's ancient kitchen. They had finished their evening meal and now began to exchange stories. Isabelle was told of the various comings and goings that had taken place during her absence and was of course asked much about her time in Italy.

"Did you meet any sexy boys?" asked her younger sister.

"No, Lilly," replied Isabelle. "Just lots of very sexy men."

They all laughed before suddenly remembering their father laying ill upstairs. Guilty looks were exchanged as they fell into silence. After a while, Isabelle's mother broke the stillness.

"Isabelle," she said. "Jacques is still single. I seem to remember that the two of you were quite sweet about each other for a while. Perhaps, you could call in on him whilst you are home?"

"Why are you telling me this, mama?" Isabelle asked.

"Well," sighed her mother, "perhaps, it's time you stopped running around and settled down. Got married and maybe even make me a grandmother. Jacques is a good man. You could do a lot worse."

Isabelle hissed as she glared angrily up at the kitchen's high, yellowed and flaky ceiling. "God, mama!" she spat in a whisper. "I have only been home for a few hours and already you begin with this, this merde! Now, please, just leave me to live my own life the way I want to live it. It's mine, not yours. OK?"

Her mother looked downcast. "OK, Angel," she replied softly. "If you want to spend your life being passed around from one man to another then that's your choice. But," and her mother's demeanour and voice suddenly hardened. "Don't you dare come crying to me when no one wants you anymore!"

Isabelle quickly stood to stare down at her mother. "I think it's time I went to bed. Simone, do you still have a laptop?" she asked her brother whilst not once moving her defiant glare from her mother's upturned face.

"Yes, why?" asked Simone cautiously.

"Because I want to facetime my English lover before he passes me on to someone else!" she spat before turning to leave the kitchen.

"I'll bring it to your room," Simone called after her.

Before going to her room, Isabelle looked in on her father again and was surprised and pleased to see he was awake.

"Ah, my little Issi," wheezed her father. "I heard your mother shouting and so I guessed you had arrived home. It's so wonderful to see you."

"It's wonderful to see you too papa but, it makes me sad that you are unwell," said Isabelle as she leaned forward to kiss her father's face before reclaiming the chair she had occupied earlier. "You must be good and take plenty of rest and very soon we can go for long walks through the countryside, just like we used to."

"Ah, my Issi," her father rattled. "It is a dream, a wonderful dream, yes, but it will never come true." He paused to catch his breath. "But you must promise me, Issi," he continued. "Don't be bullied by your mother, she means well but we have just one life and at the end of it, we must be happy with the way we have lived it. Always be true to yourself."

Isabelle started to sob and her father raised a weak hand to brush away the tears that had begun to stream down her face.

"Hush, my darling," he croaked dryly.

After a while, Isabelle raised her face and asked, "Papa, are you happy at the way you lived your life?"

Her father's yellowed eyes looked sadly at Isabelle as if searching her face for something he could not quite find.

"I have lived a good life, Issi," he said. "The kind of life that many wish for. My wife, my children and especially you, my Issi, what man could ask for more."

At that moment, Isabelle's mother quietly entered the room.

"Come on, Issi," she said softly. "Your father needs to rest now. You can talk again tomorrow."

"Goodnight, papa," Isabelle said as she gently kissed him again. "Goodnight, mama."

Isabelle left and went to her room where she found that Simone had left the laptop for her to use.

That boy knows how to keep a lady happy, she thought fondly. "He'll go far."

At her first attempt, Isabelle could just about see but not hear Tom. Her second attempt was no more successful and when she was on the point of giving up, her laptop gave a strange tremulous beep and when she pointed the cursor to the facetime icon and clicked, Tom's image appeared vivid and undistorted.

"Hello, Issi," he announced happily. "I see you arrived home safe and sound. How's your father?"

"Oh Tom, it's fantastic to see you. Are you home?" she asked.

When Tom told her that he had arrived home just a couple of hours before, Isabelle asked him to take her on a virtual tour of his flat and so Tom obligingly carried his tablet from one room to another, providing Isabelle with a floor-to-ceiling three hundred and sixty moving vision together with his commentary.

"It looks very nice, Tom," Isabelle lied unconvincingly once the tour was over and the picture on Isabelle's laptop stabilised. "Hopefully, I shall get to see it in person one day."

"I doubt it," said Tom, who quickly continued when he saw the hurt and questioning look that immediately appeared on Isabelle's face. "I'm moving soon. It's something that was finalised before my father died and I left for Rome. Well, it just so happens that I can move into the new place a little sooner than expected."

"Oh, that's nice," said Isabelle uncertainly. She didn't know why but the thought of Tom moving home seemed to take him even further away from her. It was irrational she knew but nonetheless, the news made her feel even lonelier than she had before. "Are you excited?"

"Yes, I am. This place is a bit small and so, it'll be nice to have more room. Anyway, enough of me. How are you, how's France and how's your father?"

"My papa is dying," she said sadly. "He has wasted away and now, there's nothing left of him but skin and bone. He looked so well when I left France but the sickness seems to have taken hold of him very quickly. It's terrible, Tom, it's breaking my heart."

"I'm so sorry, Issi, truly I am."

"Tom, it would be a great comfort if you could come and stay with me here. I need your strength and besides, mama is already trying to marry me off to the local vet."

"Isabelle, you know that if that were possible, I would be there with you but on top of moving home, I need to sort out the arrangements for my father's funeral." A thought suddenly occurred to Tom. "Oh crap, I'm not even sure if my mum knows yet." Seeing the look that crossed Isabelle's face Tom continued, "They have been divorced for about twenty years but I'm sure she'd still be, well, interested, I suppose."

"I'm so sorry, Tom, I had forgotten about your father. So much has happened so very quickly and although I care about you very much, I know so very little about you."

"Likewise," said Tom. "Hopefully, things will settle down soon and then we can spend a long time getting to know each other."

"I hope so too," replied Isabelle.

"Oh, by the way," said Tom, "I have your suitcase here. Is there anything you need?"

Isabelle thought for a few moments before replying, "No, Tom, if you could please just keep it for now. I think I have everything I need here and can pick up stuff from the shops if I need to. Goodnight, Tom. I miss you."

"Hey, before you go," said Tom hurriedly. "What's all this about your mum trying to marry you off?"

"Don't worry, Tom, my mama may think he's a real catch but I don't. It's funny, he has this big hairy mole."

"As a pet?" asked Tom.

Isabelle burst into sudden laughter. "No, you clown! On his face. When you look at him, your eyes are immediately drawn to it. When I see him, I can't stop staring at his mole."

"In that case, it's a good job it's on his face and not on his."

"Goodnight, Tom!" Isabelle quickly interrupted with a laugh.

"Goodnight, Issi. I'll be in touch tomorrow."

They kissed their respective screens and ended the connection.

3
A Nun's Brief Resumé of Life, Rome and Redemption

Two catholic nuns stood side by side in the small queue at the Air Italia desk in Rome's Leonardo Di Vinci airport. One was tall and slender with graceful aquiline features, whilst her companion and sibling was short, stocky and had the blunt facial features that one might more readily associate with an ageing pugilist and not a holy sister.

The taller nun, whose name was Magdalene Malone, was of a generally patient disposition, prone to shyness, especially on the very few occasions she found herself in the company of men and as a rule, was not at all confrontational. In short, she was cut from a completely different cloth from her shorter, powerfully built and truculent sibling.

"Assumptia," began Magdalene a little impatiently. "Would you please stop swinging that suitcase about and tell me, what did you like best about our visit to the eternal city?"

Assumptia Malone stopped her agitated shuffling and turned her large head towards her sister.

"Er?" she grunted quizzically as she looked with a startled expression up into Magdalene's haughty face. "What the feck?"

Magdalene cleared her throat indignantly as she looked down her nose into her sister's bloodshot and watery eyes before responding quietly but firmly, "There's absolutely no need for that kind of language Assumptia, especially as we are here in public. Now, I just asked whether or not you've enjoyed our visit to Rome?"

Magdalene's haughty face suddenly contorted in pain and she let out a small cry as she raised a hand to rub gently at her temple.

"What's that?" Assumptia asked, her voice full of concern for her sibling.

"Oh, it's nothing," breathed Magdalene as she continued to rub two fingers in a small circle at the side of her head. "I've just a headache, that's all. Nothing to worry about. Now, Assumptia, you were just about to tell me whether or not you enjoyed our visit to Rome."

"Maggie," Assumptia responded in disbelief. "What the feck is wrong with you? In case you've forgotten, we came here because you thought it'd be a good idea to seek forgiveness from God for relieving the world of the meanest piece of gnats' piss ever to have walked this green earth and in your misguided, devout blinded opinion, this was the place to get it."

"Assumptia!" Magdalene whispered harshly. "May I remind you that our visit to Rome in search of forgiveness for poisoning our father to death was indeed your idea, not mine!"

This outburst took Assumptia Malone by surprise. It was most unlike Magdalene and there was a fiery hardness deep within her sister's glare that she didn't quite recognise. However, following a few moments of uncertainty Assumptia continued regardless of her sister's protestation.

"Let's just have a quick run-through, shall we? First, we go to the Vatican and pray for forgiveness at the altar of the blessed St Peter. We asked God to send us a message and he certainly did that, alright, didn't he, Maggie? And what was the message that God sent to us Maggie?"

Magdalene cleared her throat uncomfortably before turning to stare resolutely ahead so as to avoid Assumptia's challenging glare.

"I believe we both recall what the message was, Assumptia and I really do not see the necessity to ever mention it again."

"Do you not, Maggie? So, if someone were to ask me why my breath smells of shite, I'll just tell them that it's me toothpaste, shall I?"

"Assumptia, now you're being ridiculous and would you please lower your voice down and stop making a show of yourself?" Magdalene admonished in a hushed and urgent whisper. "People are starting to look."

Some of the passing travellers milling around the concourse were throwing interested and concerned looks in their direction and Magdalene was starting to feel increasingly uncomfortable.

"Feck 'em!" Assumptia responded loudly as she glared about her in challenge. "Let 'em look! So," she continued unabated, "to forgive is divine, is it? Well, if that's what the divine tastes like, you can shove it up ya arse! Then, we have the audacity to have a spot of lunch and I get poisoned."

Magdalene huffed. "Assumptia, you drank enough wine to float a gondola, I don't know why you were surprised to be feeling a little fragile. There's no one to blame but yourself."

"And to top it off," Assumptia continued as she effortlessly lifted the suitcase she was holding to shake it under Magdalene's upturned nose. "Some French tart swapped her suitcase full of dirty fecking knickers for our five million quid!"

Magdalene calmly lifted her hand to the suitcase and eased it away from her face. "Do you know, Assumptia, I fear to say this but feel I must."

Magdalene breathed in deeply through her long thin nose in readiness for the declaration she was about to make.

"I have of late been questioning whether you're entirely suitable for a life devoted to God. There, I've said it now."

Magdalene turned her haughty face away from her sister to stare resolutely and unseeingly into the middle distance, cutting, what she hoped, was the very image of justified hurt and disappointment.

Assumptia stared at her sister in open-mouthed astonishment. "You are fecking kidding me, aren't you, Maggie?" Not waiting for or receiving a response, Assumptia continued, "I didn't choose a life devoted to God; it chose me! And Maggie, deny it if ya will but it chose you too. No one, I repeat, no one wanted us after mammy died. Certainly not that old bastard of a father and no aunts, uncles, distant cousins or even, foster homes. We were left out on the street like a couple of old and unwanted armchairs." Assumptia sniffed.

"So, there you have it, if it wasn't for the convent I don't know what would have become of us and so, I'm eternally grateful for their intervention. Don't get me wrong, Maggie," Assumptia continued with a huff. "I'd have survived because life provided me with the necessary equipment to get by," she said this whilst rolling her powerful shoulders.

"But you? Not a chance in hell. Now, I'm not pretending to be perfect and I don't mind admitting that but I've done me fair share of kneeling and praying and what not but you're not perfect either are you, Maggie?"

At this, Assumptia once again glared at Magdalene and this time, she screwed her face up in accusation.

"What on earth are you talking about now?" questioned Magdalene, who had now refocused her stare to rest upon her sister's belligerent face.

Assumptia huffed and sniggered as she tilted her large head up towards Magdalene and sneered, "You know exactly what I'm talking about, Maggie Malone and don't you go pretending you don't. I've seen the way you look at the fellas. You're like a bitch on heat!"

Magdalene flushed brightly; her eyes wide with shock. "That's just too ridiculous, Assumptia and you know it!" she whispered harshly.

"Oh, I know it alright, Maggie and so, don't you go on preaching at me like you're some kind of saint because we both know you're not. And not forgetting the almighty great elephant in the room, we were both complicit in murder, patricide no less."

Magdalene cleared her throat. "Are you quite finished, Assumptia?" she asked and without waiting for a response continued, "good because it's now our turn."

Smiling warmly at the woman behind the Air Italia desk, Magdalene said, "Good afternoon, we would like to purchase two tickets for your next flight to Paris, please."

"And another thing," interrupted Assumptia. "Just how long have you had a credit card?"

Magdalene turned to gift her sister with a slight smirk. "I acquired it on the day that Marks and Spencer came to Dublin."

"So, we get to Paris. What then?" asked Assumptia.

"Well, you have the French woman's suitcase and that has an address label. So, we get to Paris and then on to Aigurande, where hopefully, we shall be able to swap cases and reclaim our money."

Assumptia nodded in slow satisfaction. "Maggie, you're not all bad really. What with me good looks and charm and your brains, we'll go far." Assumptia's face suddenly creased into a frown. "Maggie, when you say Paris, you're not thinking of us visiting Notre Dame and asking for forgiveness again, are ya?"

"Certainly not!" responded Magdalene primly as she again placed two fingers against her temple and began to slowly massage the point of pain. "I don't care for the taste of it either."

4
Of Nutcrackers and Pizza

Tom Harrison sat at a table in the Good Samaritan Public House, a traditional watering hole situated on Turner Street, immediately behind the Royal London Hospital in Whitechapel. He looked at the young woman who sat opposite him and once again exclaimed his incredulity at her change in appearance.

Gone were Zoe's jet-black spikey hair and dark ghoulish makeup and her face and ears were no longer cluttered with piercings. She still had piercings but not nearly so many as she'd displayed when she and Tom had first met, immediately following the death of Tom's father.

Her hair was now blond, parted in the centre, with a small neat bun on either side. Her makeup was bright and cheery, which seemed to enhance the sparkle in her green eyes. She wore red dungarees, the legs of which finished at her shins, white pumps and a smart blue and white striped shirt. She looked very different but very good too, albeit in a very unusual way.

"You look like a nutcracker," said Tom. "The type you get at Christmas. Don't get me wrong, you look good, much better than before but still a bit—unusual. Very singular."

Zoe's pretty elf-like face creased into a grimace as she absorbed Tom's latest critical review of her new look.

"Oh, that's rich, let's all follow the unique fashion advice of mister perfectly boring bleeding normal, too scared to wear brown in town. Why don't you just shut up and get on with the story?" she huffed before prompting. "So, you and Isabelle are now on a train travelling from Rome to Milan. Then what happened?"

"I have occasionally worn brown shoes to work," Tom replied defensively whilst gazing down at his shiny black brogues and dark blue suit trousers. He brushed his dark fringe from his forehead and made a mental note that he was overdue a visit to the barbers. "Just not today and anyway, there's nothing wrong with fitting in."

"Whatever," said Zoe. "Now, you reached Milan, then what happened?"

"Well, there's not too much to add really. When we got to Milan, Isabelle decided to call home and let her mother know that she'd left Luca and Rome behind her. Whilst I only understood a little of what was being said, it was quite obvious that something was wrong. It transpired that Isabelle's father was very ill and that she had to return immediately to France. Luckily enough, there was a flight that afternoon and so we went straight from the station to the airport. It was all very rushed and frantic; we only just made it. A quick au revoir and there she was, gone. She even forgot to take her suitcase."

"And you're still in contact?" asked Zoe.

"Yes, we're very much still in contact. She wanted me to meet her in France but I couldn't because I have to sort out my dad's funeral arrangements, register his death and all that."

"How are the arrangements going?" Zoe asked.

"As well as can be expected I suppose," replied Tom. "My dad has or had this whole new family or step-family, I knew nothing about. And my poor mum, she didn't even know my dad had died. I still need to get the death registered and I have an appointment tomorrow at Islington Town Hall to sort that out. Yes, there's quite a bit I still need to do," he concluded before adding, "Well, at least I got the flat move out of the way, that's one less thing to worry about."

"You've moved home?"

"Yes, I've moved into a bigger place and actually, now, I even have a spare room."

"Hm." A thoughtful look suddenly clouded Zoe's face before being replaced by a bright smile. "When you think about everything that happened in Rome, you did pretty good," she said with enthusiasm.

"Well," replied Tom, "I did have a major injection of luck but that said, I did manage to find my dad's lost wartime lover as well as a half-brother I never knew I had."

"And a sexy French girlfriend," Zoe threw in. "Have you ever thought of writing a book about your adventures in Italy? I'm sure it'd make a great read and who knows, someone might even want to make a film of it." Zoe leaned forward with an excited look on her face. "If they did, which actor would you like to play you?"

"Donald sodding duck!" grunted Tom.

"Oh, you miserable old git!" exclaimed Zoe with a laugh. "Now, come on, you promised to take me out and show me a good time. Where are we going?"

"Pizza Express?" ventured Tom.

"Get me a stuffed crust and I'll let you shag my brains out."

Zoe said this as Tom was in the process of gulping down the last of his beer, which he immediately choked upon spraying the beer directly into Zoe's mischievously smiling face.

"Oh, you bell end!" she cursed in shock. "And, you do know that that was a joke, right? After all, you're old enough to be my dad!"

"Sorry," apologised Tom handing Zoe a paper handkerchief. "Shall we go?"

5
A Humid Wait for Riches

Roxy Pasternak nee Agnes Buff slouched miserably upon the ornate faux leopard skin couch that dominated the living area of the Pasternak's small condominium apartment. It was a stifling hot evening in Florida and the air conditioning had broken down again. She languidly waved a tired hand in front of her sweat-glistening face in the faint hope of generating some cool air but soon gave up to sink back into a state of motionless despair.

Horace sat a few feet away at the kitchenette's small white table. He was wearing nothing but his underpants and a stained, once white, vest that stretched tightly over the large bulge of his stomach. He tapped away furiously at the laptop's keyboard, ending with a theatrical flourish that put Roxy in mind of a concert pianist.

"Who're you writing to, Horri?" Roxy asked tiredly.

"The legal guys," responded Horace grumpily. "They got to do something about those damn limeys, so as to make them pay what they owe me for the fire."

"But the fire was two years ago, Horri and the insurance fellas say you started it yourself and so that's why they're not going to pay you a dime."

"They can say what they like, Sugar but they still got to prove it and there's no way they're going to do that here in Florida, in court."

"Are you sure?" drawled Roxy sulkily. "It's been a long time now and things haven't been like you promised me before we got married. I've had to pawn almost everything you bought me and you got to admit, this apartment is, well, it's not nice Horri."

Horace removed his thick-rimmed spectacles and tiredly rose from his chair to join Roxy on the couch.

"I know it's been hard for you, Sugar, but I promise, I'll make it up to you a million times over. We're going to be so rich, so very rich."

He lent towards Roxy intending to plant a sweaty kiss on her hot mouth, but Roxy moved away from him and held out an arm to fend off any further advances.

"It's too hot, Horri," she moaned. "Be a good boy and fetch me a cool drink."

Horace climbed disappointedly to his feet and made his way towards the fridge. He stopped and glanced back at Roxy. "I don't suppose you fancy taking a shower, do you, Sugar?"

"I might take one later and if you're good, I'll let you watch."

This news brightened Horace's mood as he set about making a couple of cocktails.

How did I let it come to this? Thought Roxy as she looked at the baggy-arsed end of Horace's underpants. This was not the life she'd contemplated when accepting his marriage proposal. Still, no pain no gain, she mused. For whilst the insurance pay-out was taking far longer than originally expected, Horace had convinced her that his plan would eventually succeed and as soon as it did well, she had plans of her own.

"Hey, Sugar," Horace called as he rummaged through the sparse contents of the refrigerator. "I thought you went to the grocery store today. Was it closed?"

"No, why do you ask?"

"I heard some people complaining that the grocery store keeps randomly closing for an hour or so each day and it doesn't look like we got much to eat."

A sly and secretive smile spread slowly across Roxy's face as she watched Horace move some jars around as he continued to search for a snack.

"Well, Horri, some of us could do with shedding a little timber and if we don't have it, then you can't eat it."

Horace turned to stare dully across the room towards his wife. "If you're not buying any food, why do you keep going to the grocery store?"

Roxy's face contorted in sudden anger as she snarled at Horace, "OK, Horri, I'll fill up the damn refrigerator tomorrow. Then, you can eat until you explode for all I care!"

With that, Roxy folded her arms in a petulant display of hostility before turning away from Horace to stare at the wall.

Hurt and confused by this sudden outburst, Horace tried to mollify her. "Sugar, I'm sorry. It's just all this stuff with the insurance company, it's making me a little edgy and I like to eat when I get anxious."

Roxy turned back towards him and slowly looked him up and down, a hard mocking expression covering her otherwise attractive features. "Well, Horri, all I can say is that you must surely have a lot of anxiety issues."

Roxy could see that her insult had cut Horace deep but she felt no remorse. "All I've asked you to do today is to fix me a drink," she continued coldly. "And you can't even manage to do that without criticising the way I do things."

Horace saw his chance and grabbed at it.

"I'll fix you the best drink ever," he said as he closed the fridge door and made for the cupboard where their supply of liquor was stored.

He'd just opened the cupboard door and reached in for the bottle of bourbon that lay hidden within when Roxy declared spitefully, "And, if you think for one minute that you'll be watching me in the shower later today, you can forget it!"

Horace's spirits plummeted yet again as he lifted the bourbon bottle from the cupboard and loosened its top. If only those damned limeys had paid his claim like they should have, then none of this would be happening. Roxy would be happy and so, he concluded miserably, and so would he.

6
Work and the Rise of the Lodger

Tom sat at his desk in the offices of Mallory Syndicate 333. The thick and untidy file of papers that rested in front of him related to a suspicious fire claim concerning Pasternak's Original Home Furnishings. The fire had occurred some two years previously and the circumstances surrounding it had, as Tom liked to put it, more red flags than the Chinese army. Tom leaned back in his chair and again mentally ticked off the circumstances that had led to his or rather Mallory Syndicate's, declinature of the claim and the legal proceedings that had swiftly ensued.

There existed a universal number of fraud indicators that, if found, required an insurer to undertake further and more in-depth investigations. However, although the Pasternak claim ticked most, if not all of the boxes, declining a claim for fraud in Florida was an extremely risky undertaking. The courts in Florida were notoriously uncompromising towards insurance companies. And, the potential financial implications for an insurer losing a fraud case could be excessive.

So, Tom thought to himself, one last time, *what are the facts?* Tom held out his left-hand palm upwards. A fire occurred shortly after the risk had been insured for the very first time and this fire had completely destroyed the premises and its contents. Tom folded his thumb into his palm. The value of the risk had been massively overstated. Tom's index finger joined his thumb. The cause of the fire remained unidentified but all possible legitimate causes had been thoroughly investigated and ruled out.

Tom's middle finger went down to join his thumb and index fingers. The business was failing and its owner had fallen out of favour with his creditors and the only person with out-of-hours access to the property was its owner, Horace Pasternak. Tom's ring and little finger folded and he now held a clenched fist.

There was also Pasternak's divorce and its financial implications. And finally, Pasternak's cell phone call to his divorce lawyer was made immediately before his call to the emergency services.

Motive, means and opportunity, thought Tom. Surely, we now have all the components needed to comply with Floridian law and to prove that this is indeed a case of arson and insurance fraud.

Conversely, in the face of such damning evidence, why had the Floridian judiciary taken no action against Horace Pasternak? Tom used his pen to scratch his head and again pondered upon the possibility that he might be missing something important. He puffed out his cheeks and wondered what, if anything, that something might be.

Given the weight of evidence that strongly suggested that Horace Pasternak had torched his own business in an attempt to commit insurance fraud, Tom was amazed that Pasternak had not run for the hills but had instead, acquired legal representation and issued proceedings against Mallory Syndicate.

Tom's thoughts were interrupted by the arrival at his desk of his supervisor, Charlie.

"Do you have any update on the Pasternak claim?" Charlie asked bluntly.

Tom straightened in his chair and looked up at the large overweight bulk of the man that was Charlie Prescott. Charlie could be an awkward sod but once you got to know him a little, you'd find that he had a heart of gold and that he was one of the best claims men in the business. He also looked much older than his sixty-one years.

"Morning, Charlie, good to see you too. How was your weekend?" Tom goaded.

"Do you have an update or don't you?" Charlie asked irritably.

"Well, Charlie, seeing as you asked so nicely, yes, I do have an update. The update is that Pasternak is not backing down and so the case is still going to trial in the US Federal Court in Tampa. The trial is scheduled to begin next Monday and is set to last for three weeks. What's more, we need a representative in court for the duration."

"Well, sunshine," said Charlie with a wicked smirk. "In that case, you'd best pack your bags and get yourself over to Tampa and Tom," Charlie bent and leaned his head in close to stare uncompromisingly into Tom's eyes. "Don't screw it up."

With this, Charlie turned and stepped away in the direction of a line of four dully silver doored lifts, presumably, Tom thought, to provide senior management with details of the first case Mallory was to take to trial for more than a decade. Tom chewed his bottom lip as he watched Charlie's wide back recede. Three weeks in Tampa didn't sound too bad and if nothing else, attending trial would be another life experience to add to his recently expanding list. Any further thoughts were interrupted by the telephone's ring, the phone's display telling him that the call came from Mallory's ground floor reception area.

Tom reached for the receiver. "Hello, you're through to Tom Harrison. How may I help you?"

"Hello, Thomas," said a voice etched with a slight West Indian undertone. "I have a young lady waiting in reception for you, she says it is urgent."

"Oh, really, did she give her name?" asked Tom.

"Hello, love," Tom heard the receptionist say. "Who shall I say is calling?"

"Tell him it's Zoe and tell him it's urgent," said Zoe, adding, "Please," as an afterthought.

"She said—"

"I know," interrupted Tom. "I'll be right down."

Standing and lifting his jacket from the back of his chair, Tom made for the lifts and hit the down indicator. Several seconds later and seeing that none of the lift floor indicators had moved, he hit the button again, only this time harder. Still no movement. Sighing, Tom pulled on his jacket and made for the stairwell.

When he reached the reception area, he was greeted by a forlorn-looking Zoe standing next to a large suitcase.

Tom went over to her and asked; "What's up, Sally?"

Tom had occasionally taken to calling Zoe, Sally. This was on account of the heavy way in which Zoe had taken to applying her makeup in what she liked to refer to as her 'new look'. It reminded Tom of a character in an old TV adaptation of the children's classic, Wurzel Gummidge, which told the story of a scarecrow that came to life. Silly old Wurzel was in love with Aunt Sally, a brightly painted fairground attraction that children of a certain era threw stuff at. Aunt Sally also came to life when not being used as a target.

Zoe's face was one of abject misery and as she looked at Tom her bottom lip started to tremble and her eyes filled with tears.

"I've been thrown out!" she wailed, drawing several startled looks from the blue and grey suited business people waiting either individually or in small tight-knit groups within Mallory's reception area.

"OK," said Tom quickly taking the suitcase in one hand and Zoe's elbow in the other and guiding both towards the door that led out onto Bishopsgate. "Let's go and grab a coffee and then you can tell me all about it."

Ten minutes later, they were sitting opposite each other in a coffee shop situated within Liverpool Street train station.

"So," said Tom. "You've been kicked out of your room. Do you want to tell me why?"

"It's that bloody Gary," she sobbed. "He tried it on with me the other night and I told him to get lost. Since then, he's been pestering me in a really creepy way. I've been so scared that at night I've been staying in my room with a chair wedged up against the door."

Tom already knew that Gary was the guy who owned the house in which Zoe rented a room but Gary was married and his wife lived there too.

"But what about Missus Gary, where does she fit into all this?" asked Tom.

"They had a massive row about something and so she went to stay with her sister for a couple of nights. When she came back, Gary told her that I'd tried to jump into bed with him and that was it! Bloody furious she was and she wouldn't believe a word I said. She made me pack my bags up and get out right there and then. Didn't want to stay anyway but now, I've got nowhere else to go."

Tom passed Zoe a paper napkin taken from the small silver container that sat in the middle of the table. Zoe took the proffered napkin and noisily blew her nose. "Why don't you go back home?" he asked gently.

"Because, Tom," she retorted angrily. "They don't want me neither. Nobody wants me, not even you."

This comment confused Tom, who frowned slightly as he considered its possible implications. The look on Tom's face was enough for Zoe who stood as if about to leave.

"Oh, don't you fret, Tom," she spat vehemently. "I'll not put you to any trouble, I'll find a hostel or sleep under a bridge, it won't be the first time."

"Don't be a plonker, Zoe," Tom said softly. "Calm down and drink your coffee. There's a spare room at mine and you can stay there until you've sort yourself out."

Tom took out a pen from his Jacket's breast pocket and wrote his address on another white paper napkin. He passed this to Zoe together with his door keys.

"Have you got money?" he asked.

Zoe nodded.

"OK," continued Tom. "I can't come with you just yet but get a cab and I'll join you at home as soon as I've finished work."

Zoe sat down and started to cry again. "Thank you, Tom," she sobbed. "I promise, I'll not be any trouble and I'll find somewhere just as soon as I can. I'll never forget this, Tom."

"Me neither," Tom said tiredly as he got up. "I'm sorry, Zoe, but I really must get back to the office, I'll see you later, OK?"

"I'd rather you came with me, Tom," Zoe replied. "Carpe Diem and all that," she said repeating the phrase that Tom had previously used when lamenting his choice not to accompany Isabelle to France. "Seize the day and all that," she concluded.

Tom paused and considered these words for a moment before sighing in defeat and sitting back down. "I'll need to call the office and let them know I'll not be back today."

"Oh, thanks, Tom!" Zoe beamed. "That's so kind."

Tom left Zoe in the coffee shop whilst he called the office. Charlie was less than pleased to begin with but Tom thought he'd finally managed to mollify him. He then picked up a few groceries and a couple of bottles of wine before collecting Zoe and heading up the escalator to the taxi rank. Half an hour later, Tom was showing Zoe around his apartment.

The flat was situated above a betting shop in East London. It had a large split-level lounge, a decent-sized kitchen, a bathroom and two bedrooms. It was newly decorated in a modern style, with walls of on-trend soft grey with contrasting metro tiles in the kitchen and bathroom. The deep and luxurious carpets in the living room and bedrooms were of darker grey, whilst the hallway, kitchen and bathroom had dark faux wooden floors.

"This is very nice, Tom," said Zoe approvingly. "Very stylish."

"Thank you. The room at the end of the hall is yours. There's wardrobe and drawer space but I need to make up the bed as I wasn't expecting guests," Tom said awkwardly. It felt a bit weird Zoe being in his home but he guessed he'd get used to it and after all, it shouldn't be for too long.

"If you just give me the bedding, I can do that," said Zoe.

"It's all in there, so why don't you go and sort yourself out and I'll put the kettle on."

Seconds later, Zoe called to him from the bedroom. "Tom, what should I do with this old suitcase that's on the bed?"

Zoe was obviously referring to Isabelle's case which had been the room's sole occupant since he'd moved in.

"Just shove it under the bed for now," he called back.

"It's heavy," called Zoe. "What's in it?"

"Just Isabelle's stuff. It's the case she run off and left me with in Milan. I'm keeping it safe for her."

"Have you had a rummage?" asked Zoe.

"No, I haven't," said Tom. "And neither are you. It's private!"

"Suit yourself, MOG, I'm not that interested anyway," lied Zoe.

"MOG?" questioned Tom.

"MOG," replied Zoe. "Miserable Old Git!"

*

Later that evening and having finished the dinner Tom had prepared for the two of them, they both occupied the soft leather couch situated in the living room's lower tier and watched what, according to Zoe, was a must-see TV series about vampires. Tom found the show, which was set in rural USA, to be bordering upon soft pornography and he said as much to Zoe.

"I thought vampires generally limited their night time activities to a bite and a slurp. These vampires just seem intent on shagging their victims to death and sometimes, don't even bother to stop for a neck nibble and a drink."

Zoe, whose eyes were fixed on the naked humping currently taking place between, if Tom had understood the plot correctly, a vampire and a young woman who apparently contained fairy blood, whatever that was supposed to be, answered with a non-committal grunt.

"Fine," said Tom. "I'm going to my room to get ready for bed and then I'll facetime Isabelle. Goodnight, Zoe."

With that, he got up and left Zoe to enjoy the rest of the show.

*

Isabelle's face appeared immediately on the screen of Tom's tablet.

"Hello, love," said Tom. "How was your day today and how's your dad?" he asked.

"Oh, just the same," she answered tiredly. "You are late today, is everything alright?"

"I've been helping a friend. She'll be staying here for a while until she gets herself sorted out."

Isabelle's face crinkled into a sudden frown. "She? Who is this she?"

Tom breathed deeply and began to tell Isabelle about Zoe, how they had met before he had left for Italy and the circumstances leading up to Zoe's occupation of his spare room. Isabelle listened intently and never once interrupted as Tom recounted his version of events. Once he had finished, Isabelle nodded a few times before asking; "How old is this lodger?"

"I don't know exactly," replied Tom. "She says I'm old enough to be her father and so, I'm guessing, late teens early twenties."

"Mon Dieu," whispered Isabelle. "Is she pretty?"

"I've never seen her with less than five coats of makeup masking her face but yes, she's pretty," Tom answered honestly.

"And do you have feelings for her?"

"I guess that I must," said Tom thoughtfully. "But not in a sexual way, I feel, well, protective I suppose but please don't ask me why because I really don't know."

Isabelle smiled tiredly. "Tom, would you have offered this girl your spare room if she were old or ugly?"

"God, no!" exclaimed Tom. "I may be a pushover but I'm not bloody mad!"

Isabelle laughed at that. "I like you, Tom, you're a contradiction. Shallow and yet also honest and kind-hearted."

Tom was relieved to have the issue of Zoe out of the way and so, he moved on to his other news.

"The funeral is on Thursday and it'll be a relief when that's over. Then, on Saturday, I have to fly out to Tampa and the chances are, I'll be staying there for around about three weeks."

"What are you talking about, Tom?"

"It's work. I've been handling an arson case. The owner of a failing business decided to insure it for the very first time and he insured it at ten times its actual value. Then, lo and behold, a few weeks later a fire burns the place to the ground.

All evidence and we have a lot of evidence, suggests the fire had at least two separate and unconnected points of origin. We also suspect that accelerants were used."

"Accelerants?" asked Isabelle.

"Petrol," replied Tom. "So anyway, we refused to pay the claim, presented our evidence and fully expected the perpetrator to run for the hills but instead, he sued us! Prior to heading out to Italy, I'd been over to Florida on a couple of occasions and during those visits, I met with Horace Pasternak and his lawyers. He's the arsonist.

"The purpose of these meetings was to try and avoid the litigation and its cost. No matter how strong a case is, there is always a risk when you take a matter to court and this is because a jury may not understand or may disregard even the strongest evidence. To tell you the truth, I never expected the case to go this far and still hope Pasternak will see sense and do a bunk."

"He cannot retract his case, Tommy, because if he does, he will be admitting his guilt and will be hunted down and thrown into prison."

Tom was a little taken aback by Isabelle's astute insight. "Good point, Issi and you called me Tommy."

"Yes, I did, didn't I," she said with a smile. "Do you not like it?"

"I like it very much, Issi, just as like I like you very much."

"I had hoped you could come and join me but now it seems you will be going further and further away. Still, never mind, I have Jacques to comfort me. Jacques is the vet in case you have forgotten."

"No, I hadn't forgotten," replied Tom with a groan. "How's that coming along?"

"My mother invited him to dinner again this evening! She is like a dog with a bone and will not give up and as for Jacques, he is little better. He keeps looking at me with these big cow eyes," Isabelle blew out her cheeks and held her eyes wide in a comic imitation of her would be suitor. "And, he is forever suggesting we go outside or for a walk but I know him and walking is the last thing on his mind!"

"Oh dear," said Tom. "Do I need to send over a chastity belt?"

"I don't know what that is," said Isabelle. "But it sounds rude."

Tom laughed. "I'll tell you about chastity belts when we're together but suffice to say that they were the reason why lockpicks were invented."

"Lockpicks?"

"Never mind."

They wished each other goodnight, kissed their respective screens and signed off.

Tom was about to turn off his bedside lamp when there was a tapping at his door and Zoe appeared holding two steaming mugs.

"I thought you might like a hot chocolate. I did, so, I made us both one."

Zoe was wearing silky, cream pyjamas decorated with a red feathered pattern. They looked at least two sizes too big for her. The bottoms pooled around her feet, the toes of which peeped out like some brightly painted but timid form of wildlife. She had washed her face in preparation for bed and it was the first time that Tom had seen her without make-up. Without waiting for an invitation, Zoe entered Tom's room, walked over to the bed and handed Tom a mug of hot chocolate. She then walked around to the other side of the bed and climbed in, resting the duvet over her outstretched legs.

She turned and smiled happily at Tom. "How's Isabelle?"

"Zoe," Tom said. "A couple of things. Firstly, we need to discuss boundaries and there's no way you should be in my room, let alone in my bed."

"Oh, don't you go getting your hopes up. I'm just here for a chat before bedtime. No hanky spanky."

"That's as maybe," continued Tom seriously. "But in future, wait to be asked."

"I have a feeling that I might be waiting a long time. Anyway, what's next?" she asked.

"Why do you wear so much makeup? This is the first time I've seen you without it and you've a really pretty face."

"It's not all I've got that's good to look at, Tom," she said mischievously. "I might be tempted to show you but I doubt your poor old heart could take it."

"I'm being serious, Zoe, on both counts."

Zoe blew steam from the top of her hot chocolate and then took a sip.

"I hide behind the makeup," she said eventually. "It's like a disguise and I can be whoever I want to be and no one will see the real me hiding underneath."

"And what's wrong with the real you?"

"I don't want to talk about it. Can we talk about something else?"

"I'd like to hear about you, Zoe," persisted Tom. "I've welcomed you into my home and yet, I know next to nothing about you. I can detect a slight west country burr in your voice and so, how did you end up being a barmaid in the Good Samaritan?"

"A proper Sherlock Holmes you," she retorted. "Well, you're right, I'm from Bristol and my mum and dad still live there. They are not badly off either, quite well to do in fact. I have or had, an interest in archaeology. You see, Tom, you're not the only old relic that I'm interested in."

Tom huffed and cast his eyes to the ceiling. "I'm not that bloody old," he said.

"But of course you are, Tom," she continued. "Anyway, so I got good grades at school and they, my parents that is, paid for me to go to Bristol University to study for a degree in archaeology. So, things were all going swimmingly well until I met Sly. He was the singer in a Goth rock band and the sexiest thing on two legs. Trouble was, he knew it. So, I go and fall head over heels in love with Sly. I leave university and travel all over the UK with Sly and the band. We travelled from one shithole to the next.

"Although I didn't realise it at the time, the band was pretty rubbish. They were called The Vile, quite appropriate in hindsight. Anyway, we finally ended up in London and following one monumentally awful gig in which the crowd hurled all kinds of crap at them and booed them off stage, the band split. They all went their separate ways, including Sly, who left me without so much as a goodbye or a peck on the cheek. Bastard! So, I get in touch with Mum and Dad but they've washed their hands of me and don't want to know and I can't say as I blame them."

"I'm sure that's not true," said Tom. "They're just a little hurt at the moment and need some time to calm down."

"What do you know, Mister Freud?"

"Fair point," said Tom in between careful sips of his hot chocolate.

"And what about you, Tom, who are you?"

"Me, I'm Tom Harrison, a divorcee with no children and a recent collector of waifs and strays. I currently live in London together with a house guest who takes great delight in taking the piss out of my age, a thing I might add, that she knows absolutely nothing about. I'm very tired, I have a busy week ahead of me and would be delighted if said house guest would kindly get out of my bed and go to her own room. How's that?"

"Sensational," said Zoe sarcastically as she got out of bed and padded her way towards the bedroom's door.

"Oh and by the way," continued Tom. "I have to leave for America on Saturday, can I trust you to look after the place whilst I'm away?"

Zoe stopped and turned her head to look back at him. "America?"

"Yes, it's work stuff. I'll be away for about three weeks."

"Three weeks?" Zoe looked stunned. "You're going away and leaving me here all by myself for three weeks?" she asked incredulously.

"What's your problem, Zoe?"

"No nothing," she replied. "I'm just amazed that you trust me enough to leave me here alone in your home for three whole weeks. If you weren't such a MOG I'd come and give you a big kiss. I'm going now, need to organise the party invites."

With that, she gave him a cheeky grin and left, closing the door behind her as she went.

7
The Battle of Paris!

"I just don't know why people keep carping on about Paris and the bloody French," Assumptia complained angrily. "Oh, they're oh so refined and apparently, the best at everything. Well, for what it's worth, I don't think too much of them or their sodding country," Assumptia continued to grumble as she and Magdalene walked arm in arm through the milling crowds of Charles de Gaulle airport. They each carried a small suitcase, one containing an unknown French woman's clothes and the other, their own few personal belongings.

"Well, Sister," breathed Magdalene as she studied the multitude of directional signs that provided the newly arrived traveller with several helpful indicators. "I'm so pleased you've given Paris and its denizens ample opportunity to impress before providing such a damning review. Now, that sign says the taxis are to the right." Magdalene pointed a long slim finger rightward and the two sisters changed tack without breaking stride.

"There's too many people," Assumptia complained again as she waived their accidentally acquired suitcase vigorously from side to side.

"Assumptia, I know you're tired and all but we're only here until tomorrow morning, then we'll hop aboard a plane to Limoges and Aigurande, collect what's rightfully ours and then decide what to do next. Now, if we could just get to the Taxi rank without you killing someone with that there suitcase, it'd be a blessing."

The airport was very busy that evening and the queue for taxis was a long one. When they finally made it to the front of the queue, they had to let three taxis go before one arrived with a driver who was able and willing to converse with them in English. The taxi was not one of the smarter vehicles the sisters had seen whilst waiting. In fact, there was no doubt that its best days were at least a decade past.

"Ah, God, be praised," beamed Magdalene as she gave the taxi driver a warm smile. "Now, would you happen to know of a good hotel where the two of us could stay for the night? Nothing too fancy or expensive mind. We would just like a comfortable place to rest. Not too far from the airport as we intend to catch another flight first thing in the morning."

The taxi driver, who was of middle eastern appearance, slowly looked the two nuns up and down before commenting, "Yes, my brother has such a place. Please, get in the car and I will take you."

Still clutching their suitcases, the two sisters climbed awkwardly into the taxi's rear seats. The car's interior was almost totally carpeted in some form of rough material that put the sisters in mind of a doormat.

As they settled warily and uncomfortably into their seats, the nuns almost immediately started to itch and whilst Magdalene did her utmost to avoid the temptation to scratch, Assumptia hefted her extensive bottom from her seat in order to administer some relief.

"Have ya ever thought of giving this here mangy rust bucket a vacuum?" she asked loudly. The driver took no notice and instead pulled the car quickly into the busy evening traffic.

Some little time later, the taxi stopped off in a poorly lit back street outside the crumbling edifice of the grandly entitled Tunis Palace Hotel. As Assumptia got clumsily out of the car, her initial relief at escaping its irritating interior quickly evaporated as she glanced up at the two sad and dirty flags which hung limply above the hotel's grubby entranceway.

"If this is a palace," she remarked under her breath. "Remind me never to set foot in Tunis."

"This way please," said the taxi driver as he ushered them through the hotel's tarnished doors towards a reception desk that was occupied by a fat unshaven man smoking a strong and foul-smelling cigarette. There followed a quick exchange in French Arabic, following which, the fat man reached awkwardly behind him to grab a set of keys from a peg. These he placed on the desk next to an overflowing ashtray before pushing them towards the nuns. He then gestured with his hand to indicate that he wanted something in return.

"This is my brother Faruq," said the taxi driver. "His English is not so good. He needs your credit card. This is good because then you can use the bar and restaurant in the hotel and it all gets charged back to the room and he is giving you the hotel's very best room."

"And exactly how much is the cost of the room?" inquired Magdalene.

"For you, it is very cheap. Yes, you are very lucky you have met me. Lots of bad people in Paris but I look after you."

"Yes, I'm sure you will," persisted Magdalene, who had started to rub at a point of pain that was developing in her right temple. "But I'd still like to know how much we're expected to pay for the room."

"Oh, for fecks sake, Maggie!" Assumptia erupted. "I don't know about you but I'm knackered. Would you just give the man your wee bit of plastic so we can put our feet up and maybe have a spot of dinner? A drink or two wouldn't go amiss either."

"This is a credit card, Assumptia, it's not a get out of jail free. One day, I must pay for everything we buy using this so-called wee bit of plastic," Magdalene retorted angrily. "Now gentlemen," Magdalene continued as she looked around dubiously at the lobby's worn and discoloured decor. "Would you please just tell me how much you charge for one night's stay in this, this, this very singular establishment?"

There followed a long stream of French Arabic between the two men before the taxi driver eventually turned to the nuns and announced smilingly, "I have negotiated the very best price for you."

"That's good to know," replied Magdalene. "And how much would that be then?"

"Just one hundred euros," replied the taxi driver.

"Excellent," said Magdalene as she turned to smile at Assumptia, who in turn nodded her head in approval to the suggested cost.

"Just one hundred euros," repeated the taxi driver. "Each."

At this, Assumptia dropped the suitcase she'd been holding and quickly reached out a large beefy hand to grab the scrawny taxi driver by the scruff of the neck. She pulled him roughly to within a few inches of her face.

"Now, you listen to me you greasy little gobshite," she whispered fiercely. "If you want me to retain my mild disposition, I suggest you and the fat fella behind the desk there, reconsider your pricing structure."

The fat man behind the reception desk rose to his feet in alarm and said something to the taxi driver in an urgent questioning tone. The taxi driver responded in a quick high-pitched and nervous gabble; his eyes bright with terror as he stared down into Assumptia's hard glaring eyes.

"Please, madame, Sister, my English it's not good," he blathered. "I make mistakes. So sorry. The room is just one hundred euros for your stay."

"Now that's more like it," said Assumptia as she let go of the taxi driver's collar and allowed him to stumble away from her. "What time's dinner?"

*

A few hours, later the two sisters sat side by side on a bench seat in the hotel's dimly lit bar. In front of them and occupying a small and badly marked round wooden table was one partially filled wine glass together with its empty twin, an empty bottle of wine and a second bottle that was still half full. The bar's other occupants were four shady and rough-looking men who sat huddled together in a tight circle playing cards.

"I think I'll try some of that wine now if you don't mind," said Magdalene as she leaned forward to pour herself a small glass of the deep rich red wine.

"Not too much now," slurred Assumptia. "You know it gives you strange urges."

"It most certainly does no such thing!" snapped Magdalene and to prove her point, she filled her glass to its brim.

"Well, it's a good job I'm here to keep an eye on you," Assumptia persisted mischievously. "Otherwise, those four fellas over there," she continued as she nodded her head in the direction of the bar's other occupants, "wouldn't have a hope in hell of getting out of here with their trousers intact."

"Oh, Assumptia," giggled Magdalene through reddened teeth, the wine obviously having an immediate impact upon her usual sobriety. "You say the naughtiest things."

"Changing the subject," said Assumptia. "What was that we had for dinner?"

"I haven't the foggiest but it was rather delicious, wasn't it."

"Yes, all in all, it wasn't too bad although, I generally like to know what it actually is that I'm eating. What do you think those round things in breadcrumbs might have been? I didn't care for the texture of them but you seemed to be munching them back like they were going out of fashion. I was also surprised by our room. Granted, it's not the Ritz but it wasn't nearly as bad as I'd expected."

"I agree," said Magdalene as she cast an enquiring glance towards the four men, two of whom now appeared to be arm-wrestling. "It's just a shame that no one bothered to clear away all of those dead flies and as for the stains on the carpet, God alone knows where they came from."

Assumptia followed her sister's gaze and quickly took in the power struggle unfolding across the bar.

"Ah, Maggie," she whispered. "I can see money changing hands. Things are looking up." With that Assumptia got slowly to her feet and made her way over to the group of men.

"Hello fellas, would you mind some outside competition?" she asked whilst gracing the combatants with what she believed was a most ingratiating smile.

The men looked up incredulously at the nun standing before them. Then, as one, they all began to laugh. When their laughter finally subsided, one of the men looked up at Assumptia and said in broken English, "This is a competition for men," he bent his arm in front of Assumptia to display the bulge of his not inconsiderable muscle. "Not women, too weak," he concluded.

"Weak ya say," said Assumptia as she rubbed her chin thoughtfully. "Well, it just so happens that I have four hundred euros that says I can best each one of you."

"Four hundred euros," said the spokesman with sudden interest. "Show me."

"Now, you don't expect me, a weak and feeble woman to be carrying that kind of cash around with me but me and my sister there," she said with a nod towards Magdalene. "We're currently residing at this fine establishment and can quickly nip to our room and grab the cash if need be. Now, can you match my bet?"

There followed a quick and hushed conversation in French between the four men, one of whom looked Assumptia up and down before shaking his head and saying, "Pas pour moi."

The other three chuckled as they delved into their respective pockets and collectively scraped together three hundred euros. The spokesman nodded towards the reluctant combatant and said, "He doesn't want to take part and so, it's our three hundred against your three hundred but, you lose if you do not manage to beat all three of us. Agreed?"

"Sounds fair," said Assumptia as she rolled up her sleeves.

The non-combatant rose from the table and wished bon chance to all before making his way slowly across the room to join Magdalene.

"Good evening," he said to Magdalene in heavily accented English. "May I join you?"

Magdalene felt herself flush as she took in the man's rough-hewn appearance. He had a shock of thick shiny black hair and was several days unshaven. He wore dark distressed jeans, a white but grubby tee-shirt over which was a red and blue plaid shirt. The man didn't wait for a response but instead sat down close to Magdalene.

"My name is Claude," he said with a smile that revealed a stained and broken front tooth. "Tell me?" he continued. "How could someone so beautiful give themselves up to the church? It fascinates me," he went on not waiting for a response. "Have you ever known a man?"

Magdalene could feel cold beads of perspiration form and trickle down her back and between her small breasts as she fought to regain control of the torrent of conflicting emotions that had suddenly taken control of her basic automotive functions. Finally, she managed, "Well, well, well, there was Father Joseph, I knew him pretty well. He used to take mass every Sunday but sadly he's passed now."

Claude chuckled as he moved even closer to the now openly quivering Magdalene.

"No, my darling, you misunderstand me." He leaned forward and whispered into Magdalene's ear. So close that she could feel the brush of his lips and his warm breath. "Have you ever had a man inside of you?"

There was a sudden loud groan from across the room followed by Assumptia's triumphant declaration, "That's one down and two to go!"

"Inside of my what?" Magdalene giggled nervously.

"Let's go somewhere quiet where I can show you," suggested Claude as he walked his fingers slowly up Magdalene's arm and across her shoulder until his rough hand rested on the back of her neck which he began to massage softly. "You have a room here yes?"

"Well, I'm not sure we should. My sister will worry and she gets angry when she worries."

A collective groan filled the room again, only to be drowned out by another triumphant roar from Assumptia, "Two down and one to go!"

"And," continued Magdalene. "You wouldn't like her when she's angry."

Claude, his lustful intentions firmly focused upon Magdalene, took little or no notice of what was happening elsewhere in the room and instead, slipped his hand from the back of Magdalene's neck to rest upon her bosom.

As Magdalene's eyes and mouth opened wide in astonishment, Claude seized the opportunity to quickly cover her mouth with his own. His thick hot tongue darted into Magdalene's gaping mouth and she almost choked.

It was then that Claude was suddenly and violently pulled away from her and unceremoniously launched through the air to crash through the bar's ornate window and into the street outside.

"Take that ya, dirty bastard!" shouted Assumptia before turning to her sister. "Are you alright, Maggie?"

Magdalene nodded dazedly. "Yes, thank you, Assumptia, I think I'll be fine."

"That's good," smiled Assumptia warmly. "Now, I've got to sort out the other three feckers, I beat them all fair and square and now, they're refusing to pay up."

The three men, who now stood in an uncertain ragged line, cast nervous looks at Assumptia and the broken window through which their friend had disappeared. The fat man from reception who had been behind the bar now tapped furiously at the bar's telephone as Assumptia having acquired two small but heavy wooden stools advanced menacingly with one held in each hand.

"Now, take my advice boys," she offered in a low and threatening growl. "Tuck your greasy heads between your legs and kiss ya arses goodbye!"

With that, Assumptia launched herself at the trio swinging the heavy stools with no more effort than if they were feather pillows. The room was filled with screams and curses as well as the sound of breaking glass and furniture.

"For Eire!" cried Assumptia as she continued her assault.

Magdalene heard the sudden wail of police sirens and saw the blue flashing lights reflected like dancing spectres upon the bar's walls and ceiling. "Assumptia," she screamed uselessly. "We need to get out of here."

But the battle lust was upon Assumptia Malone and she was oblivious to Magdalene's cries as she wrought pain and destruction down with frightening efficiency. The first two policemen who tried to intervene were deftly dispatched, one with an uppercut and the second with a headbutt. This gave those policemen following pause for thought and reinforcements were quickly summoned.

*

Later that night the two sisters sat side by side in a police cell, their eyes still watering from the teargas canister employed by a particularly overzealous police officer.

"Ah, you know, Maggie," said Assumptia dreamily. "Paris isn't such a bad place after all. That was a grand old ding-dong to be sure. You know, I'd go so far as to say that I wouldn't mind coming back," she paused to look at her sister who slouched next to her, the very picture of abject misery. "Is your head hurting again, Maggie?" she asked, her voice soft with concern.

"Why, why do these things always happen to us?" Magdalene sobbed; her voice filled with deep despair. "I really don't know if I can take much more. Things need to change, Assumptia, they really do. I feel like I'm standing on a ledge and there's nothing that'll prevent me from falling," Magdalene sniffed loudly and cuffed at the red tip of her nose.

"I'm beaten, Assumptia and I don't know if I want to go on, even if I could. I need, what I need is a complete rest."

"Well, here's a fine thing and no mistake," Assumptia said as she placed a comforting arm around her sister's shoulder. "Things will get better, Maggie. Once we get out of here, we can shimmy down to Aigurande, collect our cash and everything in the world will be good again. Yes, everything will be as right as rain in the morning."

*

However, despite Assumptia's optimistic predictions, the next morning the two sisters were taken from their cell to appear in court before the local magistrate.

The magistrate, a middle-aged wraith of a man with a stern countenance, listened with increasing incredulity as details of the previous night's carnage were presented. Upon conclusion, he stared with open hostility towards the two sisters. He breathed deeply in through his large nose before directing a harsh barrage towards them.

Assumptia and Magdalene, stood side by side, not understanding a single word but, nonetheless, detecting from the magistrate's manner and tone, that it wasn't complimentary.

They were then led by two officers from the court and escorted to another room where they were eventually joined by their state-appointed advocate.

"Ladies," he said upon entering the room. "I am afraid that the magistrate was not pleased. He has sentenced you both to serve one month's incarceration."

"He has what," began Assumptia, only to be cut off by the advocate.

"Furthermore," he continued., "you are each fined five hundred euros. If you are unable to pay this, a further week will be added to your sentence."

"Oh!" exclaimed Magdalene. "A month. I suppose solitary confinement is out of the question?"

Both Assumptia and the advocate stared at Magdalene, their faces adorned with confusion. The advocate was the first to break the silence, "Pardon, madame, I do not understand."

Magdalene, her spirit strangely restored, smiled at a jest that only she understood. "Never mind, I'm just being foolish," she said. "Now, do you accept credit cards?"

8
Matchmaking

Isabelle had spent the afternoon sitting at her father's bedside. During that time, he had been conscious for just a few minutes before again submitting to the pull of his medication and drifting back into deep unconsciousness. Waiting for the inevitable was becoming increasingly unbearable for her and she felt trapped within the confines of the family home and the quiet town it occupied. Guilty thoughts sometimes trespassed through her head as she wished for the ordeal to soon come to an end.

It was Thursday and she knew that in England, Tom would today be attending his father's funeral. She wondered if his new lodger would be there to comfort him during this troubled time and this thought made her suddenly angry. She cursed and threw a cushion across her room to thud quietly against the wall.

Sighing heavily, she went to her window and gazed outside at the small and empty town square. The day was grey and a light misty drizzle pebbled the window. A church dominated one side of the square and its bell chimed now as it did on the hour, every hour, every day and night of every year.

God, this place is so boring, she thought. At a loss for anything else to do, she decided to take a bath but before doing so, went to fetch a bottle of wine and a glass to keep her company.

When Isabelle finally re-emerged from the bathroom with a towel wrapped around her slim body and another around her head, she found her mother was in her room looking through her wardrobe.

"Mama?" she inquired.

"Ah," exclaimed her mother in satisfaction as she removed a short black dress from the wardrobe. She held the dress up to the light and inspected it before laying it carefully upon Isabelle's bed. "Tonight, I would like you to dress for dinner," her mother said. "It's a special occasion. I always think you look especially beautiful in this dress."

"Mama, what are you up to?" asked Isabelle suspiciously. "What is this special occasion?"

"You will see," replied her mother. "Now, don't be too long."

With that, her mother smiled and left the room.

Isabelle sat down on the bed and puffed out her cheeks. What is going on? She had drunk some wine and was feeling very relaxed, so the thought of sleep was much more appealing than that of the so-called special occasion her mother had suddenly dreamt up.

As if reading her thoughts, Isabelle's mother reappeared together with a pot of coffee and a cup.

"Drink this, it will wake you up."

With that, she quickly turned about and left Isabelle to dress.

Once dressed, Isabelle inspected herself in the mirror concealed upon the inner side of her wardrobe door. She had piled her hair into a retro and now again fashionable and elegant bun on top of her head, allowing a couple of long ringlets to hang loosely to one side of her face. She wore pearl earrings and around her neck, a black choker decorated with a large pearl at its front. She had also chosen black high-heeled shoes to compliment the figure-hugging dress.

I wish Tom could see me right now, she thought. *The poor man would not stand a chance.*

She then frowned as she again wondered what had prompted her mother to ask her to go to so much trouble for dinner.

She decided to check in with Tom before leaving her room and was just about to open the laptop when her mother's voice called from downstairs. "Angel, are you ready? We are all waiting for you."

Sighing, Isabelle put the laptop down and made her way carefully downstairs. Her mother was waiting at the foot of the stairs and behind her, Simone and Lilly stood giggling conspiratorially. As she descended, they all stood back to reveal Jacques. He was wearing an evening suit and stood smiling as he presented Isabelle with a large and beautiful bouquet of red roses.

"You look stunning," he said. "I have booked a table for us at the Grande Chateau, a car is waiting outside."

Isabelle threw a furious glare at her mother, "Mama?"

"It's one night, Angel. It will make a nice change and you and Jacque can reminisce."

Isabelle accepted the proffered bouquet, held them to her nose for a few seconds before passing them to an extremely delighted Lilly.

"Well, Jacques," she said, her attention immediately pulled towards the large and hairy mole that decorated his left cheek. "It appears we have both been manipulated by my conspiring mother and tonight, we are going out on a dinner date."

Jacques smiled broadly.

"Your mother was not alone in this plot and I acknowledge my part in the conspiracy but, if this is what it takes to share some time alone with you, then I would do it all again in a heartbeat."

Isabelle raised an eyebrow as she allowed Jacques to take her hand and lead her out to the waiting car.

9
Dinner for Two

Thursday was Zoe's day off and she'd spent the morning wandering aimlessly from shop to shop in Stratford's Westfield shopping centre. Her thoughts were never too far away from Tom, as she worried about how he would be coping with his father's funeral. He had looked quite glum when he'd left the flat that morning but *then again*, she thought, *it'd be a bit strange if he were to attend his father's funeral with a big smile on his face.*

She had bought herself some new clothes and also some groceries before returning to the flat, together with the ingredients for a special evening meal she had planned for the two of them. *Can't do no harm*, she thought. *And might cheer him up if he needs it.*

Whilst alone in the flat she had been sorely tempted to have a furtive rummage through Isabelle's suitcase. At one point, she had gone so far as to pull the case out from under her bed. She had then stood for several long minutes gazing down at its battered lid before finally, overcoming the urge to peek inside, she had replaced the unopened case back below the bed.

"Bloody stupid of him leaving it here to torment me," she declared to the empty room. "Serve him right if I did have a good old snoop."

Zoe spent the afternoon in the kitchen, where she carefully prepared a beef Stroganov by closely following the recipe she'd found on the back of a packet of sauce mix she'd picked up at a supermarket. Whilst this cooked, she lay the table with meticulous precision, making sure the cutlery was impeccably polished and placed.

Discovering no wine in the house, Zoe made a quick trip to the Off-License, where she purchased two moderately expensive bottles of red wine. She opened one of these bottles to let the wine breathe and then settled down to wait for Tom's return.

After a while, she turned on the television set and watched the early evening game shows. She hadn't expected him to be this late. Once the 6 o'clock news had finished, Zoe decided to help herself to a glass of wine. 7 o'clock came and went and she helped herself to another. She soon became hungry and so decided to start dinner without him.

When Tom finally walked through the door at eight-fifteen, he found Zoe slouched at the dining room table, her face resting on a plate containing, what appeared to be, the remnants of a half-eaten beef Stroganov. Tom righted the empty wine glass that lay on the tabletop before picking up and examining the label of the empty wine bottle. "Fourteen per cent, that'd do it," he said.

On further examination, he spotted the price label that still protruded from the collar of Zoe's blouse. "Shopping too, you have been busy."

Tom gently manoeuvred Zoe away from the congealed beef Stroganov and used one of the neatly folded napkins, she had so carefully prepared, to wipe the goo from her face.

"I guess we should both be thankful that you've stopped plastering yourself in makeup," he murmured to his unconscious lodger.

That task completed; he lifted her into his arms. Zoe let out a low slurred complaint as he carried her to her room, where he gently placed her on the bed. He took off her shoes, rolled her onto her side and then pulled the duvet over her. He then went to the kitchen before returning with a plastic bowl which he placed beside the bed. He also left a hand towel and a large glass of water on her bedside table.

"Goodnight, Zoe. God bless," he said as he left the room, quietly closing the door behind him. He then headed back to the kitchen. The kitchen looked like it had been hit by a bomb and Tom took a few seconds to assess the carnage before deciding where he should begin the clean-up operation.

"First things first," he said to himself, before heading to his room to change out of his black suit and into a tee shirt and jogging bottoms. He then tried to contact Isabelle. He pulled out his tablet and made the call but there was no response. He waited a few minutes and tried again but with the same result.

Deciding to try one more time once the clean-up operation had been completed, he headed back to the kitchen.

10
The Proposal

The Grande Chateau was what the restaurant and hotel had once been but that was many, many years before. Now, it was an extremely nice venue, which people generally reserved for special occasions, such as engagement and wedding parties, significant birthdays and perhaps a secret rendezvous with their lovers.

Isabelle and Jacques sat at a candle-lit table, within the superbly elegant dining room, a nearly full bottle of fine Champagne chilling in the ice bucket beside them. The air was filled with a faint ethereal music, which subtly masked the soft chatter of the restaurant's other guests. Above them, large ornate chandeliers produce a soft warm glow that allowed the uniformed waiters and waitresses enough light to pay close attention to the needs of their guests, without ever intruding upon their intimacy.

"You haven't eaten much," observed Jacques. "Is the food not to your liking?"

Isabelle glanced up at the long hairs protruding from the mole upon Jacques' face. "I'm sure the food is fine, Jacques, I'm just not hungry."

Jacques nodded thoughtfully. "Would you like some more champagne?"

"No," replied Isabelle. "I haven't yet started on the first glass."

Jacques placed the index finger of his left hand to his mouth and nibbled at its tip, whilst drumming the fingers of his right hand on the tabletop. He stared intently at Isabelle before breaking into a warm smile.

"You have always been a difficult one to impress," he laughed. "I remember, all the boys at school wanting to be seen out with you but you were not interested in anyone."

"Not according to my mother," whispered Isabelle under her breath.

"Pardon?"

"No, it's nothing. Just something my mother mentioned when I first arrived home from Italy."

On impulse, Jacques reached across the table and took both of Isabelle's hand in his own. "Isabelle, I adore you. I have always adored you. I know you feel the same about me, you must because I often catch you staring at me."

This final comment made Isabelle's face crinkle in thought and then, the horrible truth suddenly dawned on her. "That bloody hairy mole."

"Pardon?"

"No, nothing, Jacques. A thought suddenly occurred to me." Isabelle cleared her throat awkwardly. "It's very flattering, Jacques, but I am sorry, I would like you as a friend but I am not looking for a new relationship at the moment."

She tried to retract her hands from Jacques' grasp but his hold became firmer. "We can take things slowly to begin with Isabelle. I am wealthy, I have a nice house and you," he looked from her face to her breasts and then back again. "You have everything that I have ever wanted," he said pleadingly.

Isabelle's brow wrinkled again as she applied some additional effort and finally managed to free her hands from his grasp. The whole situation was bizarre and she had an uncomfortable feeling that more was possibly planned and if her intuition was correct, it would probably be better for both of them, if it could be avoided.

"Excuse me a moment please, Jacques, I need to use the bathroom."

With this, she stood and left the dining room. As soon as she was out of sight, Isabelle changed direction and headed for the hotel's reception. When she arrived, she asked one of the receptionists to call a taxi and then, on impulse, she asked whether a Jacques Lamont had reserved a room at the hotel for that night. The receptionist consulted her screen for a few seconds before confirming, "Yes, madame, Mister Lamont has booked the bridal suite. Do you still require a taxi?"

"Thank you, immediately please," Isabelle said angrily before turning to make her way back to the dining room.

Jacques rose and smiled as he watched Isabelle's return. When she was no more than a few feet away, he fell to one knee and produced a small black box from his jacket pocket. This he opened to reveal a sparkling diamond ring. There was a hushed gasp of anticipation as the restaurant's other guests and staff realised the significance of the spectacle unfolding before them.

"Isabelle, ma chérie," declared Jacques. "Will you marry me?"

Without answering, Isabelle lifted the champagne bottle from the ice bucket and amidst the hiss of indrawn breath from those watching, slowly emptied its bubbling contents over Jacques upturned face.

"There is your answer, Jacques," she said sounding calmer than she felt inside. She then turned and walked with slow elegance towards the restaurant's exit.

One guest, a man who was obviously a little worse for wear, stood up and began to clap his hands in appreciation before being hushed into silence and dragged back into his chair by his partner.

*

When Isabelle arrived home, her mother could not hide her astonishment. "You are back!" she announced in surprise. "Where's Jacques?"

Isabelle ignored her and went immediately to her room, placing a chair against its door to prevent any further access.

She immediately grabbed the laptop and noticed she'd already missed two calls from Tom and so, without further delay, she directed the cursor to Tom's number and clicked. His face appeared on the screen after just a few moments. "Hello, Tommy, how was your day, did everything go OK?"

"You look stunning," replied Tom. "What's the occasion?"

Isabelle considered whether or not she should tell Tom of her mother's deviousness but then, on compulsion, blurted out, "Jacques has asked me to marry him." She then began to cry and to laugh at the same time. "Oh God, Tom, I miss you so much. It was horrible!"

Tom listened silently as Isabelle told of that evening's events and how she had been coerced into dinner with Jacques, her discovery of the room booking and of her revenge.

"Wow," said Tom when she'd finally finished. "Remind me never to get on the wrong side of you. Didn't think of letting him down gently then?"

"No, I was too angry. How dare he and how dare mama!"

"Well, it sounds like my day was much quieter than yours. The funeral went about as well as these things can go. It's strange really, he was my dad and I loved him but I never really knew him. I guess that's the way with parents. Anyway, my mother endured the day with supreme dignity, which is more than can be said for his step-family. A gaggle of women who made a complete show of themselves. Very embarrassing. The positive thing about funerals," he said with a smile. "Is that you get to see people that you've not seen in years and so, I didn't get home until much later than I'd intended."

"Was the lodger waiting up for you?"

Tom was warned to tread carefully as he detected the change of tone in Isabelle's voice.

"No, she was asleep when I arrived home," he said easily. "I guess that's how she likes to spend her days off work."

"What are you doing tomorrow?" she asked.

"I have to go into the office to sort a few things out. Pick up my travel itinerary, tickets, ESTA and case papers. Then, when I get home, I'll have to pack. I'm actually looking forward to getting away for a while," he said.

"I feel the same," she replied.

"Sorry, I should have asked before. How is your dad?"

"The same. The waiting is awful and if something doesn't happen soon, then I may marry Jacques just to break the monotony!"

They both laughed at that. Their call went on late into the night before they signed off in their now usual fashion, by kissing their respective screens.

*

Isabelle woke in a sudden panic. She had dreamt of Luca and now, her heart pounded as she stared fearfully around her bedroom. As realisation dawned, she relaxed a little but her thoughts were nonetheless, left clouded with apprehension and anxiety. Deciding she needed to clear her head, she quickly dressed and went for an early morning walk through the town and down to the river, which flowed languidly at the foot of the hill upon which Aigurande sat.

She stood for a while at the river's edge and watched as its dark and restless waters flowed past. She wondered at the strange twists and turns her life had recently taken and for the first time, considered whether or not her mother could actually be right and perhaps, she should settle down here, in the peace and safety of the quiet French countryside. She could marry, raise a family and be content just to watch them grow.

Isabelle turned and slowly began to walk along the river's bank, following its course eastward. She thought of Tom, a man she had known for just a few weeks and knew practically nothing about. He had helped her to escape from Luca and in doing so, had placed himself in considerable danger but why?

Perhaps like her, he too was caught in life's turbulent waters and did not know whether he would drown or be washed up somewhere. She smiled at the thought, the uncertainty didn't seem to bother Tom too much, he seemed happy just to be washed along.

She wanted to be with Tom but at the same time, she was scared. The association between Tom and her past was uncomfortable and she would sooner not be reminded of the violence and chaos of her final days in Rome. But that was not Tom's fault, she reasoned. Perhaps if she and Tom built something together, the memories of how they had begun would fade, as would the fear she still felt.

Isabelle sighed, the world was full of ifs and maybes and hindsight alone would be the eventual judge. Her thoughts then turned to Jacques and she shuddered involuntarily. Why did he not get that mole removed? This thought made her laugh out loud and her mood brightened a little. What was her mother thinking? Isabelle and Jacques had never been that close.

Prior to the previous evening, they had never been on a date. He was simply a boy she had gone to school with. Ah, his mother! That must be it, Isabelle and Jacques' mothers must have conspired together.

"Poor Jacques," she said to herself. "We are both being manipulated by conniving mothers."

Isabelle continued to follow the river's course for several miles before turning southwest to head back in the general direction of Aigurande. Her homeward journey took her through dense woodland that eventually gave way to open fields. She cut across the fields and headed towards the church steeple, which she could now see in the far distance.

When she finally arrived back home, she made herself a breakfast of bread and jam, which she washed down with some freshly brewed coffee. She then made her way to her father's room and was surprised and delighted to see him sitting up in bed and conversing with his wife. Her father beamed a smile at her when Isabelle appeared at the door. In contrast, her mother rose stiffly, pecked her husband's cheek and left the room without a word.

"Oh dear, Issi," her father laughed weakly. "Have you and mama been locking horns again?"

Isabelle approached the bed happily and kissed her father before reoccupying the seat her mother had just vacated. “Papa, you are looking so well today,” she declared honestly.

“Yes, I am feeling much better today but I fear it may be the calm that precedes the storm. Never mind, we live for today. So tell me, what has been going on between you and your mother?”

Isabelle told of her mother’s matchmaking attempts and how she had discovered Jacques’s hopeful plan to lure her into a room in the Grand Chateau.

“Well,” bubbled her father, “you cannot blame the boy for trying but if I were ten years younger, I’d be giving him a flogging right now. Still, your mother should not have done this. Her intentions are doubtless good but—ah, she’ll not change her ways now.”

“I know, papa, but it just makes me so angry.”

“And your mother also tells me,” continued her father. “There’s an English boy waiting for you. Who is he and how did you meet him?”

Isabelle told her father of her time in Italy, of Luca and his subsequent violence towards her. Her chance encounter with Tom at the hospital. Tom’s search for his dead father’s lost love and of their adventure, culminating in her escape from Luca.

During her retelling of the story, she noticed her father drift into sleep but she continued, finding strange comfort in recounting that episode of her life and in doing so, hopefully bringing it to a closure. When she’d finished, she stood up, kissed her father’s cheek and went quietly to her room.

Isabelle turned on the television set in her room in time to catch the end of the afternoon news bulletin, which included the strange story of two nuns causing a violent disturbance in the backstreets of a Paris suburb. They had been arrested following the fracas and despite being sentenced to one month’s imprisonment, were unlikely to serve the full term of their sentence.

C’est très bizarre, she thought. *The world has gone completely crazy.*

11
Legal Dealings and Backroom Antics

The offices of Church, Maypole and McTavish, occupied the first three floors of an eight-storied office building situated in the centre of Tampa. The office's large boardroom with its highly polished table capable of comfortably seating twenty-four was occupied by just three people. Horace Pasternak sat on one side of the table whilst the other side was occupied by Senior Partner George Church, together with his legal assistant Emily Rudd.

George Church had grey hair and a grey goatee beard. He was about fifty years of age and whilst slim, his face bore the rugged redness of a heavy drinker. Emily was much younger, she had dark almost black hair that she wore in a long bob style. She was painfully thin and extremely pale, apart from her nose, which was perpetually red.

"How bad is it?" Horace asked whilst shifting his large bulk uncomfortably.

"Well," George replied slowly. "Had we known the truth from day one, we would never have accepted the case. Leastways, we would never have accepted the case on a contingency basis."

George was referring to the agreement concluded between Horace and Church, Maypole and McTavish, under which Horace would pay no upfront fees but instead would cede thirty per cent of any subsequent monetary award achieved by his legal representatives.

"Why, what's wrong?" Horace asked in feigned innocence.

"What's wrong, Mister Pasternak," replied George. "Is that it's as clear as the nose on your face that you either arranged for this fire to be started or that you started it yourself. I'm not really interested in which one it was but based upon the evidence that the insurance company has, we'd have to have a jury of complete fucking idiots to win this case."

Emily gave a loud wet sniff. "The evidence is rather compelling, Mister Pasternak," she said.

Horace let out a loud heavy sigh as he pushed himself and his chair back. "So, are you pulling out?" he asked nervously.

"Fuck no," said George. "We've invested too much time, effort and money in this case already. But—" George concluded with a sad and weary shake of his head.

"But what?" asked Horace eagerly.

"We'll have to throw everything we can at this," George continued. "We need experts, experts with credibility. Enough credibility to sow doubt upon every shred of evidence they have. We've got to fight dirty, real dirty and that my friend costs money."

"What Mister Church is saying," sniffed Emily. "Is that if we are to continue, we shall need to review the contingency arrangements." She finished this sentence by blowing her nose into a large paper handkerchief.

Horace appeared to be disappearing into himself as he looked anxiously at Mister Church and asked; "What do you have in mind?"

"Fifty per cent," George responded without hesitation.

Horace was incredulous. "You want half of everything?"

"Take your time to think about this, Mister Pasternak," said George. "Don't accept my word on this. Go ask any other law office, there're more than enough firms right here in Tampa."

"But the trial starts next week," moaned Horace miserably.

"True," said George.

"I have the papers right here for you to sign, Mister Pasternak," sniffed Emily as she passed the new contingency agreement to Horace and handed him a pen. "Sign right there," she indicated with a skinny white finger.

Left with no option, Horace took the pen and angrily signed the agreement.

"A very wise decision, Mister Pasternak," said George. "Don't lose faith, we'll do the very best we can and if we win, well, you'll be a very rich man."

Emily sneezed, blew her nose and sniffed. "Let me show you out, Mister Pasternak," she said.

*

Roxy sat in the car awaiting Horace's return. As Horace approached, he noticed she was talking through the unwound window of the car to a young pedestrian. He was tall and athletically built and he smiled down at Roxy as she blew him a kiss. When he noticed Horace approaching, he quickly turned and walked off in the opposite direction.

"Who was that?" asked Horace suspiciously as he climbed into the automobile.

"Who are you talking about, Horri?"

"The young guy."

"Oh, Horri, I do love it when you get a little jealous," said Roxy whilst giving Horace her most beguiling smile. "That was Frankie from the grocery store. I was just telling him that I'll be shooting by later to pick up some stuff for our dinner."

Horace huffed as he started the car, checked his mirrors, indicated and pulled away from the sidewalk. "You seem a little grumpy," observed Roxy. "Everything still going as planned?"

"Everything's just swell," Horace replied. "Couldn't be better, we're on the home run."

When they arrived back at the condominium, Horace got out of the car but Roxy shifted from her seat and took over the driving position.

"What are you doing?" inquired Horace.

Roxy looked up at him and smiled. "Go and make yourself comfortable, Horri, I've decided to go pick up the groceries right now."

She held out her hand palm upward and Horace obediently dropped the keys into it.

"See you later alligator," she piped as she gunned the engine and sped off in the direction of the freeway.

Horace watched her disappear into the distance before turning to make his way up to their apartment. It was then that he remembered that the key to their apartment was on the same ring as the car key he'd just given to Roxy. "God damn it, could this day get any worse!"

*

The backroom of the grocery store was dark, cool and filled with stock. It was also filled with Frankie's heavy breathing and the sound of Roxy's excited gasps and moans.

"God, this is so good, Missus Pasternak," groaned Frankie as he pumped at Roxy with increasing intensity.

"Sure is," gasped Roxy who was pinned against the room's rear wall with her long legs wrapped tightly around Frankie's athletic naked hips. "Oh Frankie, Frankie, Frankie," she squealed in increasing ecstasy.

"Yes, Missus Pasternak?" Frankie gasped.

Roxy gasp and held her breath for several long seconds before sighing contentedly. "Frankie, you really are quite good at this, aren't you," she breathed as the passion of their lovemaking ebbed away. She leaned back and looked at the young man affectionately as she ran her fingers through his thick dark hair. "Now, Frankie, please don't let me leave here without taking something nice home for Horace's dinner."

*

Later that day, Horace and Roxy sat in front of the television, each balancing a tray on their laps upon which sat their evening meal of chicken and green salad. Roxy gazed intently at the television screen as she ate, whilst Horace, looked miserably down at the cold pre-cooked chicken salad, which he poked and prodded sadly with his fork.

"Why do we have to eat the same damn stuff every day," Horace complained.

Roxy turned to look at her unhappy husband. "It's good for you, Horri," she said. "And you still need to lose a few pounds."

"But this," he said holding up a limp lettuce leaf, "it's making me depressed."

Roxy sighed loudly. "OK, Horri, I get your point. Tomorrow, I'll pick up something different from the grocery store," she looked thoughtful. "Maybe meatballs. Now, eat your chicken."

"Meatballs?" inquired Horri with sudden interest.

"Yeah," replied Roxy between slow chews. "If it makes you happy, I'll get you some meatballs."

"Worth a try I guess," said Horace, a little mollified by the prospect of a dinner that didn't consist of cold pre-cooked chicken and green salad. "Maybe even a pizza, I like it real hot and spicy. The hotter the better."

Roxy, still chewing slowly, turned to gaze dolefully at her husband. "You and me both, Horri, you and me both," she said wistfully.

"Sorry?"

"Nothing, now just eat your chicken and let me watch the rest of the show in peace."

12
A Flight of Fancy

It was early on Saturday morning and Tom was sitting in his living room with his two travel bags, waiting for the taxi to arrive and take him to the airport. His mobile eventually pinged to let him know that the taxi had arrived and so he climbed to his feet and hoisted his rucker across his shoulder and lifted his suitcase.

He wondered, not for the first time, whether he should disturb Zoe and let her know he was leaving when suddenly, the door to her room opened and she emerged. She was still in her pyjamas and to Tom, she looked a little vulnerable and sad.

"Good morning, Zoe," he said uncertainly. "I was hoping I'd see you before I left but didn't want to wake you. Hey, you look a little sad, is everything alright?"

Zoe looked up at him before abruptly rushing down the hallway towards him and throwing her arms around his neck. What with the rucker and the suitcase, Tom almost folded under the soft and unexpected impact of Zoe's embrace.

"Hey, Zoe," he began but was suddenly stopped as her warm mouth pressed tightly against his lips. It was then that time stopped and they both stood frozen together, mouth to mouth and unmoving, as if waiting for a starting pistol to signal the beginning of a passionate snog-a-thon. After what seemed an eternity but was probably no more than a few seconds, the moment ended and they both stepped back.

"Bye then, Tom," Zoe said with a weak smile. "Safe travels and all that."

"Bye, Zoe," Tom replied slowly.

With that, Zoe turned around and walked back to her room without so much as a backward glance.

Tom's mobile pinged again, breaking the spell that Zoe's actions had placed upon him, a spell that had left him both dazed and confused. He looked from her bedroom door to the front door and back again before finally turning and making his way downstairs to the waiting taxi.

Now, as he sat in his large business class window seat aboard the outbound Tampa flight, thoughts of the Zoe incident continued to gnaw away at him. A small part of him was flattered that an attractive and younger woman was seemingly attracted to him but, his rational side knew that, should he decide to take matters forward with Zoe, it would ultimately be doomed to disaster. And then there was Isabelle?

Despite and in retaliation to his nagging conscience, Tom smiled conceitedly to himself as he thought back to the love drought he'd been experiencing just a few short weeks earlier.

"Never rains but it pours," he said out loud.

"Sorry, sir, did you say something?"

The stewardess assigned to Tom's section of the cabin was carrying out her duties with barely disguised petulance. Tom had overheard the young woman complain bitterly to her colleagues that she had been called in at short notice and that she was less than happy about losing her weekend off. She now fixed Tom with a hard look as she waited for his response.

Tom removed the headphones he was wearing and looked up at the vexed stewardess and smiled.

"May I please have a bourbon and coke," he said.

This request was received with ill-grace but any annoyance on Tom's part quickly evaporated when she returned with four miniature bottles of Jack Daniels, a tin of cola and an ice-filled glass.

"Let me know when you're finished and I'll bring you some more," she said with a quick cold smile, her voice edged with sarcasm. "Sorry about the snorer but you can always try turning up the volume on your headphones."

With that, she turned smartly and departed.

The snorer was an elderly and comfortably plump Asian lady in a colourful sari, who had mysteriously appeared about an hour or so into the flight and who now occupied the seat next to Tom's. The seat had, much to Tom's delight, been empty since take-off and so, although he smiled at the lady when she'd arrived, he was nonetheless disappointed to now have someone in close proximity.

Tom cracked open two bottles of bourbon and poured their amber contents over the ice. He frowned as he considered whether or not he should now ask Zoe to find alternative accommodation prior to his return to London. He knew that he probably should but he also knew that he definitely wouldn't.

He was just about to delve deeper into what lay behind his reluctance to send Zoe packing when the Asian lady awkwardly shifted her position and in the process, released a long, slow and high-pitched emission. Her exhaust fumes were heavily noxious, causing Tom to screw up his face in disgust. He glanced across at the Asian lady and was surprised to see that she was now awake and staring at him accusingly, her face a picture of repugnance.

"What are you looking at me for?" he asked indignantly.

The lady responded with a disappointed shake of the head before raising her seat back into its sitting position. She then got up and left. Unfortunately, she didn't take all of her stuff with her and Tom had to adjust the overhead air conditioning nozzle to provide a full cold blast of fresh air.

Tom finished the bourbon and opened the other two bottles before flicking on a movie about a warhorse. It was then that a small Asian boy arrived to occupy the seat that the woman had vacated a few minutes earlier. The boy, who Tom guessed was about ten years old, sat quietly as he watched something on the screen in front of him.

The sullen stewardess made a reappearance and cleared away the four empty bourbon bottles from Tom's table and replaced them with four more. She never said a word during the course of this transaction and Tom looked at her thoughtfully as she made her way back to the aircraft's galley. He saw that the young boy was staring at him and so, Tom gifted him with a friendly smile before cracking open another two bottles and pouring them into the fresh glass of ice provided by the stewardess.

"Cheers," he slurred at the boy before returning to the movie about the horse.

Sometime later, Tom felt a small hand tugging urgently at his sleeve and so, he turned to look enquiringly into the concerned face of the young boy. It was then that Tom realised that he'd been crying.

"Oh, I'm so sorry," he said to the boy as he gratefully accepted the paper hanky that the boy held out in his direction.

"I don't usually cry." The boy then handed Tom a bottle of water.

"Then why are you crying now?" he asked.

"That, my new young friend, is a very good question."

The boy continued to stare sadly at Tom. "Perhaps, you are drinking too much. It is not good if it makes you sad."

"You're very wise for a young fellow."

"Or perhaps you are sad already and that is why you are drinking so much. My father also likes to drink. When he is happy, drinking makes him happier and when he is sad, it doesn't make him so happy."

"Thank you, I'll bear that in mind."

"So, why are you crying?"

Tom wiped his eyes and sniffed, "I don't really know. I guess I've been having a tough time lately and now I'm feeling well, I think I'm feeling a little bit lost."

Tom was, by nature, a very private person and usually found it difficult to disclose his feelings, especially to a complete stranger.

"What do you mean lost. Do you not know where you are or where you are going?"

"Another very good question," Tom sniffed again. "And, it gets better the more I think about it."

"When my father is sad, my mother says it is because he keeps too much inside and that he must open his doors. This, I don't really understand because only buildings have doors and I don't know why opening the doors in your house will make you happy."

"I believe your mother is being figurative."

The young boy thought about this for a few seconds before responding, "What is figurative?"

Tom huffed. "Well, I guess that your mother is being symbolic by describing your father as a house that perhaps has too much furniture inside. Because it has too much furniture inside, there is no longer enough free space to move about happily and so, some of the furniture needs to be removed. If you are going to remove some of the furniture from the house, then you must first open the doors of the house to get the furniture out."

"I see," the boy said thoughtfully. "Perhaps you also need to remove some furniture?"

Tom breathed in deeply through his nose and sighed, "I wouldn't know where to begin."

The boy screwed up his small face. "Well, I think that is easy," he said. "We all start at the beginning and so, you must go to the start and begin from there."

Tom laughed. "Well, I don't want to start at the very beginning because this flight just isn't long enough but let's just rewind a few weeks and start from there."

"Yes, please," the boy said seriously.

And so, Tom relaxed into his seat and began to recount the story of his father's last wish and everything that had transpired since. The young Asian boy slouched quietly in his seat with his hands resting entwined upon his small stomach, the very picture of a sage old man.

When Tom eventually reached the story's conclusion, he was very tired and had a thumping headache, which he thought was probably alcohol induced.

"Well, that's about it really," he said as he turned his head to look at the boy, only to find that the seat next to him was empty.

13
A Declaration of War!

Zoe's face crumpled as soon as she'd turned her back on Tom but she somehow managed to hide her emotions until she had made it back to her room. As soon as she closed the door behind her she fell into a heap and began to sob. She heard the front door close as Tom left and then quietly screamed out her embarrassment and confusion, "Stupid, stupid, stupid, stupid cow! What did you think he would do? Bloody stupid, idiotic cow!"

She sat crumpled by her bedroom door for a long time until she became aware of a scratching sound coming from somewhere behind the skirting boards. Since moving into Tom's flat, she'd heard the scratching sound a couple of times before but couldn't identify what it was or where it was coming from. Now, with her attention focused on the scratching, she started to crawl towards its source but when she was just a few feet away, the scratching stopped.

"Shit," she whispered. Zoe waited quietly on all fours for several minutes but the scratching never returned. She was about to climb to her feet when she again noticed Isabelle's suitcase under the bed. She reached out, grabbed its handle and pulled the suitcase towards her.

"Have a rummage girl," she said to herself. "That'll cheer you up."

She lifted the case onto the bed and was just about to spring its latches when she realised, she needed to pee. "First things first," she said as she padded out of her room and into the bathroom.

Despite being alone in the flat, through force of habit, she closed the bathroom door behind her before dropping her pyjama bottoms and sitting down on the toilet.

She sat in the quiet peace of her surroundings and stared aimlessly and unfocused at the closed bathroom door, as she waited for her piddle to end. Then, without warning, a small grey creature suddenly zoomed with amazing speed from under the bathroom door, to whizz between Zoe's legs and disappear behind the toilet.

Zoe leapt up and screamed before jumping, her legs constricted by her pyjama bottoms, kangaroo-like, out of the bathroom and back to her bedroom. There, she pulled her bottoms up before again picking up the suitcase and replacing it under the bed.

"OK mister mouse," she declared. "This means war!"

Having carefully checked the bathroom before taking a shower, a refocussed Zoe quickly dressed before leaving the flat to head for the shops. If she was going to war with mouse-kind, she needed suitable weaponry.

"Give me tools and I will do the job," she said, in Churchillian mimicry, as she made her way towards the local hardware store.

14
Coming to America

The in-flight announcement of the aircraft's approach to Tampa pulled Tom reluctantly from the most peaceful and reinvigorating sleep he'd enjoyed for a very long time. He continued to scan his fellow passengers as he made his way off the aircraft and through immigration but, he saw no further evidence of the young Asian boy nor, of his malodourous forerunner.

It was raining when Tom arrived in the sunshine state. His friend and Mallory's legal representative in the Pasternak case was waiting for him at the airport.

"Hey, Tom," said Joe in greeting. "How was your flight?"

Joe Becker was originally from New York but now resided with his wife and family in St Petersburg, Florida or St Pete's as it is known locally. Joe was a smiling and witty individual who liked to play the sympathy card. At least that's what Tom thought, for he could see no other reason why Joe was, at times, so self-deprecating.

As a young man, Joe had played tennis to a pretty high level but as he got older, his stature did not develop to the proportions required to be a success in the modern game. So, whilst remaining a keen tennis enthusiast, he became a lawyer. Joe now worked almost exclusively for those Lloyd's syndicates who still took risks within Florida's extremely litigious borders.

"Hi, Joe, good to see you," replied Tom as he climbed into the front passenger seat of Joe's SUV. "The flight was pretty good albeit a bit odd."

Joe looked at him enquiringly. "What, did they run out of booze or something?"

Tom laughed. "No, quite the opposite, they couldn't give me enough of it. In fact, I think they gave me too much and I had the weirdest dream. Well, at least I think it was a dream. There was this young Asian boy."

"Stop right there!" Joe interrupted. "Listen, what you get up to in your own time is your business but I really don't want to hear about it."

Tom laughed again. "Yeah, come to think of it, that did sound pretty bad."

"I'll say," sniggered Joe.

"OK, Joe, being serious now, are we all set for Monday?"

Joe smiled. "I cannot wait, this is the strongest insurance fraud case I've ever seen. There's no way, well, I say there's no way but it's possible I guess but it'd be just plain crazy if we lost this case. No, we're definitely going to win, without a shadow of a doubt."

Tom looked at Joe dubiously as he pulled his phone from his pocket and turned it back on. Changing the subject he asked, "What's happening with the weather, did you arrange for the rain so I'd feel more at home?"

Joe had negotiated the vehicle out of the airport and they were now joining the freeway.

"It's been bad for the last couple of days but it'll improve. We're heading to downtown Tampa. I've booked us into a hotel that's only a few blocks walk from the federal court building. It's called The Retreat. It's not the best but it's convenient."

"I hope it's a bit more than convenient," said Tom as he read the welcoming texts that pinged up on his phone. "It looks like I'll be staying here for three weeks and so a bit of luxury wouldn't go amiss."

"Don't worry, it's fine and anyway, I've arranged for you to stay at the Vinoy in St Pete's at the weekends."

"Cool, why are you staying at the Retreat, what is it, a twenty-minute drive from where you live?"

"I need to be one hundred per cent focused on this case. No distractions and anyway, we have our expert witnesses staying there too."

"All staying at the Retreat?" asked Tom.

"Yeah," replied Joe. "Not for the duration and not all at the same time but yeah, it's convenient and it's cheap."

Tom looked at Joe suspiciously. "How cheap, Joe?"

Joe glanced at Tom and smiled. "Don't worry, I mean, how bad can it be?"

"Is this hotel part of that chain of hotels that you collect points with?"

"Yeah, so what?"

"So," continued Tom, "You've booked us and all of our expert witnesses into some dodgy hotel for three weeks at my company's expense, just so you can collect enough points to go on holiday next year?"

"Like I said," replied Joe, who now adopted a tone that suggested his feelings were being unjustly hurt. "It's convenient and it's only you and I who are there for the duration."

Tom was about to respond to Joe's unconvincing excuse when his phone pinged once more. It was a text from Isabelle.

"Oh, shit," said Tom as he read the text.

"Hey, what's up? It's not the Asian boy is it, wanting to know when you guys are going to hook up again?" Joe asked with a snigger—

"It's my girlfriend. Her father has just died."

"Crap, I'm sorry," Joe said as the grin fell from his face. "Do you need to call her?"

"I'll give her a call when we get to the hotel," said Tom whilst texting a quick response.

SO SORRY, ISSI. WILL CALL YOU AS SOON AS I CAN. XXX

They had now left the freeway and were travelling through Tampa. The sky was low and grey and the streets were quiet and rain-paved. The SUV stopped at an intersection and as Joe waited for the red light to change, Tom's attention was caught by a group of five middle-aged vagrants, who pushed and jostled each other in a dispute important only to them and their booze and drug fuddled minds.

One of the vagrants fell slowly and heavily backwards, like a tree being felled. He lay motionless on the wet sidewalk for several long seconds before trying unsuccessfully to climb to his feet. *God, this is grim*, thought Tom. *I really hope we're not staying anywhere near here.*

The traffic lights then changed and Joe directed the SUV across the intersection before veering sharply left to pull up outside of a cream-coloured six-story building, the sign above its entranceway identifying it as The Retreat.

"Joe? Please tell me this is a joke?"

"Don't be too quick to judge," Joe responded in mock irritation. "Let's get the cases out of the trunk and into the dry. I need to park the car in the lot opposite."

The lot opposite was surrounded by a twelve-foot-high chain wire fence. "It'll be safe there," said Joe.

Temporarily lost for words, Tom removed his case from the back of the car and made his way into the Retreat. The reception area was small, unimpressive and busy.

"Why does it smell of wet dog in here?" asked Tom.

"They allow pets," answered Joe. "And it's raining outside," he continued unnecessarily.

"Joe, did I ever tell you that I'm allergic to animal hairs?"

This information was greeted with a look from Joe that suggested that he believed Tom's latest complaint was far from true, which, unfortunately, it wasn't.

During the check-in process and mindful of the expected duration of his stay, Tom enquired about the hotel's laundry services. The harassed man who had taken charge of booking them in nodded to his left, "There's a machine just down the hallway."

"I wasn't contemplating doing my own laundry," Tom said in shocked surprise.

The harassed check-in clerk quickly glanced up at Tom, a world-weary and condescending expression showing clearly on his thin face. "Yeah, life's just full of disappointments, isn't it, sir?"

Tom threw an angry look at Joe, which Joe returned with a wicked grin; "Don't worry, Mister Harrison, we'll sort something out."

Tom collected the keycard to his room, which was situated on the sixth floor and made his way towards the elevators.

"I'll meet you back down here at seven," Joe called after him. "We'll go grab a bite to eat."

Tom pushed open the heavy brown door to his room and stepped inside. The room was gloomy with a dark red carpet and a red patterned wallpaper. The furniture looked old and Tom was sure he'd seen better in charity shops and second-hand stores. To his left was a small kitchenette, with a cooker, fridge freezer and microwave. In front of him was a small dining table with four chairs. A telephone sat on the table.

Next, there was a tired looking sofa, also red and patterned. This sat in front of a television, which was switched on but instead of displaying a welcome message, it was showing a vintage cowboy series that Tom recognised from his childhood as Bonanza.

Tom put his case down and closed the door. He went over to the television set, picked up the remote control and turned the television off. As he did so, he heard the television in the adjoining bedroom spring into life and so, went to investigate. Tom was pleased to note that the bed was a king-sized. The television was situated in a corner of the bedroom so as to allow the guests to comfortably watch it whilst in bed. It was showing Bonanza and so Tom grabbed the television's remote control, which he'd spotted on the bedside table and switched the telly off.

As he did so, the television in the adjoining lounge area again sprung into life, the signature tune of Bonanza loudly announcing the start of another episode. Tom undertook the same exercise several times but could not find a way to turn off one television without turning the other one on. So, tired and frustrated, he decided to unplug both televisions. It was then that he discovered that the wiring for both had been boxed in.

"No, this can't be right," he said out loud.

Sighing, Tom gave up and decided to call Isabelle. He would then unpack, after which, he'd hopefully get a little rest before meeting Joe at seven. He'd try tackling the televisions again later but for now, he turned the volume down as far as it would go which, unfortunately, didn't result in complete silence and Tom could still clearly hear the vintage plots unfold. He nodded, maybe not such a bad thing, it might give his mind something else to focus upon other than the Pasternak case or even, some of his more personal concerns.

Tom retrieved his tablet from the small rucker, he used to carry his important items when travelling. He went through to the bedroom where he sat on the bed and was relieved to find that the hotel internet provided a strong signal and so, he logged in and dialled Isabelle. He hadn't known what to expect and so was apprehensive in his greeting when her face appeared on his screen.

"Hello, Issi."

"Hello, Tom," she greeted him with a weak smile. "So, you arrived safely. How was the flight?"

"Everything is fine, Issi, how are you bearing up?"

"To be honest, Tom, it's a relief. I know that makes me sound wicked but it was horrible to see him so ill." She gave a sudden agonised gasp and started to quietly cry, "I'm sorry, Tom, I can't do this right now, I must go."

"OK, Issi," Tom began but the screen went blank as Isabelle ended the call. Tom turned off the tablet and lay back on the bed. He felt guilty about not being with her and he felt sad. He wondered whether there was anything else he should try to do to help but couldn't think of anything.

After a while, Tom's thoughts returned to Zoe and the strange event that had taken place just before he'd left for the airport. He hadn't seen Zoe on Friday as he'd left for work early and she still hadn't resurfaced. Zoe worked the late shift at the Good Samaritan on Friday and so, he was already in bed when she'd arrived home. Why hadn't he waited for the taxi outside?

Tom chewed his lip as he again agonised about how he should deal with the unforeseen event that had unfolded that morning. Perhaps he should phone Zoe now, just to clear the air or perhaps he shouldn't.

15
The Gun

Horace placed the black automatic pistol on the kitchen table. He sat and stared down at it, mesmerised by its oily dark sheen. He then quickly snatched it up and aimed it at the kitchen's white wall.

"Go ahead, punk, make my day," he mimicked before squeezing the trigger. He smiled as he heard the satisfying metallic snap of the pistol's hammer. He then spun the gun on his index finger before replacing it on the tabletop. Several seconds later, Horace repeated the entire routine.

A few feet away, Roxy relaxed on the ornate faux leopard skin couch with a cool drink in one hand and a magazine in the other. She peered over the top of the page she was scanning and took in the sight of her husband, naked but for his socks, vest and underpants, confronting imagined enemies armed only with her unloaded automatic.

"Who are you planning to kill, Horri?" she asked languidly.

Horace looked at his wife and smiled sheepishly before straightening and adopting what he believed to be a very fearsome countenance.

"Whoever gets in my way sweetheart," he said in his best Bogart imitation.

Roxy smirked. "That'll be the day. Now, when you've finished playing cowboys and Indians, would you please put the gun back where you found it."

Horace looked longingly at the gun in his hand. "It really is quite beautiful," he said wistfully. "Strange to think that something so cold and cruel can look so good."

The irony of Horace's remark was not lost on Roxy as she stared dully at her husband. "I think it's time you put the gun away, Horri, you're starting to sound a little bit weird."

"But I like holding it, Roxy," Horace wined.

"Who's holding who?"

Horace gave Roxy a confused look before returning his stare to the pistol he held in his hand.

"Well, I think you've held it quite long enough," said Roxy, her voice taking on a harder tone. "Now, put it back in my drawer where you found it and don't ever take it out again without checking with me first. I don't want you to kill yourself or anyone else for that matter." Roxy lowered her voice until it was barely audible, "Leastways, not just yet."

"I don't know why you have a gun anyhow," said Horace glumly as he made his way into the bedroom to return the weapon to Roxy's bedside draw.

"Because I'm a poor defenceless woman," Roxy called after him. "You poor stupid bastard," she concluded quietly under her breath.

16
Settling In

On Sunday afternoon, Joe took Tom to meet his colleague, Randolph Bird. Tom had met Randy several times before. He was a nice enough guy, especially considering the gibes he was forced to endure from his British clients, many of whom employed a less than complimentary translation of his name.

Randy was a tall and gangly Afro-American who Joe liked to describe as beaver faced, in reference to his facial similarity to the river-dwelling dam builders. If Randy had a good personality, Tom had never quite managed to discover it, as Randy liked to keep himself to himself and didn't get involved in any non-business-related chats.

Thankfully, the rain had cleared overnight and it was a gloriously hot and sunny day in Florida. Joe had arranged for them to meet Randy somewhere on the coast and now the three of them walked slowly along a stretch of golden sand. The initial greetings were quickly dispensed with, the three of them turned their full attention to the impending trial.

"A lot of time and money has been invested in this case," said Joe. "The investigation was as thorough as it could possibly be. We've looked at everything from every possible angle and there's no way that Pasternak or someone hired by Pasternak, didn't start that fire."

"They may turn that on us and say that we're trying to buy a verdict by throwing so much money at it. They could say that we looked too hard to find a reason to deny Pasternak's claim for any reason," Randy opined.

"Damned if you do, damned if you don't," Tom chipped in.

"Randy will be doing most of the questioning and cross-examination at the trial and I'll get involved when I need to," said Joe.

"Why do I have to be here for three weeks?" Tom asked, not for the first time.

"Because the jury expects it. It shows you care," replied Joe.

"Do they though," said Tom, who remained totally unconvinced on this point.

"Yes, they do!" Joe and Randy responded together and in almost perfect harmony.

"Well, listen, guys," said Tom resignedly. "I'll spend the first week in the Retreat but after that, you need to find me something better."

"Pussy," jibed Joe.

"Seriously, I'm hoping my girlfriend will soon come and join me and there is absolutely no way I am going to inflict the Retreat upon her."

"Message received and understood," said Joe with a weary smile. "I'll book you both into the Vinoy."

"More points?" asked Tom.

"Oh yes," Joe replied with a smirk.

After an hour or so, Randy made tracks home and Joe treated Tom to lunch at a fish shack just off the beach. The food was very fresh and delicious. After lunch, Joe dropped Tom off at the Retreat before heading home to spend time with his family.

*

Tom went back to his dismal room where the Cartwright family were waiting for him on the television screen. One of the Characters, whose name was Horse Cartwright, was speaking to a pretty and saintly-looking young woman. By now, Tom knew that the impossibly good and pretty young woman would either be colluding to double-cross the guileless Horse, or, was about to fall in love with him. If the latter, the poor woman was definitely doomed to die a horrible death prior to the episode's end.

Tom considered the various options for her possible demise and decided that if it were by gunshot or Indian arrow, he would find a bar and drink beer. If death turned out to be as a result of her being thrown from a horse, illness or, some other non-violent cause, he would find a bar and drink spirits.

As it turned out, the woman was a confidence trickster whose dastardly plot was uncovered just in the nick of time. *Crap*, thought Tom. *That means I'll be drinking wine.*

Tom grabbed his tablet, went into the adjoining bedroom and sat on the bed. He called Isabelle and was eventually greeted by her sad and yet smiling face.

"Hello, Tommy," she said. "It's late. What's the time there?"

"It's five in the afternoon here and so, am I right in thinking that it's 1 o'clock in the afternoon in France?"

"No, Tom, it's eleven at night."

Tom thought about this for a few seconds before realisation dawned. "Oh sorry, I went back instead of forward."

"What's that music I can hear?"

"Bonanza," replied Tom and then went on to tell her about the issue with the television sets.

"The hotel is not very nice then?"

"Well, let's just say that they serve a breakfast buffet in the morning and a dinner buffet in the early evening. The plates are paper and the cutlery is plastic. Apparently, the highlight of the culinary week is Wednesday."

"Why?" asked Isabelle with a giggle. "What happens on Wednesday?"

"Wednesday is hotdog and beans night."

"Magnificent!" proclaimed Isabelle with a laugh. "At least, you'll not be getting fat. Tell me, Tommy," said Isabelle turning suddenly serious. "How are you feeling, really?"

Tom thought for a time before answering, "Shouldn't I be asking you that?"

"No, I know exactly how I am feeling and now I want to know how my Tommy is feeling."

"Well, in that case, I hate being here, Isabelle. I'm forced to be somewhere I don't really want to be at this moment in time, doing something that I don't really want to be doing just now. I'm not a control freak or anything like that, it's just that I find my current situation—," he struggled to find the word or words that would best describe how he was feeling.

"Frustrating?" Isabelle interjected.

"Yes, I guess so. It reminds me of when I was sixteen, me and two school friends wanted to join the army. Because we were all so young, we had to first obtain our parents' permission. My parents refused to sign the papers we'd been given by the recruitment place and when I asked them why, they told me that it was because they believed that I wasn't suited to army life. They said that I had the wrong temperament and also, that I had issues with authority. In hindsight,

I'm glad that they didn't sign the papers but I've always struggled to fully agree with their reasoning, until now that is."

"So, you don't like being told what to do?"

"Steady on, Issi, is this a therapy session?"

"No, I am still getting to know you that's all."

"Well, to an extent I guess that could be true although, most people dance to someone else's tune on a daily basis. Walk, don't walk. Talk, don't talk. That's fine because we all need rules but this is another level and well, I guess I'm just not that used to it. Sorry to whinge but this has just come at the wrong time for me that's all and now, as you say, I'm finding things a little frustrating."

"What happened to your friends?" asked Isabelle.

"Their parents signed. One, James, well, even I knew back then that he was far too soft-hearted for the army and I was right. It wasn't too long before he bought himself out. The other, Ron, he was a bit of an oddball anyway and he stayed in the army for some time. Actually, when he left the British army, he went and joined the French Foreign Legion. I'm not sure how long he lasted in that but the last thing I heard about him, he was cleaning windows."

"What does that mean, cleaning windows?"

"Sorry? Don't the windows in France ever need cleaning, you know, soapy water and a sponge and all that."

"Incredible," Isabelle murmured softly and then, following a thoughtful pause she continued, "Well, Tommy, this just isn't good and so, if you cannot be with me and it's making you frustrated, then I must come and be with you."

"That'd be wonderful," said Tom excitedly. "If you can come out to join me here in Tampa, then I'll transfer hotels to somewhere much nicer."

"I would like that very much, Tommy, but first, there is the funeral and so, I will not be able to come to you until possibly Saturday but most likely Sunday."

"You seem brighter," said Tom.

"Yes, the same as you, Tommy. There's been too much happening in such a small space of time and I think that during the past days, everything has caught up with me and of course, there is papa." Isabelle sniffed and Tom thought she was about to burst into tears but she rallied and breathing in deeply through her nose was able to continue, "So, tell me, what have you been up to?"

When the call ended, Tom checked his watch. It was now just after six and so Zoe should be home from her evening shift at the Good Samaritan. He somewhat reluctantly decided to call her and swapped the tablet for his work phone. The phone rang a few times before it was picked up and Tom heard Zoe's cheery tones on the other end of the line.

"The Harrison residence," she chimed in an adopted snobby posh accent. "The lady of the house speaking."

"Hello, Zoe. How's everything?"

"Oh, it's you," said Zoe in her customary west country burr. She sounded vexed and a little accusatory. "Nice of you to let me know you landed safely and everything. Wouldn't have taken you more than a few seconds to send me a text or something would it? No, too much bother for you I guess."

"Zoe, you're my lodger. Not my mother."

This was greeted with silence until Tom said, "I'm sorry, Zoe, it was completely thoughtless of me. Is everything OK?"

"Well," she sniffed. "We have a mouse problem landlord."

"Please don't be like that, Zoe and we have a what problem?"

"A mouse problem," she answered slowly as if talking to a particularly dim-witted child. "To start off I thought it was just one but now, I've two confirmed kills since you left and when I arrived home tonight, I saw a particularly big fat old mouse waddle across the kitchen floor. Now, I might be wrong but I reckon she could have been pregnant, in which case, we'll soon be inundated with the little buggers."

"I didn't know we had mice."

"Don't you go fretting landlord, I've mobilised defences and have placed chez Harrison on a war footing. I have every confidence that Harrison Towers will be cleared of enemy forces before you return. I'm actually quite enjoying the challenge."

"I can tell."

"Yes, I've put up a chart on the kitchen door and it has about twenty mouse faces on it. Every time I get a confirmed kill, I put a red cross through one of the faces. I need just four more kills before I attain ace status."

Tom chuckled. "I'm glad you're happy, Zoe."

"Me? Yes, I'm over the moon, Tom, but I do need to tell you something and I'm being serious now."

Tom began to feel a little uneasy. "OK, Zoe, fire away."

"Now, what happened yesterday when you were leaving and I kissed you? No, shut up, Tom and listen, I've been thinking a lot about this and I need to get it off my chest. Whilst I tried not to show it, I was hurt but it was my own stupid fault and I don't want it to come between us. The thing is, you've been ever so kind to me, Tom, kinder than anyone I can remember and you've never asked nor expected anything in return and that's confusing the hell out of me. At the moment, my feelings are all over the place but I'll sort them out because, well, you've got Isabelle and anyway, you're far too bleeding old for me."

"Thank you, Zoe, I think. Well, I'm glad you've got that off your chest and at least one of us is feeling better as a result. Anything else been happening?"

Zoe started giggling. "Oh, Tom, you're not going to believe this."

"Try me."

"There was this fella in the Samaritan today. He was old like you but not so devilishly handsome. Anyway, back in the day, he says that he played in some punk rock band. They were called pussy something or other. I think Pussy was the female lead vocalist. Anyway, it turns out that although the band never made it, Pussy went on to forge quite a career for herself in children's television. Bet you can't guess who Pussy became?"

"Go on, Zoe, amaze me."

"Well, according to this guy, Pussy only went on to become a Telly Tubby!"

"You are kidding me," laughed Tom.

"No, straight up. Who would have thought it?"

"Not me," said Tom.

"What's that music?" asked Zoe.

"It's Bonanza," Tom replied with a sigh. He then went on to repeat the saga of the television.

They chatted for a while longer before saying goodnight.

Once Tom had disconnected the call, he decided against venturing out in search of a bar and instead settled down in front of the telly with a cup of tea. Although he'd admit it to no one, he was starting to find Bonanza quite addictive.

17
The Trial Begins

Tom and Joe met for the buffet breakfast at seven the next morning. Tom found his porridge and coffee so surprisingly good that he briefly reconsidered Wednesday evening's hotdog and beans extravaganza.

Following breakfast, they set off on a leisurely stroll towards the Federal Court building, which was situated several blocks away. The Federal Court they were to attend was situated on the seventeenth floor of a building resembling two shoe boxes, the first lying flat, with the second standing vertically upon its lid.

As expected, security was tight and virtually identical to that employed at international airports. Having successfully passed through security, they took the elevator up to the seventeenth floor, with Joe making small talk with the lift's other travellers, most of whom disembarked prior to the elevator's arrival on the seventeenth.

"Good job these lifts move faster than those in the Retreat," commented Tom. "Otherwise, it'd take us most of the day to reach our destination."

"Listen, Tom," said Joe. "I'm getting you moved to the Vinoy on Friday. I can't take much more of your bitching."

"Really," replied Tom crossly. "If the Retreat is so great, where the bloody hell were you last night?"

Joe had the courtesy to look a little shame-faced. "I was there, I just arrived late."

"Bullshit."

"Bye, fellas," Joe said to the lift's remaining occupants when they left the elevator on the seventeenth floor. "Geez, Tom, that was embarrassing, swearing like that in a crowded elevator."

“Yes, sorry,” conceded Tom. “I’m suffering from the effects of sleep deprivation and stress. What’s more, the signature tune to Bonanza is on a constant loop in my head. It’s driving me bonkers. ”

They were now walking along a corridor, one side of which was completely glazed and if Tom glanced to his left, he could clearly see Tampa’s urban sprawl laid out before him. They took a right turn and then Joe went immediately to a door on their left.

“This is the war room,” he said whilst opening the door.

The room was quite small and contained tea and coffee-making facilities, slabs of fizzy drinks, trays of sandwiches and a large assortment of fruit and some chocolate bars. It also contained Randy Bird and two junior members of staff from Joe’s law offices.

Joe introduced Tom to an arrogant looking well-built young man named Scott and to a plump friendly faced young woman, whose name was Mary. The lawyers began to talk amongst themselves about aspects of the forthcoming trial, whilst Tom was left to fill his time as best he could.

At eight, they were summoned into the courtroom, which was found by exiting the war room, turning left and passing through two large doors. There was a long central aisle with seats situated on either side.

At the end of the aisle was a small open square with the jury area situated on the left side of the square and the witness box on the right. Straight ahead were two tiers of seats. The first tier was occupied by the clerks and officers of the court and the second and higher tier by the judge. On the wall behind the judge was a massive eagle-headed emblem with star-spangled banners draped at either side.

Tom and the team representing Mallory occupied the seats to the left of the Isle, whilst team Pasternak personnel were situated on the right. The judge was a blond-haired woman of about Tom’s age whose name was Appleyard.

Following some initial introductions and pleasantries, the morning was taken up with procedural and administrative issues. There was to be a fifteen-minute break at eleven and an hour’s break at one. The court would adjourn every afternoon at five and the jury would then be released for the day. Away from the jury’s ears, the judge would review and rule on matters arising that day, with teams Mallory and Pasternak, both being provided with ample opportunity to present their respective arguments.

This was to become the daily pattern of the next three weeks.

After day one's morning break, the jury was summoned, questioned individually by counsel from both sides and either accepted or replaced. Tom found the jury to be unremarkable with one exception, being a man of about thirty years of age, with a military bearing, who from the very start appeared pernickety and overzealous.

"I think that guy is going to be a problem," Joe whispered to Tom as they sat in the front seats on the left of the aisle, which gave them the right-side profile of each of the jurors.

"Any particular reason?" asked Tom just as quietly.

"No," responded Joe. "He just comes across as being a right royal pain in the arse."

The judge announced a break for lunch and Tom was just about to stand when George Church approached him.

"Hello, George," said Tom, who had met George several times before during pre-trial mediations and depositions.

"This is for you," said a stone-faced George as he handed Tom an envelope.

"Thank you, George," said Tom as he accepted the proffered envelope. "What is it?"

"It's a subpoena," replied George with a wicked smirk. "You'll be here for the duration."

Although Tom had expected and indeed planned for a three week stay, he was nevertheless miffed at being compelled by the court to stay somewhere that he didn't want to be. This, in effect, cut off any escape plans he may have been developing and meant that the Judge's permission was required before he could contemplate leaving Florida.

During the afternoon session, Randy presented Mallory's case and so began the long and excruciating process of witness and expert witness testimony, questioning and cross-examination.

At one point during the first afternoon of the trial, Tom found himself exploring the pockets of his suit jacket in search of anything that might provide some relief from his mounting boredom. To his great delight, his hand came across a boiled toffee wrapped safely within its golden-papered confines. He quickly removed the wrapper, popped the toffee into his mouth and sucked quietly as the chief fire marshal gave his summary of events.

Whilst listening to the fire marshal's description of burn patterns, Tom was unconsciously folding and refolding the small golden toffee wrapper. The fire marshal's recounting was suddenly interrupted when the juror previously pinpointed as a potential nuisance, raised his hand. The judge politely asked the fire marshal to wait before asking the juror what his issue was.

"It's that guy over there," said the man as he stood and pointed directly at Tom who was seated about ten feet away from the vexed juror. "He keeps fiddling with a sweet wrapper or something and I can't hear the testimony."

Joe quickly snatched the sweet wrapper from Tom's hand and threw it over his shoulder.

"I apologise, ma'am," said Joe addressing the Judge. "My client didn't realise he was making such a loud and disturbing noise."

"Neither did I, Mister Becker. May we please continue," said the judge as she looked above her spectacles at the complaining juror.

"Told you he was going to be a pain in the arse didn't I," whispered Joe.

18
Fool's Gold

"Hey, Zoe, be a darling and fetch me another pint of Guinness," said the grey-haired man who propped up the bar that and every other lunchtime in the Good Samaritan.

"Coming right up," Zoe answered brightly, as she took a fresh glass from below the bar and tilted it under the Guinness tap. "Now, Michael, my love, you know I'm not one to pass judgement but you do seem to be pushing the boat out a bit this afternoon."

"Is that right," the grey-haired man replied mildly. "Your concern is flattering, but there's no need to worry. This will probably be my last for today."

Zoe placed the glass of dark stout beer on the counter in front of the man and collected the ten-pound note he held out for her. "What are you celebrating then?" she asked with a smile. "Is it your birthday?"

"No, I don't tend to celebrate those anymore. I've had too many and so, I've stopped counting." The man lifted the drink to his lips and took a long luxurious glug that left him wearing a white foam moustache, which he quickly sucked up by extending his underbite and slurping noisily. "No, I heard some news today that has put me in a contemplative frame of mind. Now, I don't know about you but I do my best contemplating over a few drinks."

The lunchtime rush had come to an end and so, Zoe and the other bar staff could slow down a little as the pub shifted to a more relaxed and laid-back ambience.

"Good news I hope, Michael?"

"Neither good nor bad but it did bring back some memories and set me thinking about what might have been and perhaps, what might still be." Michael's voice took on an intriguing edge that piqued Zoe's interest away from the polite and into the slightly more attentive.

"Please tell me more," she coaxed as she handed Michael his change.

"Well, you may not believe it now when you look at me but back in the day, well, some might say that I was blessed with the good looks of a film star."

"Lassie," suggested Zoe with a wicked smirk.

"Ach! Get away with ya you cheeky wee thing. No, you may laugh now but I could have had my pick of the young ladies. Leastways, that's how I remember it. Anyway, I went and got myself smitten and she was bad news."

"We've all been there," Zoe interrupted. "How do you think I came to be working behind a bar in a London pub instead of studying archaeology in Bristol?"

But Michael's thoughts had become lost in the past and he gave no acknowledgement of Zoe's flippant contribution but instead stared with unfocussed eyes back through the mists of time.

"Trouble was she was married and to a hard man too. If I'd known that when we'd first met I wouldn't have got involved and I would have probably run a mile in the opposite direction. But I didn't and like all young men, I did my thinking through my underpants."

"Steady on, Michael, you'll be making me blush if you carry on like that," Zoe chirped in light-heartedly, whilst waving a hand in front of her face in feigned embarrassment. "Would you like some nuts?"

"Now, this was back in the eighties," Michael continued doggedly. "And there'd been a big bank job in which countless safe deposit boxes had been stolen. The papers were full of it at the time and the police, well they launched a massive manhunt."

Zoe looked at Michael wistfully. "Yes," she sighed, "I'm thinking about launching one of those myself."

Michael turned to glare angrily at Zoe. "Do you want to hear my story or don't ya?" he spat. "Because if you do, would you please do me a service and cut out the smart comments."

Zoe pouted before giving Michael a two-fingered scout's salute. "I'm sorry Michael and promise not to interrupt you anymore. Please, carry on."

Michael huffed at her contemptuously before continuing with his story. "As it turned out, they arrested Dolly's husband and several others but the police never found a single one of those safe deposit boxes."

"Dolly?" Zoe asked. "I take it that Dolly was the smiter, the one you fell for?"

"That's right, Dolly was my one true love," confirmed Michael.

"So," said Zoe. "A bit of a result really. Dolly's old man getting nicked and being banged up in prison. The coast is now clear for movie good looks Michael to steam in and have your wicked way."

"You'd think so, wouldn't ya, but Dolly was fiercely hurt by the sudden turn of events and she dropped me like a ton of hot bricks when her old man got sentenced. She said she couldn't be unfaithful to him whilst he was locked away inside. Strange because we were at it like rabbits before he got arrested."

"How long did he get then?" asked Zoe.

"He got thirty-five years! It's always amazed me how the authorities seem to dish out longer sentences for financial crimes than they do for murders."

"I can't see Dolly holding out for thirty-five years," Zoe announced incredulously.

"No, she lasted about two months. Right up until it came out in the press that her husband had been banging some stripper from up west."

Zoe puffed out her cheeks. "Sounds like everyone was getting plenty of action back in the eighties. So, did you and Dolly reunite then?"

"Once or twice," said Michael. "But then she ran off and headed up to Manchester with a used cars salesman."

Zoe rested her head on her hands and looked dully at Michael. "Michael, I hope there's a point to this story because you've just taken away ten minutes of my life that I'm never going to get back again."

Michael looked back at Zoe; his brow furrowed in irritation. "Of course, there's a bloody point to the story otherwise I wouldn't be telling it now, would I?"

He raised his glass and took another long slurp of Guinness before continuing, "Well, before it came out about his dalliance with the stripper, Dolly went to visit her husband in prison a couple of times and it was on one of these visits that he tells her where the safe deposit boxes were hidden. Then, following a particularly exuberant session in the sack with me, Dolly tells me everything."

"So," said Zoe, her interest rekindled. "You knew where the safe deposit boxes were hidden?"

"Not exactly, Zoe, my love. It's more accurate to say that I know where the safe deposit boxes are hidden."

Zoe laughed as she started to polish a glass she'd just taken from the washer. "Come on, Michael, there's no way that they've not been found yet. Dolly would have told someone else, the used car salesman for one and then there's her husband, he must be out of prison by now."

Michael drained his pint and banged the empty glass down upon the bar. "Well, Zoe, that's where it gets interesting. Dolly and her fancy man never quite made it to Manchester. Their bodies were found in a burnt-out car just twenty miles outside of London. They'd both been shot in the back of the head and her husband never made it out of prison."

Zoe raised a questioning eyebrow. "You sit yourself back down, Michael and I'll fetch you another Guinness, there's no way I'm letting you leave here until you've finished telling me this story."

Michael smiled and resumed his position on the barstool whilst Zoe set about refilling his glass.

"Here's your pint, Michael," she said as she placed the refilled glass on the bar in front of him. "Now, you can carry on."

Michael took a long and agonisingly slow draught of his beer, smacked his lips together and continued, "I read in the papers some years past that Dolly's murderer had made a deathbed confession. He had cancer or something and wanted to unburden his soul before meeting his maker.

"Anyway, he pinned the blame squarely upon Dolly's husband, said he'd arranged the whole thing. He'd found out about her shenanigans and understandably became worried that she'd do a bunk with some fancy man or other and steal the safe deposit boxes into the bargain. So, he took the most obvious course of action and had her done away with."

"Wow!" exclaimed Zoe. "OK, so Dolly's out of the picture and her husband is banged up in prison, so the coast is clear for you to get your hands on the loot?"

"Not, likely," responded Michael. "I'm far too much of a coward! Although Dolly's husband's sentence got extended on account of the murders; well, he obviously still had an influence that stretched far outside of the prison and anyway, he was going to get out of there at some point regardless. So, the truth is, I just didn't want to spend my entire life looking over my shoulder or shitting myself every time someone knocked at the door."

Zoe nodded sagely. "Nice image, Michael, I couldn't have put it better myself."

"But it's not over yet, is it, because," said Michael in sudden urgency as he pulled out a folded newspaper from the back pocket of his trousers and opened it onto the bar. Once the paper was unfolded, Michael's finger jabbed at a headline which read, **RONNIE WISHBONE DIES IN PRISON.**

"That's him," said Michael, "that's Dolly's husband."

Zoe frowned. "So, if the coast is now clear, why are you here and not off collecting the loot?"

"Because I need help. I need to find someone I can trust and I also need someone with a car." Michael fixed Zoe with a hard-eyed stare. "Can I trust you, Zoe?" he asked, his voice tight with the force of his words.

Zoe leaned over the bar and whispered to Michael conspiratorially, "Does the Pope shit in the woods? Of course, you can trust me, Michael. Now," Zoe straightened herself to look directly into Michael's watery blue eyes, "tell me, what exactly do you have in mind?"

19
Tom's Mis-Adventures in Tampaland

The Wednesday morning court session was brought to a conclusion and those in attendance were just preparing to leave when the judge announced that the start of the afternoon's session would be delayed until three. This was because she had a number of criminal cases upon which she was required to pass sentence.

"Do you know," Joe whispered into Tom's ear. "She can send you to the electric chair."

"Seriously," replied Tom. "Do you guys still use the electric chair?"

"How the hell should I know," said Joe.

Tom looked at Joe in stunned disbelief. "Joe, please remind me to fire you just as soon as this case is over."

"Gee, Tom, you're such a grouch," countered Joe as he stood and made his way out of the courtroom.

Tom had decided not to leave the court building that afternoon but instead killed time by walking up and down the long corridor whilst occasionally casting his eyes over the Tampa skyline in search of something of potential interest. His gaze had just become focused upon a group of people happily frolicking around the rooftop pool of a building far below when his consciousness suddenly became aware of a strange jingling sound. It was coming from the direction of the elevators and was becoming louder.

There then appeared a line of eight men, all wearing bright orange jumpsuits and manacled together by long silver chains. The chains made it impossible for them to stretch their legs to the extent they would if they were to walk naturally and so, they all shuffled along together, each with their right arm stretched forward and clasping the shoulder of the man in front. They were accompanied by two officers, each brandishing a pump action shotgun.

Tom pressed his back against the window so as to provide the maximum possible distance between him and the passing procession of malcontents, all of whom looked thoroughly defeated and devoid of any hope. Tom continued to gawp as the procession shuffled its way passed him and into the courtroom and so, he didn't see Horace Pasternak following in its wake.

"Hey, Mister Harrison, how are you doing?" Horace asked cheerfully. "Who knows, you could end up like those guys once this case is finished."

Tom was a little surprised by Horace's demeanour as, from Mallory's perspective, the case seemed to be progressing pretty well. "I don't know why you're looking so pleased with yourself," he said to Horace bluntly. "I don't think anybody actually likes arsonists."

Horace turned towards Tom and gave him a comradery pat on the shoulder. "I know, I know," he chuckled. "But the crazy thing is, they like insurance companies even less."

With that, Horace left Tom and made his way towards the restrooms, still chuckling as he went.

This encounter left Tom feeling puzzled and uneasy. What did Horace Pasternak have up his sleeve? However, Tom's misgivings were quickly forgotten when he learned later that Thursday's court session would not begin until two in the afternoon. What's more, he and Joe were going out that evening for drinks and dinner.

*

When Tom got back to the Retreat, he quickly showered and changed before facetiming Isabelle.

"Hello, Tommy," she greeted him with a smile. "You are looking like you are off somewhere."

"Yes, Joe and I are heading out this evening. He thinks I need a break from Bonanza."

She laughed. "He is probably correct, Tommy. I have been noticing a certain, how you say, twang in your voice of late."

"Why I don't rightly cotton on that, ma'am," Tom said as he smiled and mimicked doffing his hat.

"Still, you mustn't get too—how you English say, mouse bummed, because it would not look good if you turn up at the court tomorrow looking all sick and dishevelled."

"Sorry, what did you say, Isabelle?"

"I said, you mustn't get too mouse bummed tonight."

"Why on earth are you talking about a mouse's bum?" Tom couldn't have hidden the bewilderment from his face or voice had he tried and he didn't try.

"Have I made a mistake, Tommy?" Isabelle asked uncertainly. "My brother Simone, he overheard two English speaking yesterday about a friend who had drunk too much alcohol and he told me that they said he had got mouse bummed. Tommy, why are you laughing at me?"

It took a little while for Tom to compose himself enough to answer and he only managed to do this when Isabelle started to get annoyed.

"I'm sorry, Issi, but it is very funny. What your brother must have heard the people say was that their friend got rat-arsed." Tom started laughing again and this time, Isabelle joined in with his hilarity.

"Listen, Tommy, we must be serious for a moment," she admonished gently once their laughter had subsided. "Papa's funeral is tomorrow and so, whilst you cheer me up and make me forget, it is inappropriate for me to fill the house with laughter."

"Agreed," said Tom solemnly.

"I have a flight booked for Saturday. It is not direct and I must change but all being well, we should be together by Sunday evening."

"That's absolutely fantastic news, Issi," Tom said earnestly. "I am so looking forward to seeing you."

"Moi aussi, Tommy. Now, tell me about your day."

"This afternoon," began Tom. "I saw both Missus Pasternaks, the old and the new. The new Mrs Pasternak is certainly eye-catching."

"Really, Tommy? Please remember who you are speaking with."

"Yes, sorry, Issi," apologised Tom. "But in the real world, there's only one reason a woman like that would be with a man like Horace Pasternak and that's money."

"I am getting the picture but there is also a saying that love is blind."

"Yes and that beauty is in the eye of the beholder. I'm not buying it. Anyway, this afternoon Missus Pasternak the elder, took the stand. Earlier we'd heard from a former employee that the warehouse was rat infested and unsafe.

However, according to Missus Pasternak, it was a sweet place where she and her husband had watched their children grow up."

"In a warehouse?"

"She went on to say that Mister Pasternak had called on the night of the fire and that they had desperately clung to each other whilst watching all of their hopes and dreams perish in the flames."

"This is the ex-wife, yes?"

"Yes, it was terrible. Their lawyer, a snotty and snivelling woman who the judge kept reprimanding for getting things wrong was feigning tears as she asked the questions. I looked up at the jurors and there wasn't a dry eye in the place!"

"Oh, mon Dieu."

"Exactly," said Tom. "I felt myself sliding lower and lower in my seat as I tried to disappear. Then old Randy Bird starts the cross-examination. He asks Missus Pasternak whether she knew if Mister Pasternak had called anyone else that night whilst watching the fire at the warehouse. She said she didn't and so, Randy continues by asking if Missus Pasternak would be surprised to learn that five minutes before calling her, he had called his divorce lawyer telling him to advise the court that he could no longer make the alimony payments."

"The poor woman."

"Indeed, the whole mood in the courtroom changed and suddenly, I was sitting bolt upright in my chair again. It was amazing!"

"It all sounds very cutthroat," said Isabelle. "Interesting but horrible."

They chatted some more before saying their goodnights. Tom was looking forward to an evening out and so he quickly gathered up his stuff and made his way to the lifts that would take him down to Joe who was waiting in reception.

The lift was a long time coming and Tom regretted not using the stairs but just as he turned to find the stairwell, the elevator binged to announce its arrival. Tom did a quick about turn and headed back to the lift.

Inside waiting was a blond-haired woman who Tom estimated to be in her late thirties. She was holding a half-empty wine glass and it was quite evident that it was not her first, second or probably even third glass of wine. She was surrounded by three young children, the cutest of which was a young girl of about five years who, upon Tom's arrival, hid shyly behind her mother's skirts. The other two children were older boys, perhaps twins and Tom guessed they were between ten and twelve years old.

Tom smiled down at the shy girl and asked, "Hello are you heading out somewhere nice?"

"Hello, mister," replied the girl. "Are you Australian?"

"No, I'm English," replied Tom.

The girl looked up at her mother who quickly gave a slurred but accurate synopsis of what being English meant.

"Oh," said the girl. "I'm sorry."

Tom wasn't sure what the little girl meant by this but decided to let it go and responded by saying, "That's quite alright, I'll get over it."

"Hey, mister," the girl said again as she looked up at him through two large dark eyes. "I like your bracelet."

Tom was wearing a Help for Heroes blue rubber band decorated with the union flag, which he now took off and offered to the little girl.

"Here you are," he said. "It's my gift to you."

At this, the little girl tried to bury herself deeper within her mother's skirt but following some slurred coaxing from her mother, she reached out and shyly took the bracelet.

The lift finally reached the ground floor and Tom wished the family a good evening and set off happily in the direction of the hotel's reception. He had gone no further than two or three steps when he heard a voice behind him.

"Hey, mister!"

Tom turned around to see the two boys staring at him.

"We like your watch." With that, they both laughed cheekily before turning and running off to catch up with their mother and sister.

*

Tom woke early the next day and so, with hours to kill before he was required at court and feeling in need of some exercise, he set off in search of the hotel's gym. In a previous life, when married to Helen, Tom had been an avid, almost obsessive gym goer. However, that aspect of his life had waned over the years and whilst he still had a static bike at home, he struggled to muster enough enthusiasm to regularly exercise.

So, dressed in a grey tee shirt, shorts and sporting Adidas trainers, Tom followed the signs that eventually led him to the hotel's gym. It was empty, which pleased him and the gym was larger than expected or so he thought.

He walked into the room making for the cross trainer when his attention was taken by a large and dubious-looking stain upon the gym's carpeted floor. It was then that he collided painfully with the mirrored wall, the impact making him reel backwards in shocked agony. It was only once his vision had cleared that he realised that the gym was actually quite small with just a few pieces of assorted equipment and that his senses had been tricked by the mirrors.

Again, cursing Joe for booking him into such a dump, Tom began his workout. He struggled at first but once his muscles had warmed up, he started to enjoy himself and exerted more and more effort into his workout, which continued unabated for almost two hours. When he finally decided to stop, he surveyed his reflection in the mirrored walls and was proud to see his now dark grey and sweat-drenched tee shirt and shorts. Gathering his stuff together, he headed out of the gym and back to his room for a shower and a relaxing soak in a warm bath.

When Tom arrived at the court that afternoon, he found that Mallory's legal team was already in the war room. He leaned across the room's small table to grab a tin of cola and it was then that he first felt his body complain.

"Are you OK?" Mary asked as Tom winced.

"I hope so," replied Tom. "I spent a couple of hours in the gym this morning and I think I might have overdone things a little."

The afternoon session passed blessedly quickly and Tom made his increasingly stiff and painful way back to the hotel. Thursday night was a sleepless ordeal and by Friday, Tom could barely move.

Friday passed in a blur of witnesses, statements, questions and cross-examinations, ending with the conclusion of Mallory's defence of the case prosecuted against it by Mister Pasternak. The following week would be Pasternak's turn. Joe had told Tom that Pasternak's counsel intended to cross-examine him at some point the following week but was unsure on which day this would actually take place.

"Try not to worry about it," said Joe. "The way you're looking, you'll probably be dead by Monday anyhow."

"Thanks, Joe, you really are a great comfort."

"No, you'll be fine," continued Joe. "We'll go back to the Retreat; you can pack and then I'll get you checked into the Vinoy. Isabelle will arrive on Sunday and everything will be good."

"I admire your optimism, Joe, truly I do."

"Gee, Tom, you're a complete mess. Just a couple of hours of exercise and you can barely walk."

"Joe."

"What?"

"Sod off."

*

The Vinoy Hotel was situated opposite St Pete's small marina. It was a building of Victorian grandeur and elegance, carefully mixed with the kind of southern hospitality that gently and quietly exudes peace and comfort.

Tom sat alone in one of the hotel's popular and busy restaurants. It was still relatively early and yet the place was buzzing and it appeared that a private party was taking place. In the hope of numbing his pain-wracked body, Tom had ordered a rib-eye steak and a bottle of Merlot. The steak had been delicious and now Tom slowly enjoyed the wine whilst surveying the restaurants other occupants as well as the drinkers that crowded its centrally located bar.

Whilst stationary, he could easily forget his pain, which he hoped would disappear completely before Isabelle arrived on Sunday. With that thought in mind, Tom decided to call it a night, picked up the bottle of merlot and made his way slowly and painfully back to his room.

The room itself was large, pristine and elegantly furnished. It had a balcony that looked out onto the marina with its collection of gently swaying sailing boats. Tom pulled open the patio door and stepped outside. He took a deep breath filling his lungs with the warm and aromatic night air. *Tomorrow,* he thought. *I shall feel much better tomorrow.*

*

Saturday dawned grey and miserable, a combination that perfectly suited Tom's falling spirits. His agony showed no sign of abating and so he decided that following breakfast, he would go in search of a chemist and medication. Tom asked the concierge what direction he should take to find the nearest chemist and was told he would find a CVS some four blocks away if he turned right when leaving the hotel.

So, walking like a mummy brought back to life following five thousand years of death, Tom set off in the direction indicated by the concierge. The going was slow and painful, especially when stepping off and onto the sidewalk. As Tom hobbled along with, for reasons unknown, the words and music of Wombling Merry Christmas invading his thoughts, he was continually overtaken by happy runners who, Tom quickly gathered, were undertaking a charity fundraising event organised by a local church.

One of the runners, a skinny moustachioed man in his mid-fifties, with a mop of curly brown hair, which was held in place by an illuminous orange headband, slowed to a virtual jog on the spot next to Tom.

"Hey, man, how are you doing today?" the jogger asked affably.

"Not at my best," replied Tom. "Over did it at the gym and am now paying the price."

"Sorry to hear that man, I thought you were moving a little," the jogger paused as he searched for the most appropriate word. "Rustily."

"Yes, I do feel like I need oiling," replied Tom as he continued to slowly shuffle along.

"You should just stop," announced the jogger. "And shake yourself loose." The jogger with his legs continuing to pump up and down started to shake himself like a wet dog. "Come on stranger," he continued. "Run with me and we'll run with Jesus!"

At this, Tom gave the jogger a testy look. "Why don't you and Jesus run on ahead and I'll try to catch you up later," he offered.

"OK, man," the jogger responded happily. "But you'd best get a hustle on because the rains coming."

The jogger turned his head to the sky behind Tom and nodded before smiling and waving goodbye. Tom watched the skinny man disappear into the distance before glancing behind and upwards. An ominously black cloud was heading swiftly in his direction and so, gritting his teeth, Tom tried hard to pick up the pace.

A hundred yards or so further on, the rain hit like a hammer blow. It was heavy and cold but mercifully short-lived. Tom could not have been wetter had he taken a bath whilst fully clothed. Dripping wet and shivering, he started to laugh to himself, it was either that or cry and he didn't care much for crying.

"I must have been really horrible in a previous life," he muttered to himself. "Maybe I was Hitler—"

He eventually made it to the CVS store, where he hoped to purchase some Ibuprofen and codeine. Unable to find what he wanted, Tom asked for help from the pharmacist. Upon hearing his request, the pharmacist gave Tom a withering look before stiffly and loudly informing him that codeine was not readily available in the USA and that Tom would need a prescription. Tom noticed that other CVS customers, including a police officer, were now all staring disapprovingly at him.

"Sorry, I didn't know," he muttered as he moved away from the pharmacist to continue his search for suitable and available medication. Tom collected some Ibuprofen, a tube of muscle rub, a bottle of water and some chewing gum. These were all placed in a thin white plastic bag at checkout, where the friendly operative asked how he was feeling that fine morning. "I'll be much better once I dry out," said Tom as he collected his purchases and left the CVS.

Tom had been to St Pete's a number of times before and so was familiar with the area around its marina. He particularly enjoyed visiting the pier with its fast-food outlets, arcane shops and amusements. On sunny days, there was often a band playing and children would buy buckets of white fish, which they used to feed the numerous pelicans that populated the area. Also, if lucky, it was possible to spot the occasional dolphin.

As Tom headed back out into the grey and stormy weather, he doubted there'd be any dolphins spotted that day but on the plus side, the pier should be empty. With this in mind, he formulated a plan which consisted of him making his slow and torturous way to the end of the pier. Once there, he would find a sheltered spot, take a couple of Ibuprofen and apply the muscle rub. He would then peacefully sit and watch the ocean for signs of life and perhaps, he'd check in on Zoe and see how the mouse hunt was going.

Tom slowly retraced his steps but instead of continuing towards the Vinoy, he turned right at the marina and made his slow way along the path that would eventually lead him to the pier.

The wind continued to blow in wet gusts that agitated the angered and restless waves that churned around the pier's deep footings. Although the pelicans remained, they were hunched like miserable old men atop ornate iron rails, waiting patiently for the sun and the free fish to return. Tom, continuing his shuffling rhythmic hobble, in time with his unwittingly adopted marching tune of A Wobbling Merry Christmas, made his way resolutely and surprisingly, not unhappily, towards his goal at the pier's end.

As expected, the pier was deserted and Tom had the whole place to himself. He found a sheltered bench on which he slowly lowered himself, not caring that a loud groan escaped as he did so.

"At last," he breathed as he withdrew his phone from his pocket. It would still be quite early in England and he wanted to catch Zoe before she headed off to work.

"Field Marshall Zoe Montgomery at your service," Zoe said in her now undisguised west country accent.

"Hello, Zoe," said Tom with a smile. "How's the war going?"

"All quiet on the western front," she replied. "I got five of the little buggers and so, I'm still one short from becoming an ace. Although, I know there's a least one of the blighters left, so there's still hope. How's it going over in Florida? Bet you've got a nice tan by now."

"The weather's awful today," said Tom as he took the bottle of water from the plastic bag and undid its lid whilst holding the phone between his ear and raised shoulder. "And, I've managed to do myself a bit of an injury."

"What happened?" asked Zoe but just as Tom was going to relate his series of unfortunate events, a strong gust of wind took the now much lighter plastic bag and lifted it from where it sat on the bench next to Tom. Momentarily forgetting his pain and discomfort, Tom quickly stretched his arm into the air and grabbed hold of the bag.

However, the white tube of Ibuprofen escaped the bag and fell to the deck of the pier and began to roll away pushed by the wind.

"Hold on a second, Zoe, I've just got to grab something," groaned Tom as he raised himself and set off in slow and painful pursuit of the rolling tub of painkillers. The tub's momentum was slowing and Tom was closing in on it but when he was no more than eight or ten yards from recapturing his purchase, a pelican flumped down onto the deck like a soggy wet dumpling and scooped the tube up into its bill.

Having captured what, it must have thought was a fish, the bird hopped, skipped and jumped inelegantly into the air and soon disappeared into the grey and storm-shrouded sky. Tom stood aghast and forlorn as the wind and rain tugged and pulled at his hair and clothes.

"Zoe," he sighed into the phone. "There's no way you'll ever believe what's just happened to me."

20
Missed by Air Miles

Assumptia and Magdalene sat in the rear of the taxi they'd hired to transport them from Limoges Airport, to the address provided on the label of the suitcase they had unintentionally acquired in Rome. They had been released from custody after ten days but had been warned that they would face a much harsher sentence should they instigate or become involved in any further wrongdoings.

During their incarceration, the two sisters had decided, after much arguing, that upon release, they would immediately make their way to the village of Aigurande, swap suitcases and then return home to Dublin and St Mary's. There, they would take stock and try to work out how best to spend the rest of their lives, as well as the five million euros they had acquired upon the untimely death of their father.

Assumptia had tried to persuade Magdalene that they could do a lot worse than a trip to Las Vegas. However, Magdalene's plans revolved around a dating site she had discovered on the internet, meeting a suitable man or three, picking one and then settling down into a life of domestic bliss.

"The countryside hereabouts is quite pleasing to the eye, wouldn't you say, Assumptia?"

"There's certainly a lot of it," Assumptia replied dourly. "I haven't seen too many people though. Have you noticed that, Maggie? It's as empty as a synagogue when the collection plate comes around."

Magdalene, who Assumptia noticed had recently developed an odd facial twitch, now lent forward and tapped the taxi driver on the shoulder. "Excuse me, sir, could you perhaps tell us, where are all the people?"

"Pardon?" asked the taxi driver.

"Où est tout les people?" asked Magdalene slowly, her hand raised to massage a point of pain that had returned to her right temple.

"Ah," responded the driver. "Où sont tous les gens."

"Yes, that's it," said Magdalene excitedly. "Où sont tous les gens."

At that, the taxi driver started to softly sing and whilst the sisters could not understand the words, the tune was clearly that of the Beatles classic, Eleanor Rigby.

"Well, that went well," chuckled Assumptia smugly. "And ya fellas got a half-decent voice at that."

"Oh, do shut up, Assumptia, on occasions, you can really be quite tiresome."

It took the taxi the best part of an hour to reach the small town of Aigurande and to find the address provided by the sisters.

Assumptia levered herself out of the car and stood gazing around her, taking in the town's square, its church and the small gathering of houses and shops. "Hey, Maggie, would you just take a look at this; it's deader than Minane Bridge on a wet Sunday in February."

"I've asked the driver to wait and so, there's no time for sightseeing, Assumptia," Magdalene said irritably as she approached the large house indicated by the driver.

Climbing the three steps up to its front door, she pushed the ornate and grandly fashioned doorbell. A few moments later, a woman of perhaps sixty and dressed all in black answered the door. She looked at the two sisters, crossed herself and did a small courtesy before indicating that they should step inside.

"Oh thank, thank you," fussed Magdalene as she stepped into the hallway. "We shan't keep you."

"English?" inquired the woman.

"Certainly not!" exclaimed Assumptia. "We're Irish and proud."

Madame Girardet eyed the two nuns uncertainly. "Why are you here?" she asked.

"We are looking for Isabelle," said Magdalene. "We met briefly in Rome and somehow our suitcases have managed to get mixed up. Here," she handed Isabelle's suitcase to Madame Girardet. "Now, if you'd be so good as to provide us with our suitcase, we'll be on our way and leave you in peace."

Madame Girardet took the proffered suitcase and checked its label. "Yes, this is Isabelle's but she is not here."

Assumptia moved Magdalene to one side and stepped close to Madame Girardet, who took an involuntary step backwards.

"Where is she," Assumptia asked in a low and menacing voice.

"Well," said Madame Girardet who was suddenly feeling quite flustered and uneasy. "You just missed her. She has left here yesterday, for America."

This took the wind out of the sisters' sails and Magdalene swooned before falling into the arms of a surprised Madame Girardet.

"Are you unwell, Sister," she asked in concern as she helped Magdalene steady herself. "Come into the kitchen and I'll make us some coffee."

Assumptia followed Madame Girardet, who was still supporting Magdalene as she made her way into the Kitchen. Madame Girardet deposited Magdalene into a sturdy kitchen chair, pointed to another for Assumptia and then set about filling a kettle.

"There must be something very valuable in the suitcase for you to come all this way," said Madame Girardet. "But Isabelle never brought the case home with her from Italy."

"Is that right?" asked Assumptia. "Wouldn't happen to know what she did with it then, would you?"

"It hasn't been easy here," Madame Girardet continued with a sniff. "Isabelle returned home in a rush because her father was dying. He, my husband, he's gone now. Mort. And Isabelle, she has left again but as I said, she did not have a suitcase with her when she returned home."

They sat in silence for a while as they waited for the kettle to boil.

"And she, Isabelle, has now gone off to America you say?" asked Assumptia.

"Yes, she left yesterday. She is going to meet her boyfriend. He is English and is in America working at the moment. They met in Rome"

"Small world," mumbled Assumptia with barely concealed frustration.

The doorbell chimed and so, Madame Girardet excused herself and went to the door. She returned a few moments later. "Sisters, it is the taxi driver. He wants to go but you need to pay him first."

Magdalene slowly stood like a combatant resigned to defeat and just waiting for the knockout blow to fall. She turned her sad face towards her sister, a sudden and uncontrolled twitch contorting her usual superior countenance and making it look as though she were giving her sister an exaggerated wink.

"Shall we go, Assumptia?"

"Please, Sisters, you should wait," interrupted Madame Girardet.

Assumptia and Magdalene both turned to stared at her in surprise.

"Isabelle promised she would call me just as soon as she arrives safely in America. When she does, I'll ask her about the suitcase."

Suddenly brightening Assumptia and Magdalene looked at each other and smiled warmly.

"That'd be just grand," enthused Assumptia. "Maggie, you'd best go settle up with Paul McCartney. Missus Girardet, is it? Would you happen to have some whiskey in the house? I find it helps with the coffee."

21
The State of the Reunion

They embraced tightly, as a now relatively pain-free Tom lifted Isabelle from her feet and spun her around in a slow circle. "Oh, Tommy, it is so good to see you," Isabelle laughed happily.

"Much better than kissing my tablet," said Tom between kisses. "I have missed you so very much."

"I can't believe it," enthused Isabelle. "Here we both are, together again and in America." Then suddenly pouting Isabelle looked down intently into Tom's eyes and said, "Promise me, Tommy, you must stay with me, always."

They kissed some more before Tom eased his hold on Isabelle, letting her feet slide softly down onto the floor of the arrival's hall at Tampa airport. "Don't you worry, Issi," said Tom seriously. "There's nowhere I'd rather be than with you."

They embraced, squeezing themselves tightly together again.

When they parted and Tom reached out to take the handle of Isabelle's suitcase, she tugged at his sleeve. "Wait a moment, Tommy, I called Mama whilst waiting for my luggage to arrive and she told me that two nuns are at my home. They have followed me from Rome because of a mix-up with the suitcases. Do you still have my, no, their suitcase?"

Subconsciously, Tom raised his hand and rubbed the top of his head before checking his watch. He had suddenly started to feel uneasy but didn't know why. "I'll call Zoe once we're back at the hotel," he said.

"No, Tommy, please call her now, Mama says she doesn't like the feel of these strangers. She wants to help but she wants them gone too."

"OK," said Tom as he reached into one of his pockets and pulled out his mobile. "I'll call Zoe now. We might just catch her before she leaves for her evening shift."

The phone rang just once before it was picked up. "Hello, Tom," chirped Zoe. "What a lovely surprise!"

"How did you know it was me?" asked Tom.

"Because it's always you, nobody else ever calls the landline. Actually, I'm surprised you still have one. Every other landline in Britain left with the Romans in about 400AD."

"Oh, I see," said Tom, screwing up his face but otherwise ignoring Zoe's jibe. "Listen, Zoe, would you please do me a favour."

"That's more like it, lover, thought you'd never ask," Zoe responded cheekily. "Do you want me to talk dirty to you?"

Isabelle flushed and raised her eyes to the ceiling. "Mon Dieu, we must have words about your lodger."

"Who's that?" asked Zoe.

"It's Isabelle, I'm just picking her up from the airport."

"Sorry, Tom. Tell her I was just having a laugh, nothing more to it than that."

"I'll do my best, Zoe, but for now, could you please take a look at that suitcase under your bed and let me know whether it's got a name and address tag on it."

"Roger, will do; oh, by the way, I got number six and number seven, so I am now officially a mouse ace!"

"Now please, Zoe."

"OK, MOG, just wait a sec."

Tom turned and smiled weakly at Isabelle. "She's very mischievous," he said.

Isabelle just tilted her head to one side and raised an eyebrow. "Do I trust you, Tommy?"

"Hey, Tom," Zoe's voice interrupted. "The luggage label says it belongs to a Patrick Malone. There's a Dublin address."

"Right."

"Is there a problem, Tom?" Zoe asked.

"Hold on a second, Zoe," Tom turned to Isabelle. "Did you hear all of that, Issi?"

"Oui, hold on I'll call Mama."

Whilst Isabelle conversed with her mother, Tom chatted to Zoe about the mix-up with the cases and the nuns that had turned up at Isabelle's home.

"Must be something very valuable in that case for them nuns to troop all the way from Rome to get it back," ventured Zoe.

"Hold on please, Zoe," said Tom. He turned to Isabelle questioningly.

"The nuns would like an address from where they can collect the case," said Isabelle.

"OK," said Tom. "Just give me a moment." He placed a finger to his lips in a gesture indicating silence and pointed at Isabelle's phone. Isabelle nodded and tapped the mute button on her mobile. "Zoe, I'm putting you back on speaker so please behave and keep it clean."

"OK, landlord," replied Zoe.

"Zoe, the nuns want to come and collect their suitcase. Now, I don't know why but I've got an uneasy feeling about this whole thing. So, I don't want them to know where we live. Would it be possible for you to take the case with you to the Samaritan? If so, I'll give the nuns the address of the pub and they can collect it from there."

"Sounds like a decent plan, landlord. Leave it with me and I'll take it to work with me this evening."

"Thank you, Zoe. Let me know once it's collected."

"Will do! TTFN and love to Isabelle."

With that, the connection was ended and Tom asked his mobile for the address of the Good Samaritan before turning to Isabelle.

"The address is The Good Samaritan, Turner Street, London E1."

Isabelle related the message to her mother before ending the call. "It is so bizarre, Tommy, what can possibly be in that suitcase that would lead them to follow me all the way home to France?"

"That, we shall never know," replied Tom as he again subconsciously rubbed the top of his head. "Let's get to the hotel, I've booked us a table for lunch."

"There are lots of reasons why I want you to take me back to the hotel, Tommy," said Isabelle silkily as she pulled herself close to Tom and whispered into his ear, "And lunch is not at the top of my list."

22
Backroom Lover

Roxy's head was cushioned by her arm and her arm rested against the rear wall of the grocery store's back room. Her dress was rucked up to her waist as Frankie worked himself deeply and slowly into her from behind.

"Is this any better, Missus Pasternak?"

"Yes, Frankie, that's r—real nice," gasped Roxy.

Frankie quickly discovered that the best way of keeping Roxy happy was to move in time with the rhythm of *I Miss You* by the punk band Blink 182, which he sang quietly to himself during this stage of their lovemaking.

"I think I love you, Missus Pasternak," Frankie said rhythmically. Despite sometimes overwhelming urges to the contrary, he somehow managed to stay focused and diligently kept to the requested pace.

"T—that's nice Frankie."

"You know, I'll do absolutely anything for you. You do know that, don't you, Missus Pasternak?"

"You're d—doing exactly w—what I want you to do right now, Frankie."

"But if there's anything else, anything at all, you just let me know."

"I—I w—will, Frankie. You could just pick up the pace a little bit now."

"OK," said Frankie as he changed his imagined jukebox track to Staying Alive by the Bee Gees and increased his rhythmic thrusting. "My dad's been receiving complaints about me from customers. He wants to know why I keep closing up the store," he panted.

"Oh, God!" Roxy gasped urgently. "Faster, Frankie, faster."

Frankie quickly whizzed through his mental record collection until he landed on the woowho chorus of Song 2 by Blur. "He says that if I keep closing the store, then he'll find someone to replace me. Someone who can keep it open when it's supposed to be."

Roxy suddenly arched her back and let out a long and strangled cry of ecstasy before relaxing once more. “You can stop now, Frankie,” she said. She then turned a dreamy flushed face towards her young and panting lover. “Thank you, Frankie, that was very, very nice. Sorry, Frankie, did you say something?”

“But I’m not finished yet,” Frankie complained.

Roxy looked up at Frankie and gently stroked his face before kissing him on the cheek.

“Poor, Frankie, you need to learn that life is all about timing and if you get the timing wrong, well, darling, you just miss out.” She gently tapped his cheek twice. “Now, you’d best pull up your pants and open up the store.”

“Gee, Missus Pasternak, you can be harsh,” Frankie said sulkily as he sorted out his clothing.

Roxy pulled the lower half of her dress down from her waist before taking a compact mirror from her handbag and checking her face. “I’m sorry, Frankie, I’m pushed for time today but I promise that I’ll make it up to you,” she said as she reapplied her lipstick. “I may even let you do something really very naughty to me.”

Frankie grinned as he rezipped his pants; “That’d be so cool, Missus Pasternak, my friends say it’s the best.”

Roxy smiled back at him; “In that case, we should try it,” she said. “But I may need you to do something for me first.”

23
Pillow Talk

The days following Isabelle's arrival passed agonisingly slowly for Tom, who resented every minute he was forced to be away from her.

In contrast, the evenings and nights simply sped by in a haze of unbridled happiness. Hand in hand, they would go for long walks on which they would follow St. Pete's gentle coastline. They would visit the town's waterfront bars and restaurants and sometimes listen to the live music of the local entertainers. Then, they would return to the hotel and make love long into the night. Tom could not remember ever being so happy and Isabelle wholeheartedly shared these feelings of warm contentment.

"Where shall we go when this is over?" Isabelle asked one evening as they lay in bed together.

"Back to London, I suppose," said Tom. "I'll miss this, the sound of the sea and the warm evenings. But I'll certainly be glad to get tomorrow over and done with."

"Are you worried about being cross-examined in court tomorrow?"

"Yes, I don't want to spoil things. We've all worked so hard on this case but a jury can be a fickle bunch and Pasternak's legal team is doing a very good job."

Isabelle shifted her position so she lay on her side and could look at the profile of Tom's face. "How so?" she asked.

"They're cunning," replied Tom as he also moved, finally settling into a position in which their noses almost touched. "There's this woman, Emily Rudd and she does most of the questioning. She looks really ill and seems to have a constant cold. Also, she keeps getting things procedurally wrong so the judge reprimands her at least a dozen times a day."

"I don't understand," said Isabelle.

"The jury looks at this feeble, unwell young woman who keeps getting told off by the big mean old judge and they feel sorry for her. They want to help her. The whole thing is a damned theatre. And then, there's Horace. Today or rather yesterday now, the judge allowed him to use the courtroom like some kind of personal promotional stand.

"He waltzed about the place telling everyone about how he brings work and money from all over the states into Florida and this enables him to provide the good people of this state with jobs so they can afford to feed their families. Me, on the other hand, am the representative of a foreign insurance company who, doesn't mind taking their money but when it comes to paying out claims, I try to make out that they're criminals."

"Poor, Tommy," said Isabelle with an exaggerated pout.

Tom quickly moved his head forward and nipped the end of Isabelle's nose. "Ouch! That hurt me, Tommy," she giggled and writhed as Tom's fingers tickled her stomach.

"Serves you right," said Tom before again returning to the subject that was playing upon his mind. "And guess what, the other day, Pasternak approached me and asked how I thought the case was going. He was all smiles and bon amie, it was so weird."

"What did you say?"

"I said that at the end of the day, people just don't like arsonists."

"No, seriously? That's very brave of you. How did he react."

"He smiled at me, slapped me on the back, all friendly like and said that whilst generally, he agreed with me, it just so happens that people in Florida like insurance companies even less."

Isabelle started to giggle. "Oh, Tommy, I like this man, he is very funny."

"And that's the trouble, Isabelle. I like him too and worryingly, so does the jury and therein lays the problem."

"Still," Isabelle said as she turned to lay on her back and stare up at the room's ceiling. "There is nothing you can do about that and so, there's no point in worrying yourself. All you can do is to try your very best and if that is not enough to convince the jury—well, c'est la vie."

Tom turned on to his back and joined Isabelle in staring up at the ceiling. "I guess you're right, Issi. Still, it's very daunting."

Deciding to change the subject, Isabelle asked, "Have you heard from the lodger?"

"She does have a name you know and yes, I received a message earlier today. She wanted to borrow my car."

Isabelle returned to her previous position to look at Tom. "You have a car?" she asked.

"Yes, it's a bit old but it's comfortable and fast."

"A bit like yourself, Tommy," Isabelle said with a smirk.

Tom turned his head to look at her and poked out his tongue. "Anyway," he continued. "I said no. I'm not sure whether my insurance would cover her and anyway, she said she needed it to help someone she'd met at work. Some cock and bull story about safe deposit boxes or something. It all sounded very odd."

Tom went on to relay the story that Zoe had told him but his storytelling was interrupted by a sudden quiet snore that told him that Isabelle had fallen to sleep.

24
Tom Takes the Stand

"Mister Harrison, would you please approach the bench and raise your right hand."

Tom had seen this a thousand times before on television but actually playing a part in this real-life drama was something completely different. Once Tom had been sworn in by an officer of the court, he was ushered into the witness box.

The witness box directly faced the jury, the two tiers occupied by the judge, the court reporter and the clerk of the court were to Tom's right and the area in which Mister Pasternak's legal team sat was immediately to his left, with Tom's own legal team sat to the left of the jury. Tom sat in the box and adjusted the antenna like microphone that snaked up immediately in front of him.

"For the court, would you please state your name, title and who you represent here today."

Trying his best to feel and exude confidence, Tom cleared his throat and leant towards the microphone. "My name is T."

The court reporter, a very flamboyantly camp man who Tom guessed was close to seventy years of age, threw up his hands and turned an aggrieved, wrinkled but precisely manicured face up towards the judge. "He's just too loud Ma'am, he's deafening me," the reporter complained bitterly.

The judge sighed apologetically before turning to Tom and asking him not to speak so loudly into the microphone or to distance himself a little from it. Tom apologised and sat back in the chair before continuing, "My name is Tom."

The court reporter again winced before removing his headset and turning to complain to the judge once more. "I just can't hear a single word he is saying, Ma'am, this is just too ridiculous!"

"Yes, thank you, Mister Stenner. Mister Harrison," said the judge, again turning her attention to Tom. "If perhaps you could adjust your position so you're a little closer to the microphone?"

Now, feeling acutely embarrassed, Tom apologised once more before adjusting his position by leaning awkwardly into the middle distance between where he sat and the microphone. "My name is Tom Harrison," he cast his eyes in a nervous sideways look towards the judge's bench, and received an encouraging nod of approval from Mister Stenner. "I am here today as a representative of Mallory Syndicate at Lloyd's of London, England."

Tom was then asked to tell the court a little bit about Lloyd's and its structure and how Mallory syndicate fitted into that structure. He was also asked to divulge information about himself, his education and his position within Mallory. Thankfully, he managed this whilst maintaining his awkward and uncomfortable stance within the witness box. Then the cross-examination commenced in earnest and this was undertaken by George Church.

"Mister Harrison, would you please take a look at the screen behind you."

Tom looked desperately at George Church. It had taken him three attempts to get his position exactly right for the court reporter and now he was being asked to look behind him.

Trying to retain his position, Tom swivelled his upper body awkwardly to his left but there was no way he could see the screen without giving up his stance and so he conceded and turned.

"Mister Harrison, can you please tell the court what this document is."

Tom carefully returned to his position and responded gingerly, whilst again giving the court reporter a sideways glance. "It's an insurance application form."

"Mister Harrison," George Church announced. "Would you please speak up so the good people of the jury can hear you?"

Tom swallowed and tried again. "It is an insurance application form."

"For the benefit of the jury," George Church loudly proclaimed. "Mister Harrison informs us that the document now shown on the screen is an insurance application form. Mister Harrison, can you see the date on which that insurance application form was signed."

Tom again turned in his chair to look back at the form shown on the screen behind the witness box. Having accomplished this, he turned back to face George Church.

"Yes, I can," said Tom.

George Church pulled a face like someone compelled to deal with an imbecile. "Well, Mister Harrison," he continued theatrically. "Perhaps you'd be good enough to share the date with the court."

"So, you heard that OK?" asked Tom with feigned innocence.

"Loud and clear, Mister Harrison."

"Surprising," said Tom. "The date is the first of February."

"The first of April," continued George Church. "Three whole months before the fire, which you Mister Harrison of Mallory Syndicate at Lloyd's of London, England, is alleging that my client started himself in an illegal and despicable attempt to defraud Mallory Syndicate at Lloyd's of London, England. Wouldn't you say that three months is a long time to wait if, as you allege, the sole intention of Mister Pasternak when purchasing the insurance policy provided by Mallory Syndicate at Lloyd's of London, England, was to commit a fraud?"

"Mister Church," interrupted the judge. "I believe we have sufficiently established who issued the insurance policy and who Mister Harrison represents here today. Would you please refrain from doing whatever the hell it is you think you're doing?"

"Yes, ma'am. I apologise. Mister Harrison, would you please answer the question."

"No," said Tom.

The court reporter let out a screech and tore the headset off before throwing it down. "I'm sorry judge," he whinged. "He's just too close to the microphone again."

"Mister Harrison," the judge said sympathetically. "Would you please do your best to ensure you don't deafen Mister Stenner?"

Tom nodded and apologised once again.

"Mister Harrison," continued George Church. "So, you've told the court that you don't believe that three months is a long time for my client to wait before perpetrating the crime that you," George Church took this opportunity to point an accusing finger directly at Tom, "that you Mister Harrison allege that my client has committed—"

"Yes," Tom said carefully.

"Yes, what?" asked George Church. "Yes, you believe it is a long time to wait or yes you don't believe it's a long time to wait?"

"No, I was answering your question by confirming that I did not believe three months was a long time for Mister Pasternak to wait before he burnt down his business."

"OK, thank you for clarifying that, Mister Harrison. Now, do you believe it strange that if my client did as you allege and committed arson and thereby insurance fraud, do you believe it's strange that he hasn't been arrested and thrown into prison?"

Tom thought about this before responding. "Possibly."

"No conjecture here, Mister Harrison, it's either a yes or no. Do you understand that?"

"Yes," replied Tom.

"So, Mister Harrison, you do believe it's strange that if, as you allege, my client has committed arson and is now attempting to commit insurance fraud, that it is strange that he has not been arrested and thrown into prison?"

"No," responded Tom. "I was confirming that I understood that conjecture isn't allowed."

"Very amusing, Mister Harrison," said George Church as he threw a disgusted look at Tom, who sat stone-faced and totally unaware that he'd been in any way amusing.

Close examination of the various insurance documents continued wearily throughout the long morning before George Church changed tack to focus on the circumstances surrounding the fire. "So, Mister Harrison, during your deposition you stated," at this point, George Church read from a batch of documents he was holding. "That the only possible method of entry to the premises on the night of the fire was via a security door to which, my client alone knew the security code."

George turned a thoughtful face towards Tom. "Why do you believe that no one other than Mister Pasternak knew the security code to the door?"

Tom was getting tired and wanted to be just about anywhere other than where he currently sat. With a sigh, he answered, "Because that's what he told us during his deposition."

"Who told you, Mister Harrison?"

"Mister Pasternak," answered Tom.

"So, did you dust for prints?"

"Why would I dust for prints?" Tom responded a little tetchily. "Mister Pasternak's prints would be on the security lock because it led to his office and if we'd found any other prints, so what, according to Mister Pasternak, no one other than him had the passcode."

"So, just to reiterate what you've told the court under oath, Mister Harrison; No, you did not test for prints. Is that correct?"

"Correct," responded Tom.

"Mister Harrison," George Church continued. "When you carried out your investigations into the possible cause of the fire, did you consider spontaneous combustion?"

"Now, that's just ridiculous!" The fact that Tom was beginning to lose his patience was now becoming clear by the tone of his responses. "So, are you suggesting that stuff in various locations throughout the warehouse miraculously self-combusted all at the same time?"

"Mister Harrison, may I remind you that I am the one asking the questions here today," Mister Church answered smugly. "Am I'm taking it from your response that you did not consider spontaneous combustion?"

"Correct," Tom responded stiffly.

"So," George Church continued. "Is it fair to say that your investigations were incomplete at the time of your decision to decline my client's claim?"

"Incorrect."

"How so? Please advise the court how, in the absence of a full and thorough investigation, including dusting for fingerprints and consideration of spontaneous combustion, you can consider the investigations that you instigated and directed on behalf of Mallory Syndicate, as complete?"

"The court has heard from our experts," said Tom tightly. "And, it was based upon the findings of those experts and certain other information that came to light during the course of our investigations that we finally made our decision to decline Mister Pasternak's claim."

George Church turned to the jury, sighed and shook his head in feigned disappointment before turning to look back at Tom. "No further questions at this point in time," he said before returning to sit with his colleague Emily Rudd and a smiling Horace Pasternak.

"Man, you were funny," said Joe once Tom had sat back down next to him. "The jury thinks you're a fucking clown or something and the court reporter would like to tear your guts out and use them as earrings. But the good thing is, you did no damage. Come on, let's get some food."

They stood up and made their way out of the courtroom and towards the war room, where they found Randy Bird waiting by the door. The other members of Mallory's legal team were already standing silently inside.

"Would you give us a moment, Tom," said Randy as he ushered joe inside before closing the door in Tom's face.

"Who needs enemies when you've got friends like that?"

Tom turned around to see Horace Pasternak smiling at him. "They do that to you a lot. I wouldn't trust them if I was you."

"It sometimes feels that way," replied Tom.

"I guess you don't like being here anymore than I do?"

"It's OK when I'm not in court. I'm staying at the Vinoy in St Pete's, which is a really nice hotel. Yes, I'm happy when I'm not here."

"It'll soon be over, Mister Harrison," said Horace as he patted Tom on the back. "Then you can go home but take my advice, you'll need to start looking for another job."

"How so?" asked Tom.

"Because I'm going to make Mallory pay millions, you just wait and see and when I do, they'll not be welcoming you back to blighty with open arms."

Tom laughed. "God loves an optimist, Mister Pasternak. Whether or not he loves an arsonist, only time will tell."

25
London Calling

"I'm tired of travelling, Maggie. The only place we stayed for more than a couple of days was a French prison and I'd not like to go back there."

The two sisters sat in the back of a black cab as it nudged and dodged its way through the busy London traffic. They had managed to get a direct flight from Limoges to London Stansted. There, they had boarded the train into London's Liverpool Street Station and upon arrival had jumped into the back of a black cab and were now heading towards the Good Samaritan Public House.

"It's awfully busy, isn't it, Assumptia?" said Magdalene, who sat with her head slightly bowed as she gently massaged her right temple. "Would you just take a look at all the people, there are so many different colours? It's a very cosmopolitan city and no mistake."

"Surprisingly enough, I like the look of it," replied Assumptia. "It's just a shame that it's packed full of English."

The two sisters turned to look at each other before bursting into laughter.

"You'll find it's packed full of more than just English," interrupted the taxi driver. "It's a league of nations out there and where you've asked me to take you, well, you could say that it's a part of London that's full of eastern promise. We're just arriving now sisters, here we are on the right-hand side."

The cab slowly drew to a halt outside of an attractive traditional-looking public house. "How much do we owe you?" Magdalene enquired with a tired sigh.

"No, call it my good deed for the day," said the cabbie. "This is on my way home anyway but I would be grateful if you'd just say a little prayer for me."

This was the first act of generosity and kindness the sisters had experienced in quite some time and they were both a little taken aback.

"Well, God bless you," said Assumptia soberly. "I never expected such kindness from an Englishman too, who would have thought it."

Magdalene was astonished to see her sister use one of her large beefy hands to wipe a tear away.

"What are you looking at, Maggie, I just have something in my eye that's all. Come on, you can buy me a drink with the money you've saved on the cab fare."

They bid the taxi driver goodbye before turning to enter the public house. It was early evening and although the pub was busy enough, it was by no means crowded. Assumptia and Magdalene stepped up to the bar and waited to be served. When they had entered a group of men standing a little further along the bar had fell silent as they took in the unusual sight of two nuns entering a pub.

"Ah, fellas, pay us no heed," Assumptia said to the group of men. "We're not here collecting for charity but just to pick up something that belongs to us."

It was at this point that Zoe appeared behind the bar carrying the battered old suitcase. "Good evening, Sisters, I believe this is what you've been looking for."

With that Zoe heaved the suitcase onto the bar and spun it around so that the handle and latches faced the two nuns. "You'd best open it up and take a look inside to make sure it's yours."

Assumptia and Magdalene quickly looked at each other and then at the suitcase. "I don't think that'll be necessary just now," said Magdalene nervously.

"Suit yourselves," said Zoe. "Now, Sisters, seeing as you're here, can I get you both a drink? On the house, of course."

"Well," said Assumptia with sudden brightness. "I think I've been doing the good folk of England a great injustice! What'll you have, Maggie?"

"A sweet sherry for me," replied Magdalene with a warm smile.

"Right you are, a sweet sherry and a pint of the black stuff for me," boomed Assumptia.

Just then there was a burst of raucous laughter from the group of men at the bar, which made Assumptia turn suspiciously towards them.

"What's so funny boys?" she asked menacingly. "You wouldn't happen to be laughing at me and my sister, would you?"

"No, no, no," said the youngest looking of the group. "Michael here was just telling a joke, that's all."

Assumptia reached out and grabbed the pint of stout that Zoe had placed on the bar for her and lifting it to her mouth, took several long swallows before returning the nearly empty pint glass to the bar. "Assumptia, you have a white moustache," whispered Magdalene.

"I like a joke myself," said Assumptia, her glare fixed upon the grey-haired man identified as Michael. "Tell me what was so funny."

"I don't think you'd like it," said Michael uncomfortably. "It's a bit rude."

"Ah," said Assumptia. "Do my ears deceive me or do I detect a note of the old country in your voice, Michael?"

"That ya do, Sister," Michael responded happily. "I'm originally from County Cork. A little-known place by the name of Fountainstown."

"Ach, I knew it!" responded Assumptia happily. "Now, unless ya want me sisterly boot up ya arse, you'd best get on with ya story."

"OK," said Michael, a little taken aback by Assumptia's forthrightness. "But let me get you another drink first. Zoe, my darling! The same again for the sisters. Now ladies, promise me you won't be offended?"

Receiving no response, Michael cleared his throat before continuing, "A bus full of nuns get killed in a road accident and now, they're all waiting at the gates of heaven to be let in by Saint Peter. Saint Peter says welcome to heaven and I just need to ask you a few questions before I can let you through the pearly gates. He then asks the first nun whether or not she's ever touched a penis."

"Oh my," said Magdalene as she stepped closer to Michael so that she could hear the story clearly above the general hubbub of the pub. "The nun," continued Michael, "says that she once touched a penis with the tip of her little finger. Go and wash your little finger in the holy water, says Saint Peter and then you'll be allowed into heaven. He then turns to the second nun and asks her the same question. The second nun says that she once held a penis in her hand."

Magdalene placed her empty sherry glass on the bar before picking up its replacement. "Oh, do go on," she encouraged Michael.

Michael cleared his throat again and gave Magdalene a nervous look before continuing, "Well, Saint Peter tells the second nun that she too must wash her hands in the holy water. Just then, Saint Peter detects some commotion and it seems that there is one nun trying to push her way to the front of the queue. What's the rush, Sister Susan, asks the Saint and she replies, well, if I'm going to have to gargle with the holy water, I want to do so before Sister Mary washes her arse in it."

Silence fell like a heavy blanket as everyone held their breath.

Then, like a dam bursting, Assumptia and Magdalene both erupted into laughter, joined shortly thereafter by a relieved Michael and his group of friends. More drinks were ordered and consumed, as a party atmosphere was brought suddenly to life.

As it turned out, Michael and his friends belonged to a darts team that had popped into the Good Samaritan on route to another venue where a match was to take place. Unfortunately, but much to Assumptia's delight, they were a player down.

"I throw a mean dart myself," she announced with pride. "Sign me up and I'll win the match for ya."

They all trooped off to the match together and the night that followed was to be one that lived fondly in the Sisters' memories for quite some time thereafter. Assumptia proved to be as good as she'd boasted and after the match was won, the victors sat around in happy and well-lubricated comradery.

"Are you OK there, Maggie?" slurred Assumptia dreamily as she watched her sister talking quietly with Michael.

"I'm fine thank you, Assumptia. In fact, I'm having a wonderful time." She beamed at Michael before planting a soft kiss on his cheek.

*

"What happened to you last night?" asked Assumptia, as she fixed her sister with two tired and bloodshot eyes.

The two sisters were waiting in yet another airport check-in queue. This one was at Stansted airport and was for the flight home to Dublin.

"The same as what happened to you, Assumptia," said Magdalene primly. "We both spent the night at Michael's home and very pleasant it was too, despite your unremitting and extremely loud snores."

"Ay," confessed Assumptia, "I think I may have had one for the road too many. Now, Maggie, you didn't get up anything you that shouldn't have, did you?"

Magdalene gave Assumptia an outraged look and blustered, "How could you even suggest such a thing? And even if I did, which I can assure you I most certainly didn't, it would have absolutely nothing to do with you!"

Assumptia had the good grace to look down, shamefaced at her feet. "I'm sorry, Maggie," she said. "It's just that you're my little sister and I've always had to look out for you."

"That's alright then," replied a slightly mollified Magdalene. "We'll say no more about it."

"Right you are," Assumptia said slowly. "Only, what did you do then?"

"Oh, it was wonderful, Assumptia!" enthused Magdalene, whose face suddenly lit up at the memory. "We, Michael and I that is, talked and talked. It was so marvellous Assumptia, I've never spoken to anyone, let alone a gentleman, about the sort of things we spoke about. It was like, like, Oh, I don't know what it was like but it was magical and I shall never forget it."

"So, you had a good time then, did you, Maggie?" Assumptia asked softly as she gently patted her sister on the shoulder.

"I had the best time, Assumptia. The very best."

"So did I, Maggie, so did I," Assumptia sighed happily before her expression suddenly clouded and the smile fell from her chubby round face. "God alone knows what's waiting for us back in Dublin," she whispered anxiously. "God alone knows."

26
The Honey Trap

Horace and Roxy sat opposite each other at the kitchen table in their small condominium apartment. Their evening meal of ham and green salad sat neglected and forlorn between them. Horace was unhappy and tonight, it wasn't just his dinner that was making him sad.

"Come on, Horri baby," encouraged Roxy. "You gotta keep your strength up. Please baby, just try to eat a little something."

"I can't, sugar," Horace replied sadly. "And anyway, you know I don't like this shit." Horace prodded the salad with his fork before letting the fork drop from his hand to clunk noisily against the plate.

"What's the matter, Horri, is the case getting to you?"

"I guess so," responded Horace with a heavy sigh. "The case gets wrapped up on Monday and then the jury will go and decide whether to make me a millionaire or and this is what worries me, send me to the cleaners. If we don't win this case, Roxy, then I'm ruined. No, we're ruined."

"Is it really that bad, Horri?"

"Yes, it's really that bad. I have next to nothing left. I can't make the repayments on the car and the rent on this place is overdue not to mention, my overdraft at the bank resembles the national debt of some third-world nation. God Roxy, what are we going to do if I lose?"

"Do you truly think it'll come to that, Horace?"

Horace looked up and into Roxy's eyes. The only time Roxy had called him by his name before was when they had exchanged wedding vows and now as he stared at her, he could see the colour draining from Roxy's face.

"It's possible but please know this," Horace said as he reached an arm over the ham salad to grasp Roxy's hand. "Whatever happens, we'll always have each other."

Roxy snatched her hand away in sudden horror.

"What's wrong?" Horace asked, his voice thick with hurt.

"No, nothing. I'm sorry, Horri, it's just that you were so certain we'd be fine and now you're saying that you're not so sure. Is there anything I can do to help?"

Horace continued to stare at Roxy for a few moments before slouching back into his chair and scratching his head. "I don't know, Sugar, maybe I'm just getting edgy because the finish line is so close. I bet that English guy is just as nervous as I am about this whole thing."

"Do you think so, Horri? What about if I go check him out, subtle like and see how he's doing?"

"What do you have in mind, Roxy?" asked Horace with sudden desperate interest.

"Well, I don't know, Horri. What do you think it'll take to definitely swing the decision in our favour?"

Horace gave this some thought. "Maybe if we could discredit him in some way. Compromise him. Roxy, I think I have an idea!"

Roxy pursed her lips as she looked down at her long red fingernails. "Fire away, Horri," she said although she was already pretty sure what Horace had in mind.

"Well, I don't quite know how to say this, what with you being my wife and all but maybe, just maybe and it's your decision but maybe."

"Just spit it out, Horri," demanded Roxy testily.

"What about if you doll yourself up and get over to the Vinoy. Perhaps you could fool Mister Harrison into thinking he's the luckiest man alive and then, just when he thinks he's reached home base, well, it's then that you cry rape. He gets busted, the case collapses and I, sorry I mean we, walk away with millions."

"How far do you want me to go, Horri?" asked Roxy, a little surprised that Horace's suggestion had taken a slight detour from what she'd expected him to ask.

"Go as far as it takes baby," said Horace gleefully. "As far as it takes." Horace looked smugly at his wife for several seconds before asking; "Well, are you going to do it or not?"

"What, you want me to go right now?" she asked in surprise.

"No time like the present," beamed Horace.

"Aren't you even a little bit jealous?" asked Roxy.

"It's tearing me apart, Sugar," Horace lied unconvincingly. "But we all gotta make sacrifices if we want to get on. And, you do like the nice stuff, don't you, sugar."

"Yeah, I do like a nice stuff, Horri," said Roxy with a strange crooked smile. "The nicer the better."

27
The Case Is Closed

"Mother Superior, Mother Superior, they're back!"

The old nun, who sat behind a large dark wooden desk decorated with a green leather inlay looked up over the top of her wire-rimmed spectacles at the plump young sister who had burst into her office without knocking.

"Sister Mary, would you please compose yourself," she said with a sigh. "Now, please tell me, what has made you burst into my office wailing like a banshee?"

The young nun flushed and bobbed awkwardly in apology. "Sorry, Mother Superior, I got a bit carried away what with all the excitement and all. It's just that Sisters Assumptia and Magdalene, well, they're back!"

"Are they indeed," said the Mother Superior as she rose tiredly to her feet. "In that case, would you please go and fetch them here to my office. And Mary, walk, don't run."

This last comment just caught Sister Mary as she headed excitedly out of the door. Once Mary had gone, the Mother Superior picked up the receiver of the heavy black telephone that was situated upon her desk and dialled a number that she'd taken from a small card that had been held under it. She listened patiently as the phone on the other end of the connection rang several times and was about to replace the receiver when it was finally answered.

"Hello, is that inspector Lawrence? Yes, hello, it's Mother Superior Hartley here. I thought you'd be interested to learn, they're back."

Having made the call, the Mother Superior sat slowly and achingly back down. Having successfully completed this manoeuvre, she began to tap her long arthritic fingers upon the desk in front of her whilst she waited for her two itinerant charges to make their long overdue reappearance. She didn't have to wait too long before and this time, following a polite knocking upon her door,

Sister Mary appeared and solemnly announced the arrival of Sisters Assumptia and Magdalene Malone.

"Ah, welcome back, Sisters," said the Mother Superior as she beckoned Assumptia and Magdalene into her office. "Please, excuse me for not rising, I'm not as young as I once was and these days, even the most mundane movements are apt to cause me some degree of discomfort. Please, put your cases down. Sister Mary, you may go now," continued the Mother Superior whilst making a quick shooing motion with one of her aged and liver-spotted hands.

Sister Mary looked piqued at the dismissal but left with no choice, she bobbed her plain plump head several times before reversing herself out of the Mother Superior's office and closing the door quietly behind her.

"Now, Sisters," began the Mother Superior. "If you'd both please take a seat," she said whilst indicating the two heavy chairs placed immediately before her desk. The sisters nodded cautiously as they awkwardly lowered themselves into the chairs as instructed.

"Good, now, if you're both sitting comfortably," the Mother Superior continued once the sisters had settled and stopped fidgeting. "Perhaps you'd be good enough to tell me where you've been and why?"

Magdalene swallowed loudly but said nothing, whilst Assumptia just stared blankly ahead of her as if in a trance.

"Well, come now, Sisters, let's not be getting coy," the Mother Superior urged encouragingly. "I believe I've waited long enough for your explanation and so, if you know what's good for you, you'd best not keep me waiting any longer."

"Well," began Magdalene nervously. "Assumptia and I thought it'd be a good idea to—" Magdalene faltered.

"To?" prompted the Mother Superior her voice suddenly adopting an impatient edge.

"To go on a pilgrimage," interjected Assumptia.

The Mother Superior raised her eyebrows in surprise.

"Yes, that's the word I was searching for," continued Magdalene. "A pilgrimage. And we thought what better place to go for a pilgrimage than to the eternal city of Rome."

"That's right," added Assumptia. "We thought we'd pop in and say hello to the Pope."

"His Holiness the Pope that is," corrected Magdalene.

"And did you?" the Mother Superior asked.

The two sisters stared back at her blankly. "Did we what exactly, Mother Superior?" Assumptia asked carefully.

The Mother Superior gave Assumptia a cold look and replied; "Did you pop in and say hello to His Holiness?"

"Oh that we did," continued Assumptia.

"So, you expect me to believe that you were granted an audience with his Holiness?" asked the Mother Superior incredulously.

"Oh no," answered Magdalene.

"And why not?" asked the Mother Superior, struggling to keep the sarcasm from her voice.

"Ah," said Assumptia. "I think he was out when we called. Isn't that right, Maggie?"

"Yes," lied Magdalene. "I think he was in Ethiopia or some such."

The Mother Superior sat back in her chair, breathed in deeply and then exhaled angrily through two flaring nostrils. The fingers of her old hands were now laced together whilst her thumbs gyrated furiously.

"So," she said at length. "The two of you just disappear without so much as a by your leave and then, reappear after, what is it, two months—"

"About six weeks," Magdalene added helpfully.

"Shut up!" snarled the Mother Superior as she slammed an aged and delicate hand down upon the desk with surprising force.

She glared at the two sisters hatefully before and with great effort, she regained control of her emotions. Retaking her previous position against the back of her chair, she looked heavenward and muttered a silent prayer before continuing, "So, you disappear for some six weeks before returning here with some cockamamie story about going on a pilgrimage to see his Holiness the Pope. Please let me know if I've misunderstood any of details or if you have otherwise forgotten to mention something. Anything, like, let's say, for instance, a violent disturbance in the back streets of Paris?"

The faces of the two sisters flushed in horror as they turned to face each other before reverting their attention to the Mother Superior's malevolent glare.

"Yes, Sisters, I know more about your, your, your so-called pilgrimage than you realise and there's still more that I would like to know. So, if you would be so kind as to do me the courtesy of desisting with your half-truths and lies!"

Assumptia and Magdalene both nodded their heads in resigned obedience.

"Now, Assumptia, Magdalene, I hate having to do this but you've simply left me with no other option." With that, the Mother Superior pushed a heavy leather-bound bible across the desk towards them. "Now, swear, swear upon the holy book that you'll be telling me no more lies."

Assumptia lay a large beefy hand upon the bible and Magdalene lay her delicate white hand upon Assumptia's. They were just about to swear the requested oath when a knock came at the door, which opened to reveal Sister Mary's plump and smiling face.

"Sorry, Mother Superior but Detective Inspector Lawrence of the Garde is here to see you."

"Excellent timing," announced the Mother Superior in an exasperated voice. "Please show him in."

The inspector was a large heavily built man in his late-fifties, who was wearing a long trench coat and a brown trilby hat, which he removed upon entering.

"Feck me, if it isn't Dick Tracy," Assumptia mumbled under her breath as she looked the inspector up and down.

"Welcome Inspector Lawrence, welcome," said the Mother Superior warmly as she climbed achingly to her feet once again and took the inspector's proffered hand in her own. "Your timing is perfect. Now, pull up a chair." The Mother Superior indicated an empty chair resting against the office's far wall. "Now, Sisters, the inspector here has a few questions he'd like to ask you."

"Thank you, Mother Superior," the inspector said in a smooth deep voice as he placed his chair next to hers. "Good afternoon, Sisters, I trust you are both keeping well?"

Assumptia and Magdalene nodded vigorously as they watched the inspector sit and pull a notebook from his pocket. He then dabbed the tip of his thumb with his tongue before flicking through several pages of notes. Having found what he was looking for, he returned his attention once more towards the two sisters.

"Sorry, Sisters, bear with me for just a moment longer, I almost forgot the formalities."

With this, the inspector again delved into a large pocket of his trench coat from which he retrieved a small tape recorder. This he placed upon the desk in front of him before pushing the red record button.

"Sisters, if you don't mind, would you please identify yourselves for the benefit of the recording?"

"Just hold on a minute," interrupted Assumptia. "Aren't you supposed to offer us a phone call or organise some legal representation or something?" "Leastways, that's what happens on the telly."

The inspector looked at her and smiled. "Please understand Sisters, I'm not placing you under caution, not yet anyway. I just want to ask a few questions, that's all. I use the recorder so as not to miss anything that might turn out to be important. Once I'm back at the station, I'll type up the notes and then you'll get an opportunity to read them and sign off on them if you're happy to do so. I'll also return the tape to you or wipe it clean, whatever you'd prefer."

"Thank you for clarifying," said Magdalene. "My name is Magdalene Malone."

"And mine is Assumptia Malone," said Assumptia.

"Thank you, Sisters," said the inspector. "Now, I believe you are acquainted with a Patrick Malone?"

"Well, I'm guessing there's more than one but yes," said Assumptia, "we are acquainted with a Patrick Malone and before you ask, the slippery toad that's the Patrick Malone we are acquainted with is our father, although God only knows what our poor sainted mother ever saw in that low life."

"Sister please!" interjected the Mother Superior. "Please do not take our Lord's name in vain."

"Sorry, Mother Superior," mumbled a duly chastised Assumptia.

"And," continued the inspector, "are you acquainted with a Connor O'Connor?"

Assumptia and Magdalene turned their blank faces towards each other before returning their eyes to the inspector. As one they nodded their heads from side to side and said, "no."

"It may come as a shock for you to learn that your father was recently found dead. His home had been ransacked. It may also come as a shock for you to learn that Connor O'Connor was also found dead at or just outside, of your father's home."

The inspector's eyes never once left the two nuns.

"Now, as we said, we don't know who this Connor O'Connor is or was," Assumptia beamed happily. "But for the record, I'd just like to say that I'm not so much shocked by Daddy's death but more, let's say, pleasantly surprised."

"Oh, Assumptia, really," admonished Magdalene with a nervous giggle. "You can be so awful."

The inspector gave the Mother Superior a surprised look, which she responded to by casting her eyes heavenward.

Sighing heavily, the inspector continued, "There is reason to believe that both your father and Mister O'Connor were murdered. Both had ingested a large quantity of poison and whilst we cannot be certain, it is believed the poison had been mixed with whiskey they had both ingested."

"I prefer to take mine with water," Assumptia added glibly.

Choosing to ignore this comment, the inspector asked, "And when did you last see your father?"

"Well, here's a funny thing," responded Magdalene. "We hadn't seen him for about twenty years or more and to be honest, we had assumed he'd died."

"In a gutter somewhere," added Assumptia unhelpfully. "Then," continued Magdalene. "About six weeks ago, give or take, we received a call from him that he wants to see us both. He was very insistent about it too. So, whilst we were less than happy at the prospect of a reunion, we thought we'd best get it over and done with."

"The alternative was that the booze-soaked old bastard would show up here and embarrass the hell out of us," Assumptia added.

"Assumptia Malone!" reprimanded the Mother Superior.

"Sorry, Mother Superior, but you must understand, that man was the devil incarnate."

"I don't care if he was Beelzebub, we'll have no swearing here if you please. Carry on, inspector."

"So," said the inspector. "Did you visit him at his home?"

"If you mean that mould-infested hovel he lived in, then yes," said Assumptia.

"Well, that confirms one eye-witness account," said the inspector. "Was he alone?"

"Yes, there were just the three of us," said Magdalene.

"And what did you talk about?"

"Nothing very coherent," Magdalene continued. "He was very drunk when we arrived. He mumbled something about regrets and so on and then passed out."

"Did he regain consciousness before you left?"

"No, he seemed very peaceful."

Assumptia looked at Magdalene with ill-disguised admiration. She hadn't before realised what an extremely accomplished liar her prim and proper sister could be.

"And was that the very last time you, either of you had any contact with your father?"

The sisters again nodded in unison before confirming the accuracy of the inspector's summation.

"OK, Sisters, I think we're making some progress. Now, did either of you take anything away with you from your father's home?"

"No, absolutely nothing," they responded as one.

"Are you sure now?"

The faces of the two sisters adopted thoughtful expressions before they again confirmed that they had left their father's home with absolutely nothing.

"Now, that is strange," said the inspector as he scratched the crown of his head with the end of his pencil. "Because the eye-witness I mentioned earlier was sure that he saw two nuns leave the address carrying a suitcase." With this, the inspector looked over to where the sisters' suitcases sat by the door. "He was most certain that a case was being carried from the residence."

Assumptia and Magdalene looked suddenly uncomfortable as their composure began to crack and crumble under the inspector's scrutiny.

"Oh, the case," blathered Magdalene. "I'd forgotten all about the case. Silly me."

"Ach the case," Assumptia joined in. "How did that slip my mind?"

The inspector raised an eyebrow before lifting himself to his feet.

"Do you mind?" he asked as he walked around the desk to where the two suitcases rested. He bent down to inspect the name tag on the first before diverting his attention to the second. "Ah, the name tag on this one marks it as the property of a Patrick Malone."

He picked up the case before returning to his chair beside the Mother Superior. Together, the inspector and the Mother Superior cleared a space on the desk before the inspector set the battered suitcase down upon it.

"Now, Sisters," resumed the inspector. "We believe that Connor O'Connor was behind a bank job right here in Dublin. A crime in which approximately five million Euros was stolen and which, currently remains unresolved. We also know that your father was known to Connor O'Connor. They had, as they say, done time together.

"Now, some of the stolen banknotes suddenly made their way back into circulation about six weeks ago. It is our current belief that these notes were used to purchase two airline tickets to Rome. A strange coincidence wouldn't you say?"

Assumptia and Magdalene's world quickly shrunk to a doom-laden microcosm as every eye in the room became focused on the battered old suitcase.

"Now, Sisters, is there anything you would like to say before I open this here suitcase?" Inspector Lawrence asked sternly.

Receiving no response, the inspector pulled the latches of the suitcase. Nothing happened and so he tried again but with greater force. "I can't seem to get this open. Sisters, do you happen to have a key?"

Magdalene, who had been praying to God and begging for a miracle which, if granted, she would repay by never doubting his glory again, suddenly looked up in devout amazement.

"No, there's no key," she said in an awed whisper.

"You see," Assumptia added quickly, seeing an opportunity she was not going to let slip by. "The suitcase used to be mine and so when I saw it at my dad's place, I decided to reclaim it from the thieving old bugger. But alas, I could never get the damned thing open."

"Assumptia! I'll not warn you again," declared the Mother Superior angrily. "Here inspector, try using this."

With that, she offered the Detective Inspector a letter opener. He took this and using no little force began to prize open one of the latches. Eventually, the latch sprung open and the inspector turned his attention to the other, which appeared to surrender almost meekly in comparison to its twin. The inspector huffed in red-faced satisfaction.

"Now Sisters, let's see what's hidden within," and with that, he lifted the lid.

28
A Lucky Encounter

Roxy sat alone at a table in the Vinoy's terrace bar. It was early evening and she could still clearly see the small boats in St. Pete's marina as they gently bobbed and swayed with the sea's motion. Roxy toyed with her cell phone as she considered the practicalities of Horace's devious plan and how to engineer a situation in which she could accomplish its goal.

She knew she was looking good in her black bobbed wig, short black cocktail dress and heels and if she had needed confirmation, she'd received it in the admiring glances cast in her direction by many of the men and some few of the women who wandered across the terrace, either entering or leaving the hotel for their evening's entertainment.

She wasn't exactly sure what Tom Harrison looked like, she'd briefly seen him in court on just one occasion and was fairly sure she would recognise him should he stray onto the terrace at any point that evening, a circumstance that was in no way guaranteed. Roxy wondered how long should she wait before investigating the hotel's other bars and restaurants and what she should do if she couldn't find him.

A waitress approached and asked Roxy if she would like another gin and tonic but Roxy declined telling the waitress that she was waiting for a friend who should be joining her soon. Perhaps she should call Frankie, she wouldn't feel so conspicuous if she had company but how would Frankie react if she told him of Horace's plan? She believed she knew how he would react if she suddenly left him to flirt with another man. No, she decided that bringing Frankie into the equation was a bad idea.

Roxy decided that she would remain where she was for a further thirty minutes. Then, if Tom Harrison didn't show, she would take a walk around the hotel and either find him or not. If the latter, she would call Horace and ask that he come and collect her. She finished her drink before holding the empty glass aloft in a signal to the waitress that she would now like a refill.

"It seems my date is running late," she said to the waitress as she provided Roxy with another gin and tonic.

The waitress smiled sweetly as she removed the empty glass and returned to her post beside the bar. Roxy took a gentle sip of the cold liquid, again surveying the bar's other guests in the hope she would soon spot Tom Harrison.

"Hi, could I have a beer please?"

The English accent was unmistakable and Roxy turned to glance behind her and couldn't believe her good fortune. Tom Harrison had taken a seat at the table immediately behind the one that Roxy occupied.

He noticed her looking at him and smiled, "Isn't it a beautiful evening," he said.

Roxy was just about to respond when an unfamiliar rock tune erupted from somewhere on Tom Harrison's person. He gave Roxy an embarrassed smile and apologised as he clumsily removed a mobile phone from his pocket. Glancing at the screen, he tapped a green vibrating icon and then held the phone to his ear. "Hi, Zoe, what's up?"

29
All Done by the Book

Detective Inspector Lawrence stared down at the contents of the suitcase before reaching in and pulling out a large paperback book. *The Lord of the Rings* by J.R.R. Tolkien, he read aloud before lifting the book and shaking it as if trying to remove some hidden content.

He placed the book on the desk and pulled out another book. *Albion, A Guide to Legendary Britain.* He placed this book atop the Lord of the Rings before continuing to rummage through the suitcase. He continued his increasingly frantic search for several long minutes before raising his head towards Assumptia and Magdalene and saying, "The case is full of nothing but books."

The two sisters sat dumbfounded as they returned the Detective Inspector's gaze.

"I said, the suitcase is filled with nothing but books," repeated the inspector.

Assumptia closed her mouth which had been hanging open since the inspector had made his discovery. She then cleared her throat before declaring, "And I didn't even know that he could read."

The inspector seemed to be at a complete loss as he looked from one sister to the other and then to the Mother Superior. "I—er, I think—er, I need to—er consider, yes, I need to consider this new evidence. Thank you, Mother Superior," he said as he gathered up his notebook and tape recorder. "Sisters, I think I've taken up enough of your time and I'll be on my way now."

"Detective Inspector," said the Mother Superior. "Will you be taking this, here suitcase, with you as evidence?"

"No, no, no I don't think that'll be necessary and perhaps the sisters' here would like to have it as a keepsake."

Assumptia and Magdalene shrugged non-committedly.

"Well," said the Mother Superior tapping the lid of the battered old suitcase with a long forefinger. "Would someone please remove this eyesore from my desk and from my office!"

Walking slowly back to their quarters and each again carrying a suitcase, the two sisters pondered what they had just experienced.

"Do you know, Assumptia, when that policeman was struggling to open the suitcase, I prayed to God. I prayed harder than I have ever prayed before and I begged, I begged for salvation. And I think, I truly think, what we just witnessed was evidence of God's greatness and mercy. It was a miracle!"

Assumptia glanced up at her sister's devoutly radiated face and sniffed loudly.

"Assumptia, what's wrong?"

"Now, Maggie, you go on and believe whatever it is that makes you happy and yes, I'll confess that I'm pleased that we're not being thrown in gaol right now but and here's the sting of it, some bastard has nicked five million quid from us and I don't have the foggiest idea who that thieving shite might be."

"Still," said Magdalene wistfully. "That money never brought us anything but misery and so, we're probably better off without it and as you say, if someone hadn't stolen it, we'd probably now both be arrested for murder."

"Ah Maggie, I'm glad you're so philosophical about the whole business."

"That I am, Assumptia, that I am."

"Well, it'll be interesting to see if you're still filled with such saintly well-being when your credit card bill arrives."

"Oh lord, what shall we do?"

"Well, I guess you could try praying again," Assumptia said sarcastically. "It did seem to work miracles the last time you did it."

"No," said Magdalene, the referential tone in her voice suddenly replaced with one of fierce determination. "I have a much better idea than that! We need to get ourselves back over to England again, right away."

Assumptia rubbed her chin as she looked quizzically at her sister. "What haven't you been telling me, Maggie?"

"Well," said Magdalene conspiratorially. "Last night whilst you were snoring your head off, Michael was telling me about some safe deposit boxes that were stolen years back, the whereabouts of which have never been discovered."

"And?" Assumptia prompted.

"And Michael knows where they are!"

"And so what?" Assumptia asked.

"And, Michael says the boxes likely contain millions in gold, diamonds, jewels and cash."

Assumptia's brow furrowed as she stared hard, up into her sister's eyes. "Maggie, how much credit do have left on that wee bit of plastic?"

"Enough."

"That's grand," Assumptia continued. "Because I wouldn't mind returning to London myself."

"I know," said Magdalene. "The people were so friendly and in truth, I would dearly like to see Michael again."

"I was thinking more about the five million quid that some bastard stole from us," Assumptia growled angrily. "I reckon that bastard and our money is still sitting somewhere in London and that wee girl at the pub is the key to it."

The two sisters stared at each other in silent contemplation.

"In that case, Assumptia," said Magdalene breaking the silence. "We'd best plan our return and God help anyone who has stolen from us."

"Amen to that!" Assumptia responded as she clapped Magdalene on the shoulder. "Now, let's get to our room and have a think about how we should do this. Who knows, if things go well, we might get our five million back and Michael's gold and jewels ta boot!"

"Greed is a mortal sin, Assumptia," Magdalene said with a wicked smile.

"Ach, let's just add it to the list," Assumptia replied. "Perhaps we should make it our lifetime ambition to complete the list."

"Oh, Assumptia, you are awful," giggled Magdalene.

"That's a fact and some wee shite in London will soon be finding out just our bloody awful I can be."

30
Pandora's Box

Zoe sat in her pyjamas, cross-legged upon the living room floor of Tom's flat. She blew out her cheeks as she surveyed the bundles of neatly stacked banknotes. She'd just finished counting them for the third time and considered the result as now confirmed. Five million, three hundred and seventy thousand euros.

Zoe still felt a little dazed by the enormity of what she had done but when Tom had phoned her and relayed the story of the nuns' epic search for their lost suitcase, her curiosity had at last gotten the better of her and upon ending the call, she had immediately returned to her room and thrown open the suitcase.

At first, she couldn't fully comprehend what she'd uncovered. There was an old newspaper article which referred to a robbery in Ireland, together with a very large amount of money, all in crisp new notes.

She had reached out and touched some of the banknotes before pulling out one of the wrapped stacks and running her thumb along its top edge. She put the stack back and then repeated the process with another stack and then another. Finally, she put all of the notes back into the case before closing its lid. She then went to the kitchen and made herself a cup of tea.

Zoe now knew that she should have then either phoned Tom and tell him of her discovery or otherwise, just forget what she had found and deliver the suitcase as promised. However, that ship had long since sailed because overtaken by a sudden and inexplicable impulse, Zoe had returned to the case, removed the money and placed it within a black plastic bin liner. She had then taken the bin liner and its contents into the bathroom and weighed it on the bathroom scales.

After this, Zoe took another plastic bin liner into which she had placed a number of paperback books taken from the bookshelf in Tom's living room. She then weighed the book-filled bin liner on the bathroom scales and after a few adjustments, placed it within the battered old suitcase.

Zoe had then liberally filled the clasp holes of the suitcase's locks with super glue. She had left the glue to dry for a couple of hours and then tried, without success, to open the case. Finally satisfied, as promised, she had taken the suitcase with her to the Good Samaritan and had subsequently handed it over to the two nuns.

Zoe hadn't actually put much thought into the possible consequences of her actions and now, as she finally did so, she was starting to feel increasingly uncomfortable. She considered several available options, including taking the money to a police station, dumping the money, running off with the money and finally, depositing the money into her bank account.

However, she didn't like any of these options which she believe were all fraught with danger and so, following yet another sleepless night and a final recount, she decided to tell Tom what she'd done and to ask him what she should now do.

Zoe climbed miserably to her feet and padded her way into the hallway and the waiting telephone.

"He's going to kill me," she said out loud. "Can't say as I blame him and I might even help him do it."

With these final words, Zoe picked up the phone and dialled Tom's number.

"Hi, Zoe, what's up?"

"Hello, Tom," said Zoe. "Are you sitting comfortably?"

"Oh, God, what have you done, Zoe?"

"That suitcase that the nuns have been looking for. Well, I took it with me to work as asked and sure enough, a couple of nights later they turned up and collected it."

"Good," said Tom. "I'm glad that's all over and done with."

"Well, not exactly."

"What do you mean, Zoe?"

"Well, I just couldn't figure out why anyone, let alone two nuns, would go traipsing all over Europe looking for a tatty old suitcase. So, I came to the conclusion that there must be something pretty valuable inside."

"You looked, didn't you, Zoe?" interrupted Tom.

"Well, yes, I just couldn't help myself, Tom. I tried not to, really I did but—well, I failed."

"I see," said Tom cautiously. "But you didn't take anything did you?"

"Well yes, I'm sorry, Tom, but I did take something."

Tom let out a heavy sigh. "What did you take, Zoe?"

"I took five million, three hundred and seventy thousand euros."

Tom sniggered. "That's funny Zoe but really, did you take anything?"

"I promise you, Tom, that I'm telling you no word of a lie, I took five million, three hundred and seventy thousand euros."

Tom remained silent for several seconds before saying, "OK, Zoe, tell me everything. Absolutely every detail and don't leave anything out."

Tom listened in silence as Zoe recounted her story. She finished by asking him what he thought she should do now.

"OK, Zoe, don't do anything just now. I need to think about this and maybe I'll even ask my lawyer friend for some advice."

"Right you are," responded Zoe. "And Tom, I am sorry, truly I am."

"Try not to worry too much about it. Goodnight, Zoe."

"Good night, Tom and honestly, I know I'm repeating myself but I am really so sorry."

"Whatever," Tom concluded as he ended the call.

"Sorry, I couldn't help but overhear," said Roxy. She had turned in her chair to pout seductively at Tom. "Everything OK back in little ole England?"

Tom looked at the unashamedly flirtatious woman who was now lounging over the back of her chair, a position that showed off most of her long and deliciously sexy legs too. Tom thought he recognised her from somewhere but couldn't quite place it. He was just about to respond when Isabelle arrived.

"Hi, Tommy," she greeted him with a kiss on the lips which she managed to artfully combine with a feral warning look towards Roxy. "I'm sorry for keeping you waiting for so long."

Smiling happily, Tom looked Isabelle up and down appreciatively before saying, "Wow, it was certainly worth the wait. Take a seat and tell me, what would you like to drink?"

"Thank you, Tommy, I would like some Champagne and," Isabelle again looked towards Roxy, "tell me, who is your new friend?"

"Sorry, we haven't been introduced," said Tom. "I'm Tom and this is Isabelle, she is my, my—"

"We are lovers," interrupted Isabelle. "And we are, how do you say, exclusive."

"Oh, yes, I understand," responded Roxy, who was a little shocked by the candidness of the warning she'd just received. "I'm just here waiting for my date to join me but he's awfully late."

"Pardon, I didn't quite catch your name," persisted Isabelle with obviously feigned politeness.

"Oh sorry, it's Agnes, Agnes Buff."

"Nice to meet you, Agnes Buff," said Isabelle as Tom raised his glass and smiled. "I hope your date will arrive soon. Now, Tom and I have much to talk about and so, if you'll please excuse us."

"Oh, yeah, of course," said Roxy with an embarrassed frown as she turned in her seat to again cast her eyes in the direction of the marina.

"That was a bit harsh," whispered Tom. "She was just being friendly."

"Seriously, Tommy, will you never learn?"

Tom waived to the waitress and ordered a glass of Champagne for Isabelle.

"What were the two of you talking about?" asked Isabelle.

"Nothing," said Tom. "I'd only just finished a call with Zoe when you arrived and you are not going to believe this."

"Try me."

Tom paused as the waitress delivered Isabelle's drink. Tom and Isabelle clinked glasses and kissed again. "Now tell me, Tommy, what has the lodger been up to now."

Tom told Isabelle Zoe's story and watched as the astonishment began to shine clearly upon her face. "Mon Dieu, five million! It's no wonder the nuns were so desperate to retrieve the suitcase and to think, we were carrying all that money around with us. What should we do now?"

"I don't know but I'm open to any ideas you might have."

"I say we run away, Tommy," Isabelle said excitedly. "We could go somewhere fantastic and live whatever life we please!"

"I'll not deny it, a similar thought had crossed my mind but we need to think long and hard about our next move. Let's get another drink."

"Well, it was a pleasure to meet you both," interrupted Roxy as she rose from her chair. "Seems I've been stood up. Anyway, I hope you'll have a very enjoyable evening." With that Roxy turned and walked away with her customary slinky feline grace.

"OK, Tommy," said Isabelle, "you can now put your eyes back into your head."

"Now, you know I only have eyes for you, my sweet," Tom responded with a comical and exaggerated lecherous leer that made them both laugh.

31
Night Shift

A broodingly silent Horace picked Roxy up from where she waited on the sidewalk opposite the front entrance of the Vinoy hotel. Roxy tried futilely to explain the circumstances behind her failure to compromise Tom but she received no response from her stony-faced husband as he drove them silently back to their small condominium apartment. Huffing in frustration, Roxy turned in her seat to face him.

"You know Pasternak, you truly are a real piece of work!" she spat angrily. "Most husbands would be relieved that their wife didn't have sex with someone else but not you. Oh no, just so long as you get your grubby fat hands on the insurance money, you don't give a damn what you destroy along the way!"

Still receiving no response, Roxy's anger increased. "And for what it's worth," she continued venomously. "I'm as disappointed as you are that I didn't get laid by Tom Harrison because I wanted to, believe me, he could have me any day, all day long!"

This last comment finally drew a reaction from Horace. "I did it for you," he said slowly through gritted teeth as if trying to keep his fury in check. "I sacrificed everything for you and you can't even do the one thing, the only thing, I've ever asked of you!"

Roxy stared at her husband in utter disgust. "Be honest with yourself for once in your life, Horace, you do nothing for anyone other than yourself." Her words dripped like poison from an open wound. "I'm not preaching from the mount because I'm no angel and I've never tried to convince you that I was."

"Oh," Horace interjected. "I think you pretend a lot of things!"

"Horace, you lie so much that you can no longer tell what's the truth and what's not."

"Now, come on!" Horace retorted angrily. "That's just bullshit that you're making up because you failed to do what we agreed you'd do to help us, us not me and not you but us!"

"Really?" Roxy interrupted. "You tell me that you love me. What kind of love is it that sends me to have sex with another man? When we first met, you had me believe that you were like Rockefeller when, in fact, you were living off the bank's money and when the bank wants their money back, what does honest Horace Pasternak do then? He burns down his own business and lies to the insurance company so he can defraud them. And you sit there telling me you don't lie and that you're doing everything for us. I tell you, Horace, you're just plain deluded."

"Well, maybe I am and maybe I'm not but one thing's for sure Roxy and that's that if we don't think of something real fast, then in all likelihood, we're both screwed!"

Roxy turned away from Horace in angry frustration and as she stared sightlessly at the road ahead, her thoughts returned to the conversation she'd overheard at the Vinoy. Five million, she could do a lot with five million. She gave Horace a quick sidelong look.

"No, just me," she whispered to herself. "Not us."

Later that night as Roxy lay awake staring at the slow-moving fan that pushed warm air around the dark bedroom she shared with Horace. She tried to imagine different scenarios in which she could ingratiate herself into Tom Harrison's life and somehow prise him away from the French woman and more importantly, the five million euros. She chewed her bottom lip and tried hard to think but Horace's deep and rhythmic snores hindered her concentration.

Suddenly the snores stopped, the abrupt silence quickly interrupted by a high-pitched and whining fart that Horace slowly ejected from his rotund body to fill the warm night air with a fruity and fetid aroma. This done, Horace's snores resumed as suddenly as they had ended and in no more than a few seconds, they had regained their pre-interruption volume and rhythm.

Roxy huffed in disgust as she finally abandoned all hope of sleep and got out of bed. She left the bedroom to wander out onto the balcony of their apartment. Her thoughts were beginning to take shape as she marshalled them into their logical sequence.

This could work but she would need Frankie's help. Roxy smiled as she thought of what she would need to do to ensure Frankie's full and committed cooperation. It wasn't difficult and she knew she'd also thoroughly enjoy the experience. Although Frankie didn't know it, he was one hell of a lover. Pulling her thoughts back to the present, Roxy set about preparing the first step and that step concerned the heavily snoring Horace.

Having showered and slipped into some wickedly sexy lingerie, a primed and perfumed Roxy returned to the bedroom. Casting a suitably seductive pose in the half-light that filtered through the room's window blinds, Roxy called out softly, "Horri baby, your Roxy is feeling foxy and she wants her man."

This declaration was greeted with a grumbling snore and another large fart. Roxy cast her eyes heavenward as she considered the life choices that had led her to this.

"Horri," she said a little louder. "Your baby wants you; your baby wants you so badly." Horace's loud snores continued unabated. "For the love of God, Horace!" screamed Roxy.

Horace jumped awake in sudden startled surprise and confusion. "What, what's going on?" He jabbered as he looked wildly around the room for signs of danger, his eyes finally focussing upon Roxy, who had resumed her pose against the frame of the bedroom door. "What's happening?"

"Oh, Horri, did I wake you?" Roxy slinked over to the bed and pulled back the light duvet to reveal Horace in his night garb of underpants, vest and socks. She leaned down and kissed him gently on the lips. It had been a long time since Roxy had shown any interest in the physical side of their relationship and now, Horace lay spellbound and hardly daring to breathe as Roxy started to do what Roxy did best.

The experience was mercifully short for Roxy and she now fumbled in the drawer of her bedside table as Horace lay panting contentedly beside her.

"Oh, my God, Roxy," breathed Horace. "I'd almost forgotten how good we can be. We should do this type of thing more often."

"Sure thing," said Roxy whilst dabbing her face with a make-up removing pad. "Tell me, Horace, your surname is Pasternak, what country does that originate from?"

"What?" asked Horace as he shifted his bulk to stare at his wife. "Why are you asking me this now?"

"I guess it was talking to that English guy, it just made me think about our roots."

"Oh, I see," said Horace. "Some place in eastern Europe I guess but I don't know for certain. I'll look it up on the internet."

"No worries, Horace," continued Roxy. "Tell me about the fire at Pasternak's Soft Furnishings and how you managed to start it without being caught."

"Are you being serious?" asked Horace. "It's like 4 AM and you want me to tell you this again?"

"Yes, it's just that it's so exciting and you were so clever and so brave. I just love hearing about how you fooled everybody, including the police."

Horace gave Roxy a generous smile before launching into the story of how he'd managed to avoid the numerous security devices both on entry to the warehouse and most dangerously, having started the fires, on exit.

"It was a close-run thing, Sugar, but meticulous planning and a cool head in an extremely challenging and dangerous situation saw me through. That and the ability to look and sound sincere whilst lying through my teeth."

"That's amazing, Horri," said Roxy as she placed the pad she'd just used to dab her face into the drawer of her bedside table, enabling her to surreptitiously stop the voice recording mode of her cell phone. "I think I'll get up now and go for a run before the day gets too hot."

With that, Roxy got out of bed and left a confused-looking Horace, to set in motion stage two of her cunning plan.

32
Lying Eyes and Last Bananas

Tom sat next to Joe Becker in the Federal Courtroom and listened whilst George Church provided the final summing up of Pasternak's case against Mallory Syndicate. Tom had received a preview of Mallory's final summary, which was quite hi-tech and very professional. In contrast, the presentation now being delivered by Pasternak's legal team appeared quite rustic and homely.

Wearing a black suit and with his almost white hair neatly combed back, to Tom, George Church resembled some kind of bible bashing preacher straight out of the American west. George's white goatee beard and moustache only added to this image.

George Church stood in a relaxed pose before the jury. He had no props, no papers and no PowerPoint presentation, he just stood there before them with his hands clasped behind his back. Following several seconds of quiet and apparently thoughtful contemplation, George slowly began his homely and ingratiating presentation.

"Good people of Florida, you are required to ensure that justice is done here today. Horace Pasternak, a good man of this State of Florida, is accused of burning down his business in order to obtain financial gain. He is accused of being a liar and of being a cheat. He is being accused and being an arsonist and a fraudster!" George Church shouted the final word whilst banging the clenched fist of his right hand into the open palm of his left.

"These accusations," he continued fervently. "Are not made by the Floridian Police Department. These accusations are not made by the Floridian Fire Department. No, these accusations are made by Mister Thomas Harrison for and on behalf of Mallory Syndicate of Lloyd's, London, England."

George Church turned his unwavering gaze towards Tom and shook his head sadly as if in great disappointment.

"On several occasions during the course of this trial Mister Harrison has, in passing, referred to my client as an arsonist. An unfounded, hurtful and deeply damaging statement. So, good people of Florida, what I am asking you to do today is to make a decision based upon what you know in your hearts to be true."

George Church sighed as he returned his gaze towards the jury. "And having heard all of the evidence presented over the course of the past ten days, that my friends, my fellow Americans, maybe the easiest thing you are ever asked to do."

George Church then looked down at his shoes. "This puts me in mind of a conversation I recently had with a friend of mine," he resumed, his voice accentuating a southern American drawl. "My friend said to me, George, did you go and take a look at what I told you to take a look at? I said, no Jake, I did not. Why not George, he asked me. Because Jake, I know it's not true. Now, good people of Florida, what you must ask yourselves here today is, do you believe what you know in your hearts to be true or, do you," at this George Church turned to point an accusing finger directly at Tom, "or do you believe Mallory Syndicate of Lloyd's, London, England and their lying eyes!"

With this final salvo, George Church bowed before the jury and returned to his seat.

Tom stared wide-eyed and open-mouthed in shocked amazement. "Can he say that?" he asked as he nudged Joe Becker in the ribs.

"Well, he just did," whispered Joe. "That was some performance, he deserves a fricking Oscar!"

*

Tom and Joe stood alone in the corridor directly outside of the Courtroom. The jury had retired to consider its verdict and there was nothing left to do but wait. The once fully stocked war room was now completely devoid of food and drink. Joe was holding the final banana in his hands as he once again predicted the ultimate outcome of the Pasternak case.

"Now, I know Randy could have done a lot better but even so, there's no way a Jury is going to find Pasternak innocent," he said whilst pointing the banana at Tom for added emphasis. "There's just too much evidence. What do you think?"

"I think they liked George Church," opined Tom.

"Yeah, George is a good guy," agreed Joe.

"I also think," resumed Tom in a tight voice, "they hated the sight of Randy Bird and to be honest, following his performance in there," Tom pointed angrily at the Courtroom doors, "I can't say as I blame them because, to be honest, at this precise moment in time, I don't like him very much either."

Tom was referring to the previous week's cross-examination of a witness produced by Pasternak's lawyers. The witness, a purported incendiary expert and apparently, nice old guy, had been torn to shreds by Randy Bird over the course of several gruelling hours. It had soon become apparent to Tom that Randy had lost the jury, who found the beating up of the kindly old fellow rather offensive.

However, despite this and Tom's open instruction to Randy during one of the breaks, to cease and desist, following the trial's resumption, Randy had nonetheless continued in his remorseless and ultimately unsuccessful attempts to find a chink in the old fellow's armour.

"OK, I get it but Randy was trying his best," said Joe defensively.

Joe's attempt at defending what they both thought was an inept and jury losing performance by Randolph Bird was interrupted by the approach of four very large and muscular Afro-American men, all of whom were wearing basketball vests and shorts. The smallest of this contingent, a man, Tom estimated to be in his mid-twenties, approximately six feet five in height and weighing somewhere in the region of two hundred and forty pounds, asked Joe if he knew where he could find a Miss Hernandez.

"Yeah, you'll find her right down the hall, fifth door on the right," said Joe helpfully, whilst indicating the direction by pointing with his banana.

The man thanked Joe before loping off in the direction indicated. Meanwhile, his three larger companions stood looming around Joe and Tom before one of them, the largest, asked Joe whether or not he had anything to eat.

"No, sorry man," responded Joe. "We're all out of food."

"But you got a banana," said the astute giant. "I can see it, it's right there in your hand."

Joe looked sadly at the banana and then up at the colossus of a man in front of him before generously handing him the banana. "It's OK, I didn't want it anyway," he lied.

The man accepted the banana and asked if Joe and Tom were both lawyers. "No, I'm a lawyer," replied Joe, "and he's my client."

The giant slowly looked Tom up and down, his face showing confusion before breaking into a large and friendly grin.

“My, oh my, but looks can sure be deceiving,” he said with a laugh. Then, their companion having returned, the four bid farewell before disappearing towards the elevators.

“Bloody cheek,” said Tom. “They think I’m a frigging criminal!”

“I’m so hungry,” Joe replied sulkily.

“In that case, you should’ve held on to that banana,” Tom said without pity.

“Well, that guy was hungry too,” Joe replied although, it was abundantly clear to Tom that the handing over of the banana had nothing to do with Joe’s intimated generosity but rather the imposing enormity of the young man who was now laughing, banana in hand, his way to the elevator.

“Yeah sure, Joe,” Tom replied sceptically. “How long do you think the jury will be out?”

“It could be days,” said Joe.

“In that case, let’s go and get something to eat.”

33
The Shopping Trip

Isabelle relaxed on a sunbed beside the Vinoy's outdoor swimming pool. She was wearing a black one-piece swimsuit, a white floppy hat and a pair of retro black and white sunglasses that were rather pointed at the top outward corners. In one hand, she held the paper-backed book, the storyline of which was puerile and yet, nonetheless, entertaining and in the other, a tall glass filled with iced water.

Setting the glass down upon an adjacent table, Isabelle closed her eyes for a few moments and enjoyed the touch of a warm breeze as it gently caressed her sun-kissed body. She was at peace with the world and wished she could stay that way forever.

"Excuse me," said a female voice that Isabelle did not quite recognise. "Isabelle?"

Isabelle lifted her head and using a finger to slide her sunglasses a little way down her nose, she peered up over their rim to see a red bikinied Agnes Buff standing next to her sunbed.

"I am so sorry," continued Roxy, "I didn't want to disturb you but, I did want to apologise for the other evening. I think we got off on the wrong foot."

Isabelle raised an enquiring eyebrow. "That's OK, just forget about it," she said quickly as she again pushed her sunglasses into place before returning to her relaxed position on the sunbed.

"It's so peaceful here," continued Roxy. "We're so lucky to have the entire pool to ourselves today. Don't you just love it?"

Receiving no response from Isabelle, Roxy spread her towel over the sunbed next to the one occupied by Isabelle. "I hope you don't mind if I join you."

"Why?" asked Isabelle.

"Why," repeated Roxy, who after a few moments of thought continued. "Because a woman on her own can attract all kinds of unwanted attention."

"I believe you," Isabelle responded irritably.

This was turning out to be more difficult than Roxy had expected but she needed to make it work if her plan was to succeed.

"If you don't mind me saying so, your Tom seems very nice."

Isabelle sighed loudly as she turned to face Roxy. "Look Agnes," she said, "What is it that you want?"

Roxy, who was now sitting on her sunbed looked sadly down at her red-painted toes and Isabelle was surprised to see a tear spill suddenly from one of Agnes's eyes.

"I'm so sorry," said Roxy in a feigned tremulous voice. "It's just that I'm so lonely. I wasn't waiting for anyone when I met you and Tom the other night. I just needed to be around people, just to feel for a while that I wasn't so alone."

Concerned and feeling a little guilty for behaving so indifferently, Isabelle sat up and faced Agnes. On a sudden impulse, Isabelle took both of Agnes's hands in her own and squeezed them gently. It was then that she noticed the wedding band on Agnes's left hand.

"But you are married?" she said.

"Yes, I am," replied Roxy and relying upon a sudden cunning instinctiveness, she continued; "But he is a wicked and cruel man and if he could he would lock me up in a cage. He hates it when I leave home, even when I go to the grocery store. He gets so jealous and sometimes," Roxy paused to look into Isabelle's concerned face. "He lashes out and becomes violent towards me."

Isabelle, who knew all about being in an abusive relationship, went to sit next to Roxy. She placed a comforting arm around her shoulders. "It's OK," she said to Agnes. "Don't be sad. He's not here now and we can spend some time hanging out together if you would like that."

"Really?" said Roxy as she blinked the faux tears from her eyes and tried to hide the elation she felt inside. "That'd be so cool," she sniffed. "Do you know what I'd really like us to do together?"

"No, tell me," said Isabelle who was relieved to see Agnes brighten a little.

"I would like us to go shopping. I can hear you are French and you dress so, so, well, so chic, I guess. I would like you to help me choose some stuff so that I could look all sexy and French too."

"Oh," exclaimed Isabelle, who was momentarily taken aback by this unexpected request. "OK," she said after a few moments, "if that would make you happy, when and where?" she asked.

"No, time like the present," Roxy replied enthusiastically. "I have my car and so, all we need do is get changed and we're good to go."

Isabelle's face dropped. She didn't really want to leave the poolside as she held the unfounded hope that Tom might finish in court early and be able to join her there. "Now, you want to go shopping right now, today?"

Roxy pouted. "Is that a problem?" she asked, her voice tinged with contrived dolefulness.

"I guess not," said Isabelle as she rose and quickly collected her stuff from the sunbed. "Give me ten minutes and I'll meet you out front."

*

Twenty minutes later, Isabelle sat in the passenger seat of Roxy's car, looking at the verandas and gardens of the grand houses they passed, with their immaculately manicured front lawns and large shuttered windows. "These houses all look very old and very grand," she said. "I think I would like to live here."

"It's a bubble," replied Roxy. "A mile or two down the road and it isn't so pretty."

"But you can say that of almost anywhere."

"I guess you can. Hey, do you mind if we pop into the grocery store? If I don't have something ready and waiting on the table when my husband gets home from work, well, it's just better for me if his dinner is there waiting for him."

"No problem," replied Isabelle. "Have you ever thought of leaving him and making a better life for yourself?"

"All of the time. In fact, I'm hoping I'll not have to put up with him for too much longer. I keep feeding him up in the hope that he'll soon die of a heart attack."

They both laughed at this. "Here we are," said Roxy as she indicated and turned left into a small shopping precinct. "I should only be a couple of minutes, why don't you join me?"

"OK, why not," said Isabelle. The car drew to a halt in one of the many empty parking bays and Isabelle climbed out of the vehicle and followed Roxy as she headed towards the grocery store. When they reached it, the sign on the door indicated that the store was closed. "Oh no," said Isabelle.

"Don't worry," replied Roxy as she knocked at the glass door. "I'm pretty good friends with the manager."

A young good-looking man came to the door and working the lock, opened it to allow the two women to enter. He then closed the door behind them and re-engaged the lock.

"Hello, I have your groceries ready out back," said the man who Isabelle thought looked and sounded a little nervous.

Roxy led the way to the back room. "Isabelle, could you come with me please, I might need a hand," she called over her shoulder.

Isabelle was starting to feel a little uneasy as she hesitantly followed Agnes into the grocery store's back room.

"Agnes, is this normal?" she asked as she stepped into the room's dark interior. It was then that a strong arm grabbed her violently from behind and a large hand clamped over her nose and mouth. She involuntarily inhaled through a chemical-soaked cloth as she vainly struggled to free herself. Then her world turned suddenly black and she passed out.

"Well done, Frankie!" exclaimed Roxy as Frankie lowered Isabelle's inert body gently to the floor. "Now, you'd best tie and gag her before she comes around."

"Why are we doing this, Missus Pasternak?" asked Frankie unhappily.

Hearing the sadness and concern in Frankie's voice, Roxy stepped over Isabelle's body so that she could hold herself softly against her young lover. She looked up at him before kissing him gently on the lips.

"Don't you worry, Frankie, no one's going to get hurt and this will soon all be over and done with."

"And then what?" said Frankie miserably.

"Then you and I can go somewhere really nice and be together always. We won't have to confine our meetings to the backroom of your father's grocery store. Oh, Frankie, it's going to be just wonderful."

Roxy moved away from Frankie and looked down at Isabelle. "OK, Frankie, tie and gag her and then you'd best reopen the store. I've got a couple of things to do and then I'll be right back."

"OK, Missus Pasternak."

"Frankie, please call me Roxy."

Frankie looked at Roxy and gave her a weak half smile.

Seeing the uncertainty on his young face, Roxy embraced him again. "Come on, Frankie, don't let me down now. We must stay strong for each other."

She looked up into his sad blue eyes and said, "Frankie, you do know that I love you don't you and that I'm never going to leave you?"

Frankie brightened a little at this and gave Roxy a tight squeeze. "I love you too, Missus Pasternak, I mean Roxy."

"So," said Roxy as she again disengaged herself from Frankie. "Let's get this over and done with."

Leaving the grocery store, Roxy returned to her car and taking out her cell phone, she called the Tampa Police Department.

34
The Fall of Horace Pasternak

Horace sat in the diner opposite George Church and Emily Rudd. The two lawyers watched mesmerised as Horace devoured his third, aptly named, Mega Burger.

"You sure do have a good appetite, Mister Pasternak," sniffed Emily as she toyed with the remnants of her ice cream pot. Her face was its customary deathly white, with the exception of the dark circles occupying the space immediately below her pale watery blue eyes and her nose, which as ever, was red-tipped.

"And some," added George in support of his colleague.

"It's the only time I get to eat anything descent," mumbled Horace through a mouth stuffed full with burger. George flinched as Horace inadvertently spat a small piece of sesame seed bun in his direction. "Every day my wife goes to the grocery store and every day she comes back with the same old crap."

George stirred his coffee thoughtfully and said, "Well, it's a good thing your wife doesn't shop at the same store as the one used by my wife. She's forever complaining that every time she goes there to do some shopping, the damn place is closed!"

"That right," said Horace. "Roxy uses the one just passed the bridge, the one on the way to the Clairmont Mall."

"That's the one," replied George. "My wife has a routine she sticks to; I think she may be a little OCD but three in the afternoon is her time for grocery shopping and recently, she's pitched up at the grocery store and like I said, it's closed."

"Weird," replied Horace. "Roxy goes around about the same time and has no trouble getting what she wants."

With that, Horace stuffed the last of his final burger into his mouth and munched happily away, his cheeks distended like those of an over-zealous squirrel preparing for a particularly harsh winter.

George and Emily's cell phones pinged almost simultaneously. "Well," said George. "It looks like the jury's back. They didn't need much time at all to reach their decision. They're ready now and so, we'd best make tracks."

"Do you think they'll find in our favour?" Horace asked anxiously.

"Yeah," answered George casually as he rose from the booth they were occupying and threw some ten-dollar bills down on to the table. "Let's go."

"Hold on just a second," said Horace as he reached for the large Styrofoam cup that contained his Mega Cola. "I haven't touched this yet and don't want to leave it behind. I just hate to waste, don't you?"

With that, Horace exhaled fully before placing his fat lips around the plastic straw protruding from the cup's lid and then, his lungs empty, he embarked upon one gigantean greedy suck.

George had been about to tell Horace to bring the cup with him but now stood spellbound as he watched Horace's fat face take on a pink hue which quickly turned to a deep purple.

"Do you think we should do something?" sniffed Emily in a concerned whisper. "He looks like he's about to have a coronary."

These quiet words broke the spell that had suddenly possessed George and he now reached out a hand with which he planned to remove the cup from Horace's now dark blue face but, just before his hand touched the cup there came a noise of rattling ice cubes combined with a wet whistling sound as Horace sucked up the cup's final few dregs of cola. Having achieved his goal, Horace loudly exhaled again before gasping for breath.

"Wow, that was cold!" he exclaimed in triumph as he rose from the booth to join his waiting legal team. He'd just made it to his feet when he abruptly stopped and clenched his chest, his face contorted in a mask of excruciating agony.

"Mister Pasternak!" Emily screeched in sudden panic as she scanned the diner desperately in a search of a defibrillator.

However, her panicked search was cut short by a loud and violent belch that ejected itself forcibly from Pasternak's rotund body. "Ahhh, that's better," Horace sighed in relief.

"For a second, there I thought you were about to die on us," George said sardonically.

"What me? Na, I'm a picture of health and vitality. I treat this," he said patting his distended belly affectionately, "like a temple. But you know, Mister Church, your concern for my well-being is very touching. I appreciate it, truly I do."

George Church brushed invisible dust away from the shoulder of his jacket on which Horace had just rested a comradery hand. "I hate to break it to you, Horace, but my only concern was and is for the payment of my bill."

With that and with Emily Rudd in tow, George turned and made his way out of the diner, leaving a glaring Horace Pasternak in their wake.

"Prick!" Horace cursed quietly under his breath. "My only concern was and is for the payment of my bill," he mimicked whiningly. "Sometimes, I think I'd enjoy losing this case just to see the look of horror on Church's arrogant son of a bitch face."

Having let off this small amount of steam, Horace slowly followed George and Emily back to the Federal Court building. When he entered the building, he found that his legal team had already passed through security and were now waiting patiently for him on the other side of the detector frame. Horace was emptying the contents of his pockets into the small grey plastic tray provided when someone tapped him on the shoulder. Turning, he was confronted by two large uniformed police officers and another smaller man who was wearing a dark suit.

"Mister Horace Pasternak?" asked the suited and stony-faced individual whilst holding aloft a badge identifying him also as an officer of the law.

Horace swallowed loudly as the colour drained from his round face. "Oh my God, is it Roxy, is she OK?" he babbled nervously.

"Mister Pasternak, we would like you to accompany us to the station," continued the officer.

"I'm afraid that won't be possible," interrupted George Church who had now passed back through the security doorway to re-join his client. "Mister Pasternak is currently due in court and the Judge will be mightily pissed if he's not there and soon."

The stony-faced officer looked coldly into the eyes of George Church before returning his attention to Horace.

"Horace Pasternak, I'll keep this brief and to the point. I'm arresting you on suspicion of arson with the intention of perpetrating a fraud. You have the right to remain silent but anything you do say can and will be used in evidence. Frank!"

"Yes, sir!" said one of the large uniformed officers.

"Cuff him and take him downtown. Mister Pasternak, there may be some other charges brought against you once we've had an opportunity to review all of the evidence but for now, you might want to consider obtaining some legal representation."

Horace looked totally shell-shocked as he was placed into handcuffs. "No, this can't be happening, there's been a terrible mistake. Please don't do this, I'm so close. George, do something!" he pleaded, the panic ringing clear in his voice.

"Now listen, officers, I'm sure there's been some kind of mistake," George said in his most reasonable tone. "And I'm sure we can clear things up just as soon as the case we are currently dealing with is concluded and that should take no more than a couple of hours. What if I personally guarantee that Mister Pasternak will attend the police station just as soon as we're all done here?"

"Sorry, Sir," said the suited officer. "We have Mister Pasternak's recorded confession to the crimes for which he is now being arrested."

"But—" George tried to interrupt.

"And," continued the officer. "We have reason to believe that your client represents a significant flight risk. In the circumstances, we are immediately taking your client into custody."

George blanched as he absorbed the full and unavoidable implications of this new development. He regarded Horace coldly, his face full of loathing. "He's no client of mine," he said before turning his back on the small group and walking away.

"George!" Horace called desperately. "George, come back! I'm innocent, you know I am—George!"

*

Joe checked the message he'd just received on his cell phone. "OK, Tom, the jury's ready. We'll know what they've decided in about fifteen minutes."

Tom nodded towards the courtroom doors, which were about six feet away. "Do you think we'll make it in time?"

Joe looked up from his cell phone and smiled. "Smart arse," he said before turning and making his way into the courtroom. Taking their customary seats,

Tom looked around at the virtually empty courtroom. “Well, for better or for worse, this will soon be over,” he said.

“Here,” said Joe. “I have something for you.” With that, Joe handed Tom a folded sheet of paper.

“It’s not another subpoena is it?” asked Tom with a smile.

“No, it’s just something I thought you’d like.”

Tom opened the paper and read:

Three weeks from now, I will be harvesting my crops. Imagine where you will be and it will be so. Hold the line. Stay with me. If you find yourself alone, riding in green fields with the sun on your face, do not be troubled; for you are in Elysium and you’re already dead! Brothers, what we do in life, echoes in eternity.

Tom looked at Joe and nodded. “This is from the film Gladiator,” he said. “It’s one of my favourites, thank you.”

“It’s been a tough slog,” said Joe. “Let’s hope we get the result we deserve.”

The Courtroom slowly began to fill and the jury returned from their deliberations to take their places within the jury box.

Some minutes later, a clerk of the court ordered all those present to stand for the Judge, who shortly thereafter entered the courtroom to take her seat at the centre of the top tier. Having settled, she asked, “Foreman of the jury, please stand.”

The foreman, the man who, during the early stages of the trial, had complained about Tom’s fiddling with a sweet wrapper, stood.

“Has the jury reached a decision upon which you all agree?” asked the Judge.

But, before the foreman could answer, George Church stood and asked, “Ma’am, I apologise for the interruption but may I please approach the bench?”

All eyes turned towards George Church. “Where’s Pasternak,” whispered Joe.

“This is most irregular, Mister Church,” said the Judge.

“I sincerely apologise, Ma’am, but I need to urgently inform you of an important development that has a significant bearing upon these proceedings.”

“Very well, Mister Church, would you please approach the bench.”

Joe looked at Tom and shrugged. “Never seen this happen before,” he said.

George Church handed a note to an officer of the court who in turn passed the note to the judge. The judge appeared to read and then re-read the note.

"Thank you, Mister Church," the Judge said. "Please return to your seat."

The Judge then surveyed the Courtroom before beginning her monologue. "I have just been informed that the Plaintiff in the case brought before this court against Mallory Syndicate at Lloyd's, Mister Pasternak, has been arrested by the police on charges that include arson and conspiracy to commit fraud. Apparently, the evidence against Mister Pasternak is quite compelling. In addition, those charges relate directly to this case and it is therefore, with regret, that I must bring these proceedings to a close."

There followed a stunned silence before the judge continued, "I regret the time, trouble and expense we have all had to invest in this matter. However, it is only right that the criminal proceedings run their course before these civil proceedings are, in the unlikely event they remain appropriate, resumed. Court dismissed! Mister Church, Mister Becker, I would like a word in private please."

Tom was waiting outside the courtroom doors for almost thirty minutes before Joe appeared. "What happened?" Tom asked.

"Procedural stuff," replied Joe as they made their way towards the elevators. "Apparently, the police received a recorded message in which Pasternak confessed to setting the fire. It was given to them by his new wife. He must have really pissed her off!"

"Wow, there's a lesson for all of us in there somewhere," said Tom.

"Yeah," continued Joe. "And we owe Roxy Pasternak big time."

"How so?"

"The Jury found against us on every count and so, Horace would have won the case, Mallory would have lost millions and you'd be looking for a new job. However, thanks to Roxy, Pasternak will likely get ten to fifteen years imprisonment, Mallory prevails and you get to keep your job. Who knows, you might even end up getting a promotion."

35
The Trap Is Sprung

Tom had tried several times to call Isabelle but his calls had gone straight through to her voicemail. He was now in a bar close to the court building, where he, together with Joe and the rest of Mallory's legal team, were noisily celebrating their victory in the Pasternak case.

"Hey, Tom, what's up?"

"Nothing, Joe, I was just hoping to contact Isabelle. It'd be good if she could come here and join in the celebrations."

"Don't sweat, she's probably run off with the pool attendant. It's the heat out here, it can affect a lady's moral compass."

"Thanks, Joe, you're a real comfort."

Smiling, Joe handed Tom another bottle of beer. "Come on, it's over and so let's get drunk!"

Tom accepted the beer and re-joined the melee of celebrants, his concerns lost amidst a sea of laughter and backslapping. Sometime later, Tom's bladder called for a time out and so he made his way through the celebrants and towards the restrooms.

Whilst in the privacy of a toilet cubical, Tom again tried to contact Isabelle, his concern growing with each unanswered ring of the phone. Leaving the restroom, Tom signalled to Joe that he was leaving.

"Come on, man, we're only just getting started," complained Joe.

"Listen, Joe, I'm just heading back to the Vinoy to collect Isabelle and then we'll be straight back. I'll be about an hour that's all."

"Alright," said a somewhat mollified Joe. "Make sure you come back. I'll be timing you."

About thirty minutes later, Tom walked down the hotel corridor towards his room. He'd already checked the veranda, swimming pool and gym en route and he now desperately hoped that he'd find Isabelle waiting for him in their room.

He flashed the key card over the lock, heard the latch retract and saw the green light blink into life and so, pushed open the heavy door. The curtains were drawn closed and the room was in darkness.

"Isabelle," he called. "Are you home?"

"Why, hello, Tom," came a silky voice. "I was wondering when you'd return. I hope you don't mind but I got a little thirsty and so, well, I helped myself to some champagne from the mini-bar."

Tom, his heart suddenly racing, fumbled for one of the parade of light switches situated by the room's door and he managed to click on three lights simultaneously. The lights revealed a red bikinied Agnes Buff, posed suggestively upon the bed and sipping a glass of champagne. Bemused, Tom just stared at her opened-mouthed before rallying his senses and asking, "Agnes, what are you doing here and where's Isabelle?"

"Oh, please call me Roxy," she answered as she slid into a sitting position on the bed. "And, I do apologise, you must think me awfully forward but I didn't want to crease my dress."

Placing her champagne glass on the bedside table, Roxy pulled off her dark wig to reveal her blond hair, rose and slinked the few paces it took for her to reach Tom, who remained frozen. She stood very close to him and raised herself on tip-toes to plant a light kiss on his cheek before moving to whisper in his ear, "You will be a good boy and do exactly as I ask, won't you?"

Tom swallowed hard before taking Roxy by the shoulders and pushing her firmly away from him. He finally recognised Agnes as Roxy Pasternak.

"What's going on, Roxy and where's Isabelle?"

"Oh, first things first. I believe a thank you is appropriate."

His anger starting to simmer, Tom grabbed Roxy by her bikini top and pulled her roughly towards him. "Just tell me where Isabelle is," he demanded.

Roxy let out a deep feline purr as she smiled up at him. "Go for it, Tommy, I like it rough too," she breathed.

Tom let go of the bikini top and pushed past her to reach the room's telephone. "OK, Roxy, last chance, you tell me where Isabelle is or I call the police."

Roxy just smiled at Tom mischievously before sliding open the wardrobe door. She pulled out the hanger on which she'd placed her dress. Glancing over her shoulder at Tom she said, "I once had a boyfriend who would get turned on by watching me dress. Weird, don't you think?"

Not waiting for a response, Roxy climbed into the dress before leaning down at the bottom of the wardrobe to collect a pair of sandals which she slid onto her feet. "Did that do anything for you, Tommy?" she asked with a grin. "No? I didn't think you looked the type."

Roxy moved over to the bedside table to collect her glass of Champagne and throwing back her head theatrically, drained the glass. She again turned to Tom, who stood, still holding the telephone's receiver in his hand. "Now, Tom," she continued suddenly business-like. "I have Isabelle somewhere safe. If you want to see her again, you do exactly what I tell you to do and you do not, I repeat, do not contact the police. Got it?"

Again, not waiting for a response, Roxy continued, "Now, all I'm asking from you in return for getting Horace out of your hair and ensuring your Isabelle remains safe until she's returned to your loving embrace is five million dollars. Don't bother trying to tell me you don't have the money because I overheard you on the phone on Saturday evening and by the way," Roxy said with an exaggerated pout. "I think your girlfriend can be quite rude."

Tom started to say something but Roxy quickly put her index finger to her lips to signify that he should keep quiet. "Five million dollars or euros or pounds, I really don't care which but it's got to be five million. Got it? Good."

Roxy moved to stand in front of Tom. "You have two days, Tom."

She then reached up to suddenly kiss him hard on the mouth but the kiss quickly turned into a spiteful and painful bite of his lower lip which made Tom pull back in pain. Tom gasped as he wiped blood from his mouth and glared hatefully at Roxy.

"Two days, Tommy; five million and then, we all live happily ever after."

Roxy walked towards the door but before opening it to leave, she turned and blew Tom a kiss. "Two days," she said once again and then, she left.

Tom was pulled out of his thoughts by the sound of his mobile, which loudly pulsed out Jumping Jack Flash by the Rolling Stones. He pulled the phone from his pocket and placed it to his ear.

"Hey, Tom, you coming back here or do I need to get drunk all by myself?" asked Joe.

"No, I need to think," said Tom as he ended the call.

Tom, whose primary reactions were not his best asset, was still absorbing what had happened, whilst trying to decide what he should do next. He opened the curtains to let the sunlight back into the room before turning off the electric lights. He then sat on the bed to weigh up his available options or rather, his lack of available options. He could call the police and risk something dreadful happening to Isabelle or, he could arrange for Roxy to receive the five million euros currently sitting with Zoe in his flat in London.

"Not exactly spoilt for choice, am I?" he said out loud as he again reached for the phone.

Sighing heavily, Tom picked up the receiver and called Zoe.

"Hello Tom," chirped Zoe. "Must I be polite or are you on your own, in which case, we can talk dirty."

"Listen, Zoe, this is really important. Do you still have the five million?"

"Well, of course, I bleeding well do and actually, it's five million three hundred and seventy thousand."

"I need you to bring it here, right away."

"Look, Tom, I appreciate a joke as much as anyone but it's getting late and I've not even had my dinner yet."

"Isabelle has been kidnapped and I have to pay five million to get her back safely."

"Are you drunk, Tom?"

Tom was quickly becoming exasperated and was struggling to find a way in which to make Zoe take him seriously.

"I swear, Zoe, I swear on my mother's life that I'm being serious. Will you please listen to me?"

"OK, Tom, you have my full and undivided." Tom detected Zoe's cautious change in tone. "But, if it turns out that you're pulling my leg, I want you to know that I'll not be at all happy."

"I'm telling the truth, Zoe, I swear it."

"OK, enough of the swearing, what do you need me to do?"

Tom outlined his plan. He would purchase a ticket for her which she could collect at the British Airways desk. He'd text her the flight details etcetera. All Zoe needed to do was bring the money with her.

"This is very important, Zoe and so listen up, if you need to pay for anything, use your credit card or cash but under no circumstances, use any of the money in that case. I'll pay you back once this is all over."

Zoe paused for a while. "I need to tell work," she said. "And I need to find my passport. Why can't I use any of the money from the suitcase? There's more than five million in there."

"Just trust me on this one. Please, Zoe."

"OK, don't get your knickers in a twist. I'll go and pack and wait for you to let me know the flight details."

There was a knock at the hotel room door.

"Thanks, Zoe, I'll be in touch," said Tom as he ended the call and went to see who was at the door.

It was a slightly drunk-looking Joe Becker.

"Hey, Tom, what's up," he said as he pushed passed Tom to enter the room. "Where's Isabelle and more importantly, where's the mini-bar?"

"Come on, Joe, we're leaving," said Tom, who was still standing by the open hotel room door. "I need to get out of here and I'd like to talk to you about something."

"Fine," said Joe as he spun on his heels to follow Tom out of the room. "Where are we going?"

"Just to the veranda bar."

Five minutes later, they were both sitting in the veranda bar with a beer. Joe was looking at Tom quizzically as over the phone, Tom purchased a one-way airline ticket from London to Tampa. "What's going on Tom, you seem strung out?"

"Hold on, just a second more please, Joe," replied Tom as he tapped out a text to Zoe. Having completed this, Tom looked at Joe and puffed out his cheeks. "Roxy Pasternak has kidnapped Isabelle."

Joe smiled uncertainly, "You're kidding right?"

"Joe, do I look like I'm kidding?"

"No, you look really pissed off. What are you going to do?"

Tom sighed heavily. "I'm not entirely sure yet about what I am going to do but I do know what I'm not going to do."

"What's that?"

"I'm not going to the police."

Joe looked suddenly animated as he raised his voice to a loud urgent whisper. “Like fuck you’re not! That’s just plane crazy, you must go to the police!”

36
The Void

Isabelle's mind swam frantically towards the surface of consciousness but each time she seemed to come close, invisible hands would grab hold of her and drag her screaming back down into the dark depths of the void. She was acutely aware of her anxiety and of the painful pounding in her head as well as a desperate thirst.

"Don't struggle, Isabelle." It was her father's voice and she called out to him and pleaded for help but her voice echoed and rebound in a myriad of nauseous undulating waves.

"Please, papa, help me. I'm so scared!" She wept but the voice was gone and she sank back down again, deep into the darkness.

Frankie's face was full of concern as he looked down at Isabelle. "I think she's dying," he said worriedly as he moped the sweat from Isabelle's brow with a cool damp cloth. "Maybe we should take her to the hospital."

"She'll be fine," replied Roxy with more confidence than she felt. "And anyway, we can't just show up at the hospital and say hey, this is a woman we've kidnapped and she appears to be struggling with the drug we used to sedate her."

Roxy saw that her sarcasm had hurt Frankie and so she went and helped him up from where he crouched to nurse Isabelle. She hugged him tightly. "Don't fret, Frankie, this will soon be over. She'll be fine and we'll have our whole lives ahead of us to enjoy doing whatever it is we want to do."

Isabelle let out a tortured moan. "It's probably best if you put that gag back on and reopen the store," said Roxy. "We're close to the finish line now."

"Isabelle, it's good to see you." The voice was dark and familiar and edged with a deep menace. "Come on, Isabelle, just a little further."

"Qui es-tu?" Isabelle's frightened question echoed and reverberated around her.

"Who am I," the voice began to laugh madly. "Who am I? Who am I? Who am I?"

"Est-ce que je te connais?" Isabelle shouted in fear.

"Do you know me," laughed the voice. "Oh yes, you know me very well, very well indeed. Don't you remember me Isabelle—how soon you forget your Luca."

Isabelle screamed, the sound tearing into her brain until it felt as though her head would explode.

"I can't gag her, Missus Pasternak, she's convulsing. Oh my God, what have we done!"

Roxy quickly knelt down and tried to roll Isabelle onto her side and into a foetal position but her efforts were hampered as Isabelle's body started to thrash and wriggle about wildly. A white bubbly sputum appeared from between her blue lips which were now contorted in a tight expression of terror.

"Frankie, stop yammering and please give me a hand here. Oh shit, she's pissing herself."

With Frankie's help, they managed to get Isabelle onto her side and held her there until the rigours that had so violently possessed her finally began to ease.

"What the fuck did you put on that cloth, Frankie?"

"Just what you gave me, Missus Pasternak."

Isabelle's breathing was now starting to calm and some of the colour that had drained from her face was beginning to return.

"I can't gag her," Frankie repeated and as if to emphasise his point, Isabelle's frame began to convulse again and this time she vomited, a small puddle of yellow bile which collected and pooled upon the floor where her head lay.

"Jesus Frankie, she's covering me in all kinds of ick. You'd best go fetch a mop and bucket."

"OK but what then?"

"I don't know but maybe if we can wake her up and get her to eat something, then she might stop pissing and puking all over the God damned place."

Frankie nodded and climbed to his feet. "I'll bring some stuff to clean her and this place up and then, I really do think we should take her to the hospital."

"One thing at a time, Frankie, one thing at a time."

37
The Lodger Has Landed

Being inconspicuous was not in Zoe's nature and therefore, whilst fairly used to being gawped at by passers-by, she'd found the entire journey, from the moment she'd checked-in at Heathrow until now, waiting at the luggage carousel in Tampa airport, an excruciatingly nerve-wracking ordeal.

Expecting to be intercepted by the airport authorities at every turn, her nerves were frayed to the extreme. Now, as she stood, dressed in spangled dungarees that finished several inches above her feet, her hair back in its two small neat blond buns and her face plastered in makeup, she waited nervously for the suitcase containing the five million euros to appear from behind the thick rubber streamers of the luggage carousel.

An eternity seemed to pass before the suitcase finally lumbered into sight and Zoe pushed through a crowd of holidaymakers to reclaim it. She cast her eyes around until she located the entrance leading to the customs checks and airport exit. Zoe swallowed audibly, her mouth almost totally devoid of moisture, she took a deep breath and grabbing the suitcase's extended handle, pulled it and herself towards the final hurdle.

Zoe almost wept when she finally passed unstopped through customs control and saw Tom waiting for her on the other side. Letting go of the suitcase, she rushed forward and threw herself at him. "Oh, Tom," she sobbed. "I've never been so scared before in my entire life."

Tom held her and gently rubbed her back. "Well done, Zoe," he said. "You've been really very brave and I want you to know that I truly appreciate what you've done for me and for that, I can't thank you enough."

They released each other and Zoe looked up at him and grinned before replying; "Well, a rent rebate wouldn't go amiss."

"But, Zoe," said Tom. "You don't pay any rent."

"Well, I'm glad we got that sorted out," said Zoe smiling as she reclaimed the suitcase with its precious cargo. "What now?" she asked.

"Now, we wait," said Tom.

Tom took Zoe back to the Vinoy, where he'd managed to book her into the room next door to the one he and Isabelle were staying in. "It's exactly the same as my room," he told her as she carried out a preliminary inspection of the room's interior. "Which is right next door."

"In that case, you should have saved yourself some money," she said from the bathroom. There followed a few moments of silence before Zoe continued. "Sorry, Tom, inappropriate given the circumstances but this whole thing is just so sodding surreal. It's like what happens in the movies or on TV but not in real life."

"I know," said Tom as he sat down on the bed. "But it's happening just the same and we'll just have to deal with it as best we can."

Zoe reappeared from the bathroom. "Yes and where's bloody Superman when you need him?"

She went over to sit next to Tom on the bed. "What with Italy and now this, you're not leading what might be described as a quiet life, are you?"

"Given the chance, I would be but none of this would have happened if you hadn't looked inside that old suitcase. The kidnapper overheard us discussing your discovery on the phone and the rest, well, it's history."

"So," said Zoe slowly. "Are you saying this is all my fault?"

"God, no!" Tom responded sharply. "This is no one's fault other than Roxy bloody Pasternak."

As if on cue, Tom's mobile suddenly burst into life.

With shaky fingers, Tom answered his phone and tapped the icon to place it on to speaker.

"Hello, this is Tom Harrison."

"Why, hello, Tom," came Roxy's silky voice. "And how are you doing on this fine day?"

Tom exchanged glances with Zoe, who looked as nervous as he felt. "As well as can be expected," he replied. "May I please speak to Isabelle?"

"I'm afraid that's impossible. She's taking a nap right now and I'd hate to disturb her."

"What do you want?" asked Tom angrily.

"Silly Tom," giggled Roxy. "You know exactly what I want. Do you have it?"

"Yes, I have it but if you think I'm just going to hand over five million euros without first knowing that Isabelle is safe and well, then I believe you're even crazier than I think you are!"

"Oh, Tom, you really are so sweet. I just wish we could have met under different circumstances; I think we could have had lots of fun. However, we are where we are and so, you have five million that I want and I have a French girl that you want. The solution really is quite simple, wouldn't you say? Now, so far as Isabelle's current welfare is concerned, well, you'll just have to trust little ol' Roxy in that respect."

"And tell me, Roxy, why on earth would I trust you?"

"Simple," Roxy giggled again. "Because you have absolutely no choice."

Tom was silent because Roxy was right, he had no choice other than to do just exactly as she asked.

"Oh, cheer up, Tom," Roxy continued. "This is nearly done with. All you got to do is give me the five million and I'll make sure Isabelle is delivered back to you in one healthy piece."

"OK, I'm listening," said Tom.

"That's better. Now, there's a boat that takes sightseers around the bay. It departs from the marina every hour and I want you and the money to be on the 4 o'clock boat."

Tom checked his watch; it was three fifteen. "That doesn't give me much time," he said.

"Well, you'd best get a hustle on. Put the money in a bag and sit at the front of the boat. Enjoy the tour and when you get off, just leave the bag with money behind. Simple enough?"

"And what about Isabelle?"

"As soon as I have the money, you get your little French poodle back. Now, I'd best leave you to it. Don't be late."

With that Roxy ended the call.

Tom looked at Zoe. "Wait here, I need to get something from next door."

Tom came back a minute or two later holding the rucker he used to carry his important stuff when travelling. Zoe had placed her suitcase on the bed and had removed the clothes she'd brought with her to reveal the tightly packed bundles of notes. Tom quickly started to pack wads of notes into the rucker whilst Zoe placed bundles of notes to one side.

"What are you doing?" asked Tom.

"Three hundred and seventy thousand," replied Zoe. "I don't see why that bitch should have it."

"Good point," said Tom as he continued to stuff the rucker with bundles of notes. "It's amazing how much money one of these things can hold."

"What are you going to do if they don't give Isabelle back?"

"Please Zoe, let's not go there."

38
Gunfire

Frankie fidgeted nervously in the passenger seat of Roxy's car. They were parked on the side of the road just outside of the Vinoy hotel. On their left was the entranceway to the hotel and on their right was St. Pete's marina. Isabelle, unbound and unconscious, slouched on the car's rear seat.

"So, Tom Harrison will soon be leaving the hotel and making his way to the pleasure boat jetty," said Roxy, her voice clinical and devoid of emotion. "All you have to do is follow him onto the 4 o'clock boat and take a seat immediately behind him. When the tour's over and everyone gets up to leave the boat, he'll leave the bag containing the money behind. You collect the bag and start walking in the direction of the pier. I'll be waiting in a different car to collect you and then, we make our way to Sarasota. Anything you want to ask me?"

"Why are we going to Sarasota?" asked Frankie, his voice dry and etched with a nervous tremor.

"Oh, good question, Frankie," said Roxy as she abruptly leant across to butt her lips against Frankie's cheek in a pale imitation of affection. "I have rented a place for us in Sarasota. We needed an address so that I could open up a bank account. We need a bank account so we can deposit the five million euros."

"Won't the bank be suspicious if we deposit all of that foreign money?"

"Yes, but I've told them to expect it. I said that I was in the process of selling an expensive piece of artwork to a very private person who wishes to remain anonymous and so, they're paying me in cash."

"And they believed you?"

"Oh, Frankie, I can be very, very convincing."

Frankie gave Roxy a strange and questioning look but asked no further questions.

"Here, you'd best take this," continued Roxy as she reached across him to access the vehicle's glove compartment. She pressed the catch on the compartment's door, which obediently fell open to allow Roxy to remove the automatic pistol that lay within. Resuming her position in the driver's seat, she handed the pistol to Frankie.

"What the hell!" exclaimed Frankie in horror.

"Schhh!" hissed Roxy. "It's just for show, security just in case Mister Harrison decides to get stupid."

"There's no way," began Frankie but Roxy cut him short.

"Like I said, it's just for show and it's a million-to-one chance that you'll need to take it out of your pants. Now, come on Frankie, we're so close to the finish line. In just over an hour, we'll be in the clear." With that, she kissed him again. "And there's a nice big soft bed waiting for us in Sarasota." She looked at him and smiled. "It'll make a nice change from your dad's store room."

Just then, Roxy saw Tom making his way down the steps of the Vinoy's veranda.

"OK, Frankie, that's our guy. I'll see you in about an hour."

A very unhappy Frankie reluctantly tucked the pistol into his belt and covered it with his tee shirt. He then left the vehicle and followed Tom down towards the pleasure boat jetty.

Roxy watched him go before turning to look at Isabelle, who seemed to be stirring a little.

"You can wake up any time you like now," Roxy said as she too climbed out of the car to make her way towards the hire car she had parked close to the pier.

The car she'd left with Isabelle was owned and registered to Horace and so, she had no qualms about leaving it behind. Roxy had decided to leave everything behind, including Frankie. The story she had told him about running away to Sarasota was largely true, the only difference being that her planned destination was Miami.

*

Zoe stood on the Vinoy's veranda and watched as Tom made his way down the path to the roadway that separated the hotel from the marina. Reaching the end of the path, Tom turned left and disappeared from view. As he did so, Zoe stepped lightly down the veranda's steps and also made her way down the path and towards the road.

It was a warm and sleepy afternoon in St. Pete's and the relaxed and contented demeanour of the few people Zoe saw, belied the seriousness of what was happening under their very noses.

Zoe reached the end of the path and turned left, she could see Tom up ahead as he approached the pleasure boat jetty, where about half a dozen or so holidaymakers waited patiently for the next cruise around the bay. She began to follow when she was distracted by a cry that came from behind her.

Turning, she saw a young woman stumble from a parked car before falling to her knees on the sidewalk. Swearing to herself, Zoe glanced in the direction that Tom had taken before turning and rushing to the assistance of the distressed woman. As she approached, the woman looked up at her through two red and tear-soaked eyes and pleaded, "Aide-moi, s'il te plait."

Zoe stared down at her aghast. "Isabelle, is that you?"

The woman looked up at Zoe as if trying to focus. "Lodger?" she asked incredulously.

Zoe smiled warmly at Isabelle as she helped her to her feet. "My friends tend to call me Zoe but Lodger will do for now."

They received some wary looks as Zoe helped Isabelle slowly up the path towards the hotel and when one person offered assistance, Zoe declined, saying that her friend had just had a little too much sun and would be fine once she was back in her room.

When back in the room, Isabelle lay on the bed whilst Zoe fetched her some water and aspirins. "How are you feeling?" she asked Isabelle.

"Like I have had too much wine last night. Why are you here and where's Tom?" asked Isabelle groggily.

Zoe quickly told Isabelle everything that had happened since her abduction. Suddenly, Isabelle sat up whilst clamping a hand over her forehead, which felt like it might burst. "Call him quickly, tell him I am safe!"

"I've tried," Zoe said miserably. "But it keeps going through to voicemail."

"Then you must go and tell him," pleaded Isabelle.

"Believe me, I would but right now he's on a boat cruising around the bay. It'll be coming back soon and so; actually, I'd best go now. Are you sure you'll be OK here by yourself?"

Isabelle made a quick urgent shooing motion with her hand. "Yes, of course, please go, be quick and be careful."

*

Tom was relieved to see that those who had boarded in front of him were taking up residence towards the rear of the boat, which allowed him to follow Roxy's instruction and sit at the front of the pleasure craft. He had cast a suspicious eye over the group but doubted that anyone of them were involved in Isabelle's abduction and ransom. However, a young solo traveller who followed him onto the boat did catch his attention and his suspicions grew when the young man took a seat immediately behind him.

The boat tour skirted around a naval base before providing passengers with brief glimpses of the impressive dream homes, lawns and jetties of the rich and famous. Had Tom not been involved in a ransom drop, he would have probably found it a very enjoyable way in which to pass an hour or so on a warm and sunny afternoon.

However, as it was, Tom's senses were on high alert as he tried to surreptitiously scrutinise his fellow travellers, who numbered about a dozen in total. As his prime suspect was seated immediately behind him, he was out of Tom's visual scope but as Tom weighed up the other passengers, he grew increasingly confident that his instincts regarding the young man were correct.

Tom's heart was beating loudly within his chest as the boat finally concluded the tour and headed sedately back towards its jetty. The cruise personnel secured the vessel and its gangplank allowing the passengers to disembark. A crew member stood at the top of the gangplank with a small Tupperware container in his hand, into which the happy tourists sprinkled coins as a token of their appreciation of the tour. Tom stood and stuck his hands into the pockets of his jeans and groaned, whilst he still had five million euros, that was all he was now carrying.

Tom looked at the young man, who was the only passenger still seated. Believing his suspicions confirmed, Tom lifted the rucker and pulled out a euro note before closing the zip and throwing the bag at the young man, who flinched as the heavy bag hit his chest. Tom leaned over the youth and whispered, "Here's your money. Tell Roxy it's over and I never want to see you or her again but if you've so much as harmed one hair on Isabelle's head, I promise you, I'll track you both down if it's the last thing I ever do and when I find you—"

Tom knew this was all bravado but the young man looked up at him uncertainly before nodding and mumbling; "OK, Mister Harrison and don't worry, she's fine."

Tom continued to stare down at the young man, fighting off the urge to punch him hard but he eventually turned and moved away towards the gangplank. The crewman smiled as Tom dropped the note into the proffered Tupperware container and then looked confused as he examined the identity of the note.

"Sorry, it's all I have," said Tom as he made his way off the boat and started his short journey back to the Vinoy.

He hadn't gone very far when the young man, with Tom's rucker, slung across his shoulder, jogged passed him. Tom watched as the man increased the distance between them. It was then that Tom spotted Zoe approaching from the direction of the Vinoy. He saw Zoe's head snap around as the young man passed her. Then and to Tom's horror, Zoe turned and set off in pursuit of the man carrying Tom's rucker.

*

Zoe didn't feel great about leaving Isabelle but as Isabelle was now safe, there was no need for Tom to hand over the five million euros and Roxy's dastardly plot would now be well and truly screwed, if only Zoe could reach Tom before he handed over the money.

So, it was with a large degree of urgency that Zoe jumped down the steps of the Vinoy's veranda and quickly made her way towards the pleasure boat jetty. As she reached the end of the path and turned towards the jetty, her attention was caught by a man running in the opposite direction. As she looked, she realised she was too late as the man was carrying Tom's rucker. Turning quickly, Zoe set off in pursuit. She didn't know what she would do if she managed to catch up with him but she was, nonetheless, determined not to let the criminal get away with their money.

Although she was running as fast as she could, Zoe was making little headway on her prey as he headed towards the pier. She was about to give up the chase when she noticed the man slow and start to look around frantically.

"Oi!" she screamed. "Stop thief and give me back my money!"

This outburst caught the attention of several passers-by who stopped to gawp at the drama unfolding before their eyes. Zoe redoubled her efforts as she resumed her pursuit.

The man had slowed to a complete stop and he now looked around desperately, panic showing clearly on his sweat soaked face. Zoe slowed and also came to a stop some twenty yards away from her target. She was breathing hard and felt a little sick, whether it was from exertion or nerves she neither knew nor cared.

"Just drop the bag and sod off," she panted and then froze as the man pulled out a gun and pointed it directly at her. "OK, you can keep it if you want," Zoe blurted out in sudden terror before too scared to look, she placed her hands over her eyes.

It was then that she felt herself barged violently to the ground and heard the heavy hard crack of two shots followed by a sudden outburst of screaming, seemingly from afar. She then felt someone fall heavily on top of her. Zoe uncovered her eyes and looked up to see a car come screeching to a halt. The man pulled open the passenger door and threw the bag inside but before he could also climb into the vehicle, the car pulled away at high speed leaving the man standing alone and dumbfounded.

He turned in quick circles trying to decide what to do before choosing a direction and setting off at a sprint, still carrying the gun in his hand.

Zoe grunted as she tried to shift the weight that was holding her down.

"I think you can get off me now," she gasped as she tried to wiggled her way out from under him. Then managing to turn her body she saw that it was Tom who had shoved her to the ground and who was now protecting her with his body.

Annoyingly, he would not respond to her pleas and shoves. She did however finally manage to get free of him. With growing concern, Zoe crawled back to where Tom lay motionless. With no small effort, she managed to push him over on to his back and her breath caught in her throat as she took in his ashen complexion and the blood that streamed from a wound on his head to soak the front of his tee shirt.

"Oh no, Tom, don't you bloody well dare die on me you rotten sod," she mumbled as she frantically searched his prone body for signs of life. "Come on do something," she urged desperately as she knelt beside him and started to pump his chest with her entwined hands. "Come on, Tom, please!" she screamed, her tears falling like rain to dilute the blood that continued to stream down Tom's lifeless face.

39
Michael Dear

It was a bright day in Dublin and Assumptia and Magdalene Malone sat together on a park bench situated within the leafy surrounds of St Stephen's Green. They had visited a nearby homeless shelter and were now taking stock prior to making their way back to the convent of St Mary's of the Blessed Heart.

They both looked peaceful and content as they sat dappled by the sunlight that danced its way through the autumn-rusted canopy above. Crisp brown leaves occasionally rustled before drifting downward in slow peace as a gentle but cold-edged breeze provided its subtle warning of winter's impending approach.

"It's a beautiful day for the time of year, Maggie," said the shorter and yet larger of the two nuns. "I like the autumn. Maybe a bit melancholy but it has a peacefulness that I appreciate. Now, show me that letter again."

Assumptia's tone had suddenly changed from one of dreamy reflectiveness to impatience as she held out one of her large beefy hands to nudge her rigid and straight-backed companion.

"Oh, for heaven's sake, Assumptia, you must have read it a dozen times or more already. Let's just pop it in the box and see what happens."

"Is that what you said ta ya man, Michael, when you were alone with him over in London?" Assumptia spat back wickedly and was pleased to see her barb strike home as Magdalene gasped in righteous indignation.

"Wash your mouth out, Assumptia Malone!" Magdalene huffed. "You have a dirty wicked way about you and should be ashamed!"

Assumptia's wheezy laugh quickly gave way to a fit of coughing which continued until Magdalene patted her sister helpfully, if perhaps a bit too forcibly, upon the back.

"Ah, Maggie, I was just pulling your leg," Assumptia wheezed. "But we've got to get the letter right if he's to take the bait."

Magdalene sniffed imperiously before conceding the point and handing over the letter for Assumptia's re-inspection. Pulling it from its pale blue envelope, Assumptia unfolded the page and began to read.

Dear Michael,

I do hope this letter finds you well.

It may come as some surprise to hear from me and it is my profound hope that you've not yet forgotten me or the wonderful time we shared together whilst in London. As you may have guessed, I am not a worldly person and given my position in life, am unused to spending time with gentlemen or indeed, entering into correspondence of this nature.

Therefore, I am uncertain whether this letter will actually make the journey to your home or whether, like its many predecessors, it will travel no further.

So, you may now be asking yourself, why am I writing to you. Put simply, I miss you, Michael. I miss you terribly and I find myself tormented by the memories of our short time together. I know you must think me foolish but for some time now, I have felt unsure and uneasy about my vocation. My confusion is consuming me from within and you Michael, are the source of my restlessness, of my dreams and of my desires.

I could go on and indeed, some of my prior attempts at writing to you were a little long winded to say the least.

Put in a nutshell, I have feelings for you Michael and I need to know whether my affections are misplaced or reciprocated.

Please write, even if it is—well, you're a clever man and so, you can work that bit out for yourself.

With affection and in hope,
Magdalene x

Assumptia chewed her lip thoughtfully. "Do you think it's racy enough or do you think we should put some of that black laced stuff in there to spice it up a bit?"

Magdalene covered her mouth with a slim hand as she giggled shyly. "I didn't know that research could be so, well, so enlightening."

"I know what you mean, Maggie, but upon reflection, I do think that dragging me along to the cinema to watch that film about the fifty shady grey bits was a bit too far."

"We did get some strange looks right enough," admitted Magdalene.

"Well, Maggie, it didn't help when you suddenly spat your popcorn out all over that couple sat in front of us!"

"It got stuck in my throat!"

Assumptia was about to add some more colour to that particular episode but thought better of it and instead reverted to the subject of the letter.

"Maggie, are you sure you want to go through with this?"

Magdalene turned to look at her sister quizzically. "Why do you ask Assumptia?" she enquired.

"Well, I know that you like this fella Michael and I don't want you getting hurt. That's all, Maggie," Assumptia said as she patted her sister's leg affectionately.

Magdalene smiled sweetly at her rough-hewn sister. "I do like Michael," she said softly. "And if we manage to help him recover those safety deposit boxes so much the better."

"Better for who?" Assumptia asked pointedly.

"Better for us, of course, dear sister, better for us."

Assumptia suddenly detected something new in her sister's eyes, something that should have remained hidden. A deep, cold and yet inscrutable gleam that left the large nun feeling more than a little uncomfortable. This was just the latest of several subtle changes that Assumptia thought she was detecting within Magdalene's demeanour. She shook her head and waved her hand in front of her face as if shooing away a fly.

"Are you alright, Assumptia?" Magdalene asked.

"Ach, yes," replied her sister. "I think I'm a little tired and am in need of some rest."

Magdalene looked down her long nose and sniffed. "In that case, we'd best get you back."

With that, Magdalene rose from the bench and without waiting, set off at a brisk pace in the direction of St Mary's.

40
Home Base

They heard the key enter the lock of the front door, which gave them just enough time to quickly rearrange their clothing and sit up straight upon the couch.

"Mon Dieu, it's like being a teenager again," whispered Isabelle as she repositioned her brassiere.

"Too much information," breathed Tom as he leaned discretely forward in an attempt to hide all evidence of the effects of their impassioned canoodling.

They had returned to England a few days earlier, their trip extended as a result of Tom's hospitalisation and the police enquiries that had followed. Luckily for Tom, whilst the shot fired in his direction had left a furrow along the left side of his head, it had caused no significant or long-term damage. As Zoe liked to point out, it was a good job that the bullet had struck Tom in the head, instead of hitting him somewhere that might have caused some serious damage.

They had remained tight lipped during the subsequent police investigation, which had thus far resulted in no arrests. So far, as they were aware, the police were treating the matter as a random event following a petty theft and in the absence of any further leads, considered the matter closed.

Isabelle's story of the drug induced nightmare she'd experienced during her abduction by Roxy, had left Tom feeling unsettled and so, following some thought, he had decided to call Rome and to speak with his half-brother, Alfredo. Whilst it was good to touch base with Alfredo and Maria, neither could throw any light on Luca's whereabouts.

However, Alfredo had told Tom that he had very good reason to believe that the corrupt police officer was in all likelihood dead. Despite Tom pressing him on the subject, Alfredo would go into no further detail as to why he strongly believed Luca to be dead.

The living room door was thrown open to reveal a red-faced and smiling Zoe. "Hello, young lovers," she beamed happily. "Look, Tom, I got you a present for your head. Just until all of your hair grows back."

With that, Zoe pulled out an Arsenal FC bobble hat from the pocket of her coat and handed it to Tom.

Tom scowled at the hat, a look of disgust plastering his face, before tossing it into the far corner of the room.

"Don't you like it?" Zoe asked mischievously.

Isabelle got up and retrieved the hat. "I actually think it is quite nice," she said as she returned to her position beside Tom on the couch. "What don't you like about it, Tommy?"

Tom knew full well that he was being baited by the two women and would not give them the benefit of rising to their taunts.

"Hello, Zoe, your timing is as impeccable as always," he said instead. "Where did you find the gooner hat?"

Zoe smiled as she leaned over and brushed Tom's cheek with a kiss. "Someone left it on the bus and as soon as I saw it I thought of you and your big head."

"Thanks, Zoe, you're all heart. How was work today?"

Zoe took off her coat and went to hang it on a peg in the flat's hallway. "It wasn't too bad actually," she said as she returned to the room and flung herself into one of two vacant armchairs. "Although," she said becoming suddenly animated. "I did learn something today that you both might find just a little bit interesting."

"Aw, colour me interested," yawned Tom as he adjusted his position on the couch.

"The nuns are back!"

Both Tom and Isabell sat suddenly upright.

"What do you mean the nuns are back?" Tom asked urgently.

"I thought that'd get your attention," said Zoe. "Now, it just so happens that my friend Michael was in the Samaritan again this lunchtime and he tells me that he and the nuns have been communicating."

"Why and about what?" Tom asked, the incredulity ringing clear in his voice.

"Well," Zoe continued. "According to Michael, he and one of the nuns hit it off when they were over to collect their suitcase. Now, I can't see it myself but

Michael believes himself to be a bit of a heartthrob. Anyway, it seems that one of these nuns had taken quite a shine to him."

"This is a joke, yes?" asked Isabelle.

"Sounds like the plot of some kind of weird porn film," added Tom.

"And exactly what do you know about weird porn films?" Isabelle suddenly demanded.

Tom was futilely searching for an appropriate response when Zoe came to his rescue.

"So anyway," she continued. "Not only is this nun sweet on Michael but it just so happens that her adoration is not entirely unreciprocated. Well, they've exchanged a few letters, which I didn't think people did anymore and the upshot is that the nuns are on their way back over to dear old London town. Tom! Don't touch your head."

Tom lowered the hand with which he'd subconsciously started to rub the crown of his head.

"Well, what's going to happen when they arrive? I mean, they are nuns after all and just in case you've forgotten, we did steal over five million euros from them," he asked worriedly.

"Oh bugger, I'd forgotten that," said Zoe, the animation suddenly falling from her face. "What the hell are we going to do now, Tom?"

41
Fish 'N' Chips

"Come on, Zoe, you're late," Harry, the manager at the Good Samaritan complained as he pushed a tray holding three plates of fish, chips and mushy peas in her direction.

"Sorry, Harry," apologised Zoe as she shrugged herself out of her heavy coat, which she placed on one of a close by selection of pegs. "My bus didn't show up and so I had to walk most of the way here on foot."

"Not my problem," said Harry dismissively. "Now, take this over to table seven."

Zoe sighed loudly as she accepted the proffered tray and made her way into the pub's restaurant. Moving with practised ease, Zoe didn't look up until she'd arrived at her destination . It was only then that she saw Michael's the two unsmiling nuns that sat opposite him. She stood rooted to the spot in sudden shocked horror. Michael broke the spell by standing to help Zoe distribute the loaded plates of food from the tray.

"Are you alright, Zoe?" Michael enquired. "You look like you've just seen a ghost."

Quickly gathering her thoughts, Zoe bid Michael and his guests a warm welcome and asked whether they wanted any accoutrements over and above those readily assembled in the centre of their table.

The blunt-featured nun was staring hard and unblinkingly at Zoe. "You're the young thing that handed us our suitcase a few weeks back, aren't you." This sounded more like an accusation than a question. Zoe swallowed hard and nodded. "Yes, that's right, Sister. I trust you got home OK?"

"Do you now," Assumptia said, her voice deep with unhidden menace. "Now tell me, you didn't happen to take anything from our suitcase, did you?"

Zoe, resembling a deer caught in the headlights of an oncoming vehicle, gaped stupidly at the large accusing nun. "Take something from your suitcase?" she echoed in a tremulous voice.

"You heard me, girl!" Assumptia growled. "Now, tell me the truth because I'll know if you're lying!"

Again swallowing hard, Zoe cleared her throat as she felt a cold bead of sweat trickles slowly down the centre of her back.

"I'll be honest, Sister," she said nervously. "I was more than a little inquisitive, what with you following the suitcase all around Europe and everything and so, yes, I did try to take a sneak peek."

Assumptia began to rise from her chair, her large head reddening with the effort and also the expectation of violence.

"But, but," Zoe quickly continued. "Try as I might, I just couldn't get the locks open."

Recalling the incident with Inspector Lawrence, Assumptia stopped and slowly eased herself back down into her seat.

"I take it that something was missing from your suitcase then?" asked Michael.

"Not only handsome but as sharp as a bowling ball," Assumptia grunted as she reached out a hand towards the salt and vinegar pots.

"Now just stop it, Assumptia," Magdalene admonished. "Let's enjoy this fine meal that Michael is kindly treating us to and stop with all of your accusations and insults."

There it was again, that cold unfathomable gleam in Magdalene's eyes. Assumptia grunted uncomfortably as she noticed that she'd inadvertently buried her fish and chips under a thick layer of salt.

"Mine's a pint of the black stuff," she announced, her thoughts suddenly clouded with anxiety for her sister. Was she imagining it or was the Magdalene that she knew and loved becoming someone different, someone cold.

Michael ordered some drinks for the table and asked Zoe to return later when she had five minutes to spare.

"That's the girl I was telling you about," said Michael once Zoe had departed. "She has a heart of gold and what's more, she has a friend with a car and we'll need a car if we're going to collect the boxes."

"And why is it that you don't drive, Michael?" Magdalene asked as she delicately gathered a small piece of fish onto her fork before placing it into her mouth and slowly chewing for several long moments.

"I've been disqualified," Michael said flatly. "And living here in the city, a car is just more trouble than it's worth. Anyway, most of the time I have nowhere to go and so what do I need a car for."

"Can she be trusted?" Assumptia mumbled through a mouth stuffed full of fish and chips.

"Oh, I'd stake my life on it," Michael enthusiastically proclaimed. "She's like the daughter I never had."

"Done," Magdalene said as she nodded her agreement.

"What?" asked Michael.

"I've accepted your wager and so, if the wee girl can be trusted, I'll not have to kill you."

Michael and Assumptia both sat back in their chairs and stared disbelievingly at Magdalene.

"Oh, Maggie," said Assumptia, breaking the uncomfortable silence that had suddenly enveloped them. "You really are quite the joker."

Magdalene could feel Assumptia urgently squeezing her leg and so she gave Michael what she believed to be a warm and ingratiating smile before continuing, "Ach, come on, Michael, you'll not be taking me seriously now, would you. I'm just pulling your leg."

Michael looked in horror at Magdalene's demonic grin and felt himself grow cold inside. "That's some sense of humour you've got there, Magdalene," he said unconvincingly. "I'll just go and see where our drinks have got to."

"A grand idea, Mikey," Assumptia beamed. "I found the fish and chips a little too salty for my taste and it's giving me a raging thirst."

Trying his best to hide his growing discomfort, Michael quickly made his way to the bar. When he arrived, he was pleased to see that Zoe had just finished serving another customer and was momentarily free.

"Zoe!" he called in a hushed urgent whisper. "Zoe, would you ever come here."

Zoe looked hesitant and uncomfortable as she made the few steps towards where Michael was standing. "Yes, Michael, what can I get you?" she asked, her voice devoid of its usual warm bright cheeriness.

"Zoe, you've got to help me, they're mad. I mean stark raving dangerously mad, the pair of them."

"Not my problem, Michael," Zoe replied with more determination than she felt inside. "They're here because of you and your, your, well, your bloody overinflated opinion of yourself."

"Now, come on, Zoe, that's a bit harsh," said Michael, his voice betraying the hurt he suddenly felt as a result of Zoe's barb. "It's just that it's been a good few years since any woman has shown even the slightest bit of interest in me."

"She's a frigging nun, Michael!" Zoe bit back angrily. "Do you think it's normal for nuns to be throwing themselves at men? No, of course, it frigging well isn't," said Zoe answering her own question. "So, don't come here complaining to me that they're mad because that was bloody well obvious from the get-go!"

Zoe turned to go but Michael stretched across the bar to grab her arm. "Please, Zoe, I don't know what to do and I need your help."

Fighting against her better judgement and because she couldn't help but feel in some small way responsible for Michael's current predicament, Zoe relented and turned to face Michael. "What exactly is it that you want?" she asked.

"Help," Michael responded desperately. "A car and someone to drive it, someone we can trust." Michael took a quick look over his shoulder and could see the two sisters deep in conversation. "Also, two pints of Guinness and a sweet sherry please."

The two nuns fell silent as Michael returned to the table with the three drinks balanced upon a tray. "Here's your sherry, Magdalene," he said as he handed her a small glass filled to the brim with amber-coloured liquid. "And here's your pint, Assumptia."

"What took you so long?" Magdalene asked bluntly, her expression hard and distrustful.

"Oh," said Michael, a little taken aback by Magdalene's tone. "I was just talking to Zoe about arranging a vehicle for our forthcoming expedition."

"Were you now and exactly what do you know about this Zoe?" Assumptia asked as she lifted the pint of dark beer to her lips and began to drink.

"Well, I know she works here for starters," Michael said with a nervous laugh.

"I believe my sister would like to know where she lives," said Magdalene.

"Oh, I see. Well, I don't know where exactly but it'll not be too far away from here."

Assumptia placed the near-empty pint glass on the table and belched. "Do you know whether she lives alone?" she asked as she wiped a moustache of white foam from her top lip.

"Ah no," said Michael. "She lives with her friend Tom. I think she's a bit sweet on him but that's going nowhere as he's just moved his French girlfriend into the flat they both share."

The two nuns turned to look at each other before returning their gaze to Michael. "And what do you know about this Tom and his French girlfriend?" asked Magdalene.

"To be honest, not too much," replied Michael. "I've never actually met him although I understand he works in the city and," Michael suddenly paused in thought. "Here's something interesting," he continued. "They, Tom that is, his French girlfriend and Zoe, well they were all recently in the United States and they got themselves into a right old pickle."

"What type of a pickle?" enquired Magdalene.

"Well," continued Michael. "The French girl got herself abducted and during her rescue, Tom got shot in the head. Now, isn't that something," Michael chuckled stupidly.

The two sisters stared at their host in blank-faced amazement.

"Oh, don't you worry, Sisters," continued Michael. "The bullet just grazed him and he's OK but they did lose the five million in ransom they had to pay the kidnappers."

Following several moments of heavy pregnant silence, Magdalene looked from Michael across the bar to where Zoe was serving another customer. "And where would the three of them get five million?" she asked no one in particular.

"Zoe told me that Tom's company paid the ransom, she said that they have insurance for that kind of thing."

"Ay," said Assumptia. "And I'm the bloody queen of Sheba."

42
Planning the Maniacal Mystery Tour

"No way, Zoe and that's final, I really don't want to get involved," Tom said as he stepped up onto the higher tier of the flat's split-level lounge come diner. Much to the annoyance and in Tom's opinion, exaggerated disgust of both Isabelle and Zoe, when agitated, he'd developed the bad habit of picking dried pieces of scab from the furrowed scar left by Frankie's bullet and which ran across the left side of his skull.

"But, Tom, we are involved," pleaded Zoe. "If we hadn't stolen their money then the nuns probably wouldn't be here now."

"She's right," added Isabelle. "Every action has a consequence. And Tommy," Tom looked directly at Isabelle, aghast at her support for Zoe's request. "For heaven's sake leave your head alone," she finished.

Tom swore under his breath as he lowered his hand. "I'm still taking medication for this," he said indicating the scar on his head, "and now you want me to get involved in some more air-brained dodgy dealings. What is it with you two, will you not be happy until I'm dead!"

"There's a thought," said Zoe mischievously. "Can I still live here when you're gone?"

"Piss off, Zoe."

"Oh, now that's just charming," Zoe responded with mock indignation.

"Oh, stop being so melodramatic, Tommy," said Isabelle. "All we have to do is to drive them to the seaside, pick up some boxes and then drive them back. Voila! Couldn't be easier and then we can concentrate on redecorating the apartment."

Isabelle's proposed redecoration of Tom's flat had been the subject of much and some heated debate over the past several days. Tom wasn't keen but both

Isabelle and Zoe were very enthusiastic. At first, Tom had been pleased with the way in which Zoe and Isabelle had quickly bonded to become firm friends. Now, however, he often became irritated at the way in which they constantly united in support of each-others suggestions and plans, many of which fell contra to Tom's own wishes.

"All 'we' have to do," said Tom as he interrogated Isabelle's last comment. "So, is that a slip of the tongue or are the two of you proposing to join the party?"

"But, of course," Isabelle said brightly. "We couldn't leave our little Tommy all alone with those wicked old nuns now, could we?"

Tom sighed. "When you say it like that it does all sound rather crazy. OK," he relented. "In that case, we'll need something bigger than my car. I'll see what a mini-bus or a large four-by-four will cost to hire. But I'm warning the both of you. If I end up dead, I'm coming back to haunt you!"

"You can put the willies up me anytime," Zoe smirked.

"That's too far, Zoe," said Isabelle reprovingly.

"Sorry," said Zoe, her face momentarily colouring in embarrassment. "Sounds like a bit of a beano," she continued happily. "Where is Frinton on Sea anyway?"

"I don't know," replied Tom. "Probably south or west I should imagine. I'll look it up on the internet."

As it turned out, Frinton on Sea was east of London and situated on the North Essex coast. According to the internet, Winston Churchill had once rented a house in Frinton and King Edward VII occasionally liked to frequent its golf course. More ominously, Frinton was the last target in England attacked by the Luftwaffe during the second world war.

"Sounds like a nice place," said Zoe once Tom had finished reading aloud from his iPad.

"Apparently, it's the ideal place to hide a heap of safety deposit boxes for over thirty years," said Tom. "The more I think about this whole thing, the less likely it all seems. Do you think Michael's making it all up?"

"I hope not," replied Zoe.

Glancing up from his iPad to look at Zoe, Tom asked, "Why?"

"Because if he is," added Isabelle. "The nuns will kill him."

"Really," said Tom. "That sounds a bit farfetched."

"Well that's what Michael believes," said Zoe.

"And when they visited my home in France, Mama said that she really didn't like the feel of them. She detected something," Isabelle paused. "Something wrong. And Mama is good at that sort of thing."

"That's a point," said Tom. "If you're coming along on this jaunt, you'd best come as someone else and someone who's not French."

"Tom's got a point, Issi, if they work out who you are, they'll probably put two and two together and work out that you had something to do with nicking their five million."

Isabelle sighed and raised her eyes to the ceiling in pseudo-despair. "What is wrong with you both?" she asked. "They got their case from you, Zoe and they know that you got it from your landlord and he got it from, from me."

They all fell silent as the truth behind Isabelle's brief assessment suddenly dawned on them.

"So," said Zoe, finally breaking the silence.

"They already know that it was us who stole their money," Tom concluded.

"Merde," breathed Isabelle.

43
The Road East

It was early evening on a chilly and wet Wednesday and the mini-bus Tom had hired rested with its six occupants in the carpark of a large DIY store. Sat angrily behind the steering wheel of the bus, Tom was the picture of frustrated annoyance. Beside him, Isabelle sat quietly and stared sightlessly at the rain pebbled windscreen.

"So," Tom breathed angrily. "Just to recap, we're on a journey to dig up a grave that's allegedly packed full of unopened safety deposit boxes and none of you thought to bring a bloody shovel!"

Tom's words were directed at Michael and the two nuns who occupied the seats immediately behind him. Zoe sat a little further back towards the rear of the vehicle.

"Ach, would you ever stop whingeing," Assumptia grumbled. "You're really starting to get on my wick!"

"Fuck off!" Tom spat back angrily. Any reverence he may have felt towards the two nuns had quickly evaporated when the plan to desecrate the grave had been revealed.

Behind him, Assumptia started to shift uncomfortably. "Let's get one thing straight, you little turd," she growled menacingly. "If we didn't need you for transportation purposes, I'd snap your neck like a twig. Now, stop belly-aching and go and fetch some hardware."

Tom bit his lip and climbed out of the bus, quickly followed by Isabelle and Zoe, they made their way miserably across the carpark and towards the store's entrance.

"Tommy, you must try to keep your temper in check," Isabelle pleaded. "That fat nun is built like, like a gorille."

"That's French for gorilla," Zoe added helpfully.

"No shit!" Tom cursed angrily. "Do you actually appreciate the kind of trouble we're getting ourselves into?"

They walked through the automatic doors and into the DIY store.

"I think we all know that, Tommy, but we should keep calm otherwise we will make them angry and then, something terrible may happen."

Tom stopped and turned to face his two companions, subconsciously raising his right hand to rub the crown of his head. "I believe something terrible will happen regardless of how we behave. I have a very bad feeling about this. That fat nun and her vampire of a sister are exuding so much malice towards us that it's difficult for me to concentrate upon driving the bloody bus."

Zoe swallowed loudly. "Oh, so you've been feeling it too. I thought it was just my imagination getting caught up in the excitement of it all."

Isabelle looked around nervously. "In that case, we should run," she said, the sudden increased apprehension she felt making her voice tremble. "I'm sure there must be a back way out of here."

"Then what?" asked Tom. "It's not like they're not going to come looking for us, is it and," Tom looked directly at Zoe. "Someone's been providing them with all the information they'd ever need to find us."

"I told Michael not them," Zoe responded defensively.

"Well, it hardly matters who you told them because they now know," said Tom as he shifted his gaze away from the two women to scan the indicator signs that hung above each of the aisles.

"What are you looking for?" Isabelle asked.

"Shovels."

"So, despite the dangers, you fear you're going through with this?" Isabelle's voice was now full of doubt.

"Look," said Tom. "I'll tell them that you fell ill and that Zoe is staying with you until you're fit enough to return home. That should give me at least two fewer things to worry about."

"No!" the two women protested in unison.

"We're in this together and we'll see it through together," said Zoe.

"Ah, here you are then," came the menacing lilt of Assumptia's deep voice. "I've just come to see what was taking you so long."

Assumptia's heavy and powerful frame was just a few feet away and yet none of them had seen or heard her approach. What's more, they didn't know just exactly how long she'd been standing there or what, if anything, she'd overheard.

Quickly gathering his thoughts Tom said, "I don't see why I should be paying for all of this stuff. Have you come to contribute?"

Assumptia stepped forward and despite his best intentions, Tom took an involuntary step backwards.

"That's right, Englishman, you'd best be quick on your toes," she said, her stare hard, evil and uncompromising. The foreboding silence that followed was broken by a tannoid announcement. **This store will be closing in ten minutes.**

Assumptia graced them with a jolly smile, "Ach, saved by the bell. Now, you'd best get your arses in gear. I've left my sister alone with Michael for far too long as it is and so, I'll be seeing you outside."

With that, Assumptia turned and ignoring the protestations of the security guard, made her way out of the store the same way that she'd made her way in, which was clearly marked, "No Exit."

"There's no way she's a real nun," breathed Zoe.

"There's no way she's a real woman," added Tom. "Come on, we'd best get the stuff and whilst we're at it, try to think of a way to get ourselves out of this mess."

"We should just call the police," Isabelle said as she followed Tom towards an aisle containing gardening equipment.

"That'd go down well," Tom replied over his shoulder. "Yes, officer, we're in fear of our lives from two nuns. And why would that be, sir? Oh, because we nicked five million quid from them."

"There's no need to be sarcastic, Tommy, it's very unattractive."

"So is being murdered," responded Tom as he picked up two green-handled shovels. "Best get a couple of flashlights too."

"What if we slip some of this into their tea?" asked Zoe as she bent to retrieve a box of rat poison.

"Seriously," said Tom disbelievingly as he turned to make his way towards the aisle containing electrical goods. "In the unlikely event, we all get out of this mess in one piece, I may well have to review your rental agreement."

Zoe and Isabelle stopped and looked at each other in shock. "That's just nasty that is," said Zoe.

"I know," agreed Isabelle. "Sometimes I don't know why I love him."

"Me too," agreed Zoe and when she saw Isabelle's brow furrow she quickly added. "I meant that sometimes, I don't know why you love him too, also, just you that is."

Only partially convinced, Isabelle nodded and the two women set off again in pursuit of Tom.

They returned to the mini-bus and threw the stuff they'd purchased into the back.

"What have you got?" asked Michael.

"Two shovels, two torches, some rubble sacks and a box of rat poison for your guests," replied Tom.

"Ach, you're a real charmer," said Assumptia as she cracked the knuckles of her right hand.

"Take no notice, Sister," Magdalene added indignantly. "After tonight, we'll never have to see him again." Then under her breath, she continued quietly, "after tonight, no one will have to see him again."

With that, Magdalene retrieved a ball of wool and two knitting needles from her bag and started clicking her way towards completion of an as yet unidentifiable item.

Tom slammed shut the rear doors of the mini-bus before returning to his position behind its steering wheel. "Everyone buckle up," he said as he gunned the engine into life and they continued their journey towards Frinton on Sea.

Sometime later, they passed a football stadium on their right, the stadium's floodlights were on suggesting that a game was either about to start or was otherwise in progress. "Who plays there, Tommy?" asked Isabelle.

"I believe it's Colchester United," replied Tom.

"I have never heard of Colchester," Isabelle responded.

"Really," said Tom. "I believe it's Britain's oldest registered town and when the Romans first came here, they made it their capital for this region, they named it Camulodunum. Unfortunately for the Romans and the citizens of Colchester, the Romans managed to get on the wrong side of the local populous and in particular, a queen of the Iceni named Boudica. The Iceni was a tribe of Celts that occupied the land north of here. They and their allies the Trinovantes, an ancient tribe of Essex, rose up against the Romans and destroyed Colchester and killed everyone in it."

Isabelle looked at Tom in amazement. "Tommy, I didn't know you liked history."

"No, neither did I," Zoe piped up above the clicking of Magdalene's knitting needles.

"We still have a lot to learn about each other, given enough time," said Tom ominously as he checked out the reflections of the two nuns in the bus's rear-view mirror.

"So," Isabelle continued. "What happened to the queen?"

"Well, her actions led to a general uprising. She and her armies went on to sack London and generally lay waste to everything Roman they could get their hands on. Meanwhile, the main Roman army was in north Wales eradicating the druids, who were the priests of the ancient Britons and generally thought to be the cause of insurrection against Roman authority.

"Anyway, when they heard about what Boudica was up to, they hot-footed it down south. It's believed the two armies met somewhere in the Midlands. The Britons were defeated and legend has it that Boudica and her two daughters escaped the ensuing slaughter but knowing that all was lost, took poison and died."

"Ah, now, that's a lovely story," said Magdalene. "A tragedy and no mistake. Did you know that the Romans never made it over to Ireland?"

"Yes I did," said Tom. "I guess they chose not to. Maybe Ireland doesn't have the natural resources they were after or perhaps they just thought it was too much trouble."

"Choice is a funny thing now wouldn't you say," Magdalene continued. "Now, for example, if you had to choose between Isabelle and Zoe, who would you pick?"

The atmosphere in the mini-bus suddenly became charged with menace and the silence grew heavy around them, broken only by the clack of Magdalene's knitting needles. The headlights of their companion traffic lit and faded the interior of the mini-bus with irregular and swift bursts of brightness.

Tom cleared his throat before responding carefully, "Isabelle and Zoe are both very dear to me and I'd not want to choose between them."

"But if you had to!" demanded Magdalene as she quickly leaned forward to place the pointed ends of her knitting needles at Isabelle's neck. Isabelle gasped in fright, her back suddenly rigid against the bus's front passenger seat.

"Tom!" Zoe called nervously from the rear of the bus. "Choose Isabelle."

Tom glanced around at Magdalene and was horrified to see the demonic look of hatred that had replaced Magdalene's more familiar countenance of pious superiority.

The mini-bus swerved violently jolting its occupants and pulling Tom's attention back to the road. "Put the needles away, Magdalene," he said through gritted teeth. "Otherwise, I'll drive us off the road."

To emphasise the point, Tom quickly moved the steering wheel which again made the bus unstable for a few seconds.

The tension was broken by Assumptia's wheezy laughter which, after a few seconds was joined by Magdalene's giggles. "Ach, that was a good one, Maggie," Assumptia chortled somewhat unconvincingly. "Ya fella there," she continued as she nodded her head in Tom's direction, "almost shat himself."

Assumptia cleared her throat before turning her head to gaze out into the night from one of the mini-bus's side windows, from which she only saw a distorted image of herself staring sadly back at her. *Dear God*, she thought miserably. *Maggie seems to be getting madder by the minute and there's not a thing I can do to stop it.*

The mini-bus soon left the main roads behind and the deeper darkness outside of its windows was now only occasionally interrupted as the landscape became emptier and more rural. The silence that had enveloped them since the knitting needle incident had become deafening, the engine of the mini-bus its lone disturber.

"OK," Tom said eventually as he slowed the mini-bus down. "We are now approaching Frinton On Sea, where would you like me to point this thing?"

"Just a minute," said Michael as he twisted awkwardly in his seat and eventually managed to retrieve a scrap of paper from his pocket. "Sorry about that, now let's have a look. No, I can't see, it's too dark."

Tom sighed as he brought the vehicle to a halt, switched on its hazard warning lights and then turned on the interior lighting.

"Ah, that's better," Michael continued. "We need to find the Church of St Mary the Virgin and that's in Old Road."

Tom tapped the information into his phone. "OK, we're only about five minutes away," he said as he re-engaged the engine and pulled out into the otherwise relatively quiet road.

44
St Mary the Virgin

They found the Church of St Mary the Virgin at the very end of Old Road, situated immediately before the Esplanade, which separated the town from its Greensward and the North Sea beyond.

The Church itself was an unimposing but picturesque building that dated back a thousand years or more. It was surrounded by a small graveyard, decorated with heavy leaning stone crossed or arched grave markers. The church and its yard was illuminated by a single spotlight that gave the ancient place of worship a ghostly, ethereal atmosphere.

Tom had no trouble in finding a parking space for the mini-bus immediately in front of the church and now, he and the bus's other occupants all sat in the warmth of the vehicle's interior and gazed out through the rain pebbled windows towards the silent church and its gothic appearing cemetery.

"Would you just look at that," Magdalene breathed in a reverential whisper. "It looks like the staged scene for some spooky horror film."

"In that case, you two should feel right at home," Tom put in flippantly just before his head was violently knocked to one side by one of Assumptia's large meaty fists.

"Let that be a lesson to you," the big nun said as she opened the mini-bus's side door to climb out. "If we're going to be digging things up I'd best get rid of that spotlight. Now, you, Zoe, pass me one of those shovels."

"Whilst I hate to spoil the party," said Michael as he too exited the vehicle. "It might be a good idea if we wait a couple of hours. We can have a look around now and stretch our legs but we'd best leave the digging until we're sure that the good citizens of Frinton are all safely tucked up in their beds."

"So, you're not as stupid as you look," Assumptia replied as she turned to look again at the little church. "Who's coming?"

"We're transportation only," said Tom. "So, we'll be staying with the bus."

Assumptia turned her large head to look intently at Tom, who to this point had remained in the mini-bus's driving seat and was speaking through the open window of the driver's door. "Now, you'll not be having any foolish ideas about driving off and leaving us stranded here would you?"

"The thought never crossed my mind," lied Tom.

Assumptia stepped over to Tom and opened one of her large hands. "Keys," she demanded.

Following a slight pause, Tom handed the mini-bus's keys over to Assumptia before climbing out of the vehicle and into the cold dampness of the night. He was quickly joined by Isabelle and Zoe and the three friends stood together in a close miserable huddle and waited for whatever was to come next.

Once they were all out of the mini-bus, Assumptia indicated the small wooden gate to the churchyard with a nod of her head.

"Lead on, Mikey," she said gruffly and they all followed Michael through the gate and along the churchyard's narrow pathway.

Michael led the small group to the rear of the church to where the spotlight didn't penetrate and there, in the near complete darkness, they found a small Garden of Remembrance. Michael stopped and pointed into the night to where they could just make out a stout brick wall of perhaps five feet in height.

"There, by that overhanging tree, in the corner abutting the wall is an unmarked grave," he whispered. "That's where we should find the boxes."

"Any idea how many boxes?" asked Tom.

"Not a clue," responded Michael. "But that's the place Barbara described to me."

"Barbara!" exclaimed Zoe. "You told me her name was Dolly?"

"Barbara, Dolly, what does it matter now?" Michael retorted.

"But you told me that she was your one true love and now, you can't even remember what her name was!"

"That's men for you, Zoe," said Magdalene with a disgusted look in Michael's direction. "Perfidious scoundrels the lot of them. Take my advice and steer well clear."

This comment raised Assumptia's eyebrows but instead of investigating the cause of her sister's obvious vexation she instead shook her head angrily and admonished the group for being too noisy.

"Quiet! You're making enough noise to wake the dead and right now, we're surrounded by enough of the feckers to make a difference."

"Are you really nuns?" asked Tom who was then quickly grabbed by the collar of his coat and lifted effortlessly from the ground by Assumptia. She pulled his face so close to hers that he could smell her warm rancid breath upon his mouth.

"We are whatever you fear," she whispered menacingly. She held him there for a few seconds more before releasing him to fall clumsily to the wet ground.

Isabelle and Zoe quickly formed a small ineffective but endearing protective shield between Tom and Assumptia as he pulled himself to his feet and brushed himself down.

"Are you OK, Tommy?" asked Isabelle.

"Yes," Tom replied quietly. "I think I now know everything I need to know."

"Alright," said Assumptia. "Let's up sticks for a couple of hours."

They returned to the mini-bus but before climbing back in, Tom asked Assumptia if she'd mind if he, Isabelle and Zoe could instead go for a walk. Assumptia studied him thoughtfully for a couple of seconds before responding.

"Like my dear sister said, you must choose. You can either go for a walk with Isabelle or with Zoe but not with both of them."

"Come on, Issi," said Tom. "We're going for a walk."

With that, Isabelle hopped lightly over to Tom and looped her arm through his. Huddled together, they turned away from Assumptia and stepped silently into the night and towards the sound of the sea.

The air was crisp and fresh and the blustering wind blew rain from the trees to cover their bowed faces with cold wet tears. They crossed an empty road and followed a path below some white-limbed trees, the autumn leaves of which rustled and crunched under their feet. Soon, they came to a series of uneven steps that led down to a long beach and the sea beyond. The clouds had begun to break in the brisk wind, allowing shafts of silver moonlight to illuminate the coastline.

"Oh, Tommy, it is so beautiful."

"Come on, let's go down to the sea," he replied and still huddled together against the cold and rain, they made their way carefully down the steps and to the beach below.

The tide was low and so they had to walk for fifty yards or so before they reached the seas edge. There they stood and stared silently out at the restless moon-kissed ocean, hearing nothing but the sound of the sea as it lapped against the land. After a while, Isabelle turned to face Tom, stood on tiptoe and kissed him gently on the mouth.

"Are you crying?" he asked as he looked into her face and watched as tears fell from her blue catlike eyes.

"No, I'm just cold," she lied. "Tommy, why do bad things keep happening to us?"

"I don't know," he said after a pause. "I believe that everything that's happened and is now happening to us is, in some weird way that I don't understand, connected."

"Are you scared, Tommy?"

As he looked down into her beautiful and vulnerable face he thought about lying but seeing her as if for the very first time, he couldn't even if he'd wanted to.

"I'm terrified," he confessed. "Those two batty nuns seemed to be spiralling and getting worse by the minute and Assumptia, well apart from anything else, is so freakishly strong. So, yes, I'm scared but believe me, Issi, if it comes to it, I'll lay down my life for you and that's a promise."

Although the tears continued to spill from her eyes, Isabelle smiled up at him before burying her head into his chest. "There is so much we still have to do," she said. "Do you know, we've never danced together."

Tom held her tightly and slowly began to sway from side to side. "Like this?" he asked.

"Yes, like this but only better," she laughed weakly as she too began to move in time with the rhythm of the waves.

They moved together in a slow circle before kissing each other deeply.

Their romantic interlude was broken by a high-pitched screech of a whistle and they turned to see Assumptia waving at them from the stairs. As they looked towards her Assumptia beckoned them in her direction.

"Last chance, Issi," said Tom. "You could run now and no one will catch you."

"Only if you run too, Tommy."

Tom shook his head. "I can't leave Zoe behind. God alone knows what the old cows would do to her if we scarpered."

"And I can't leave you behind, Tommy." Isabelle stretched up to kiss him again and then they turned and made their way back to where Assumptia was waiting.

"Get a room," Assumptia said with a chuckle as they returned to the foot of the stairs. "Bloody sex mad the pair of ya."

With that, she turned and with surprising agility, the large nun started to climb the stairs that led back to the Greensward and to the Church of St Mary The Virgin.

45
Gravediggers

When they returned to the mini-bus, they found it empty and so they made their way through the church gate and down the path to the rear of the building. The spotlight was no longer working and the moon provided the only light they had to safely navigate the path.

When they reached the rear of the church they found Zoe, Michael and Magdalene, distinct by the flashlight held in Zoe's hand. Zoe's miserable and frightened face looked towards them as they approached.

"We've not seen anyone for over half an hour," she said. "And so, they've decided to get started. Here," with that Zoe handed the second flashlight to Isabelle. "We're the designated lighter uppers."

"Shift out of the way," said Assumptia as she barged passed Tom and Isabelle. "Hand me one of those shovels and let's get cracking."

With that, Assumptia and Michael set about the arduous task of prising up the long rectangular flagstone that lay across the top of the ancient unmarked grave, whilst Isabelle and Zoe covered their efforts with the yellow beams of the flashlights and Tom and Magdalene looked on.

Once the stone was loosened, Assumptia used her immense strength to pull it free from the earth before shoving it heavily to one side. Slapping her large hands together in satisfaction, she and Michael then retrieved the shovels from where they rested against the brick wall and began to dig. The night remained silent except for the grunts and groans of their exertions, as the earth piled behind them steadily grew into a mound. Eventually and breathing heavily, Assumptia handed her shovel up to Magdalene before climbing clumsily from the hole she and Michael had dug.

"Michael, there's feck all down there," Assumptia said between gasps. "Looks like ya fancy woman was telling you porkies."

Just then, the peace of the night was shattered by the sound of an alarm. Quickly moving to the corner of the church, Tom looked back down the path to where he could see the mini-bus's lights were flashing urgently. "Looks like something has set off the bus's alarm," he said. "Assumptia, quick, give me the keys and I'll go turn it off."

Assumptia delved into one of her pockets and pulled out the keys, "No funny business, do you hear," she said. "Don't forget, we still have your little lady friends here."

With that, Assumptia tossed the keys in Tom's direction. Tom caught the keys and quickly made his way down the path and back to the mini-bus.

"I think I've found something," Michael said from where he still stood deep inside the hole. With that, he bent down and picked up a small tin box.

"Give it here," Assumptia ordered as she bent down and beckoned with an outstretched hand. Michael handed Assumptia the dirty tin box and waited within the hole.

"Lights ladies, please," Assumptia said as the women gathered around to watch her wipe damp earth from the lid of the tin to reveal the legend, ***Golden Virginia***.

"A tobacco tin," Assumptia confirmed and then began to prise off its lid. The lid came off with a satisfying pop to reveal a folded piece of paper within. Assumptia dropped the tin and gently unfolded the paper. The note read;

I'M NOT HERE BUT YOU CAN FIND ME UNDER THE MARKER, FIVE HUNDRED STEPS EAST FROM THE NEAREST TOWER.

"It's a riddle!" gasped Zoe.

"It's that alright," confirmed Assumptia. "But what the feck does it mean?"

"Would someone please help me get out of this hole?" Michael's tired voice intruded upon their thoughts.

"Tom might know," Zoe continued. "I think he's pretty good at stuff like this."

"Is that right," replied Assumptia.

"Anyone, please," Michael pleaded.

"Well," announced Magdalene. "It appears we are done here and so we'd best fill up the hole."

With that, Magdalene raised the shovel that Assumptia had passed to her, high above her head and brought it crashing down edge first to cleave Michael's skull in two with a sickening crack that exploded blood and brain matter into the night air.

A stunned silence was quickly followed by a collective anguished gasp of horror and a strange strobing of light as the two girls dropped the flashlights they had been holding and fled wailing into the darkness.

Unfortunately, their path to Tom and the mini-bus was blocked by a stunned Assumptia and Magdalene was between them and the wall, so the girls took the only route that was available to them and this led deeper into the churchyard and the darkness beyond.

Magdalene stood coldly above the open grave, her body stiff and erect as she gazed smilingly down at Michael's lifeless corpse. Assumptia, who'd been rooted in shock, slowly made her way over to her sister's side and gazed down at Michael's still twitching corpse.

"Well, Maggie," she said quietly. "I didn't see that coming."

"I loved him so much," Magdalene said coldly. "I loved him so much and yet, he rejected me."

Assumptia nodded her head stupidly. "Well, he won't be doing that again now, will he," she said.

Magdalene sniffed and smiled. "Oh Assumptia, you're so pragmatic," she said in a strange childlike voice. "Now, let's finish what we've started and go and find this stolen loot."

"That's my girl, Maggie, that's my girl," Assumptia breathed nervously as she patted her sister comfortingly upon the shoulder. "Our journey's nearly over. One way or another, Maggie, it's nearly done."

Laying in the wet earth beneath the dripping foliage of a large rhododendron, Isabelle and Zoe watched in terrified silence as the two nuns picked up the flashlights and began to cast their yellow beams around the churchyard. Isabelle was shaking uncontrollably and so, Zoe put her arms around her and squeezed her tightly into her own body, convinced that Isabelle's shaking would give away their hidden position.

"Issi, please keep still," she whispered into her ear. "We can't let them find us."

Isabelle let out a sob that Zoe quickly stifled with one of her wet and muddy hands.

"What was that?" Magdalene hissed as the beam of her flashlight waved wildly through the darkness. "Was it those nasty treacherous girls. Perfidious whores the pair of them."

The beam of a flashlight fixed directly onto where the two frightened young women were hiding and when Zoe looked up and squinted nervously into the light, she could just make out Assumptia's large squat frame behind the torch.

Assumptia breathed in deeply through her nose before letting out a long sigh and spitting on the ground. "Ach, they're long gone, Maggie," she lied. "Let's get back to the bus and see if the other fella can make head or tail of this here riddle."

With that, the beam that had been fixed upon them for several long seconds moved away from Zoe and Isabelle's position to return them once again to total darkness. The two nuns turned and slowly retraced their steps along the church path and back to where Tom was waiting in the mini-bus.

Isabelle's uncontrolled sobs continued. After a few moments, Zoe released her hold on her friend, climbed to her knees, turned her head and vomited. Coughing and spitting bile from her throat, Zoe then stood before bending to help Isabelle to her feet.

"Are they gone?" Isabelle asked shakily.

Zoe was still wondering why Assumptia had decided not to give their position away.

"Zoe, have they gone?" Isabelle repeated desperately.

"Yes, they're gone, Issa and they've taken Tom with them."

46
The Nearest Tower

Tom was just about to leave the mini-bus and return to the rear of the church when he saw Assumptia and Magdalene coming along the church path.

"Where are the others?" he asked as he turned in his seat to watch as the two sisters threw their shovels and flashlights into the back of the mini-bus before climbing in and taking their seats in the rear of the vehicle.

"We've left them there to fill in the hole," Assumptia replied. "Now, take a look at this and tell me what you think."

With that, Assumptia handed Tom the piece of paper retrieved from the tobacco tin. Tom took the paper and turned his back on the sisters so that he could switch on the vehicle's interior lights.

Tom read the message aloud;

I'M NOT HERE BUT YOU CAN FIND ME UNDER THE MARKER, FIVE HUNDRED STEPS EAST FROM THE NEAREST TOWER.

"What is this?" he asked.

"It's the only thing we found in the hole that we dug," Assumptia replied. "We're thinking it's a clue to where the booty is actually hidden."

Following a moment's thought, Tom took out his phone and tapped the internet icon.

"What are you thinking?" Assumptia asked as she leaned her head over the empty front passenger seat to watch Tom.

"I'm searching the net for towers near Frinton," he said as he waited for the results of his search to load. "Ah, the nearest one seems to be at Walton on the Naze, which is about two or three miles from here. It says it's a navigational aid built in the seventeen hundreds."

"That'll be it then," Assumptia said as she gave Tom a comradery slap on the shoulder.

"OK, let's wait for the others. They shouldn't be too much longer," he said as he looked anxiously out towards the empty churchyard.

Magdalene's sudden high-pitched screech made Tom flinch in fright.

"We're going now!" she screamed maniacally, her knitting needles clenched threateningly in her hand. He quickly turned and for the first time, saw the two nuns illuminated by the mini-bus's interior lights. His stomach lurched as he took in the sight of Magdalene's blood and gore covered face.

"Oh my God," he stammered. "What have you done?"

Magdalene made an aggressive move towards him but was held back by one of Assumptia's strong arms.

"Listen to me carefully, Thomas," Assumptia's words were slow and deliberate. "I swear to you that your two friends are unharmed. They're safe. Poor Maggie here," she indicated her still struggling sister with a nod of her large head. "Is feeling a little under the weather. She's not quite herself at the moment and the best thing you can do, is to do just exactly what I tell you to do. Do you understand me?"

Tom looked from Assumptia's blunt but sincere features into the mad raving eyes of Magdalene and back again.

"What do you want me to do?" he asked nervously.

"Take us to the tower and no funny business otherwise," Assumptia turned her head in Magdalene's direction before returning her gaze to Tom. "Well, as they say, least said soonest mended."

Tom nodded, turned off the vehicle's interior lights before gunning the engine into life. Tapping the tower's location into his phone, he turned on the mini-bus's exterior lights and pulled the vehicle away from the kerb.

"So where are Isabelle and Zoe?" he asked as the vehicle proceeded down Frinton's dark and deserted high street.

"Buggered if I know," replied Assumptia. "They scarpered when they saw Maggie cave Michael's head in."

Tom swallowed hard and Magdalene started to giggle inanely.

"You're kidding right?"

"I wish that I was Thomas, I wish that I was."

It took little more than ten minutes to make the journey to the Naze Tower. They had to leave the mini-bus by a lowered barrier that restricted any further approach to the tower outside of certain prescribed opening hours. However, they could just discern the tower's erect outline as a deeper shadow within the darkness of the night and so, armed again with shovels and flashlights, they carefully made their way towards where it stood, approximately five hundred yards distance from the barrier.

Tom pointed the flashlight he was holding up at the tower's brick exterior which disappeared high above them into the night. The light disturbed some gulls who were perhaps taking shelter from the stormy night in some nook or cranny hidden away from the searchers gaze. They plaintively cried out their protests, their white forms weaving and spiralling in and out of the light's beam.

Tom breathed in the ozone enthused air deeply through his nostrils, *will this nightmare never end*, he thought to himself as his gaze switched from the gulls to the two unlikely nuns who stood close together, their garments pulled and tugged by the strong north easterly wind that was blowing in from the sea, bringing with it spiteful slaps of icy rain.

Assumptia, the powerfully built sister, was gazing up at the tower through squinted eyes.

"It doesn't look hundreds of years old," she commented. "But I guess that it's hard to tell in this light. Now, which way is east?"

Tom pointed towards where he could hear the sound of waves crashing angrily against the shoreline.

"Towards the sea," he said whilst manoeuvring his back to the tower and setting off with long measured steps in the direction he had indicated. However and long before he reached the count of five hundred steps as proclaimed within the riddle, he could see that he was running out of land. Soon after he had come to the realisation that there were no five hundred steps eastward from the tower, the flashlight beam picked out a yellow cliff edge sign which, on closer inspection, warned the unwary traveller to beware of the unstable cliff edge.

Battered and buffeted by the wind and rain, Tom and the two sisters stood in the blackness of the night at the broken edge of the cliff, the sea pounding relentlessly below them as they stared disconsolately at the sign revealed by the yellow beam of Tom's flashlight.

After what seemed like an eon of silence, Tom cleared his throat and asked, "What now? The land and whatever was on it or under it has gone. There's nothing but the North Sea now."

A growing high-pitched alien whine, like the whistle of a steam kettle coming to the boil was cutting through the natural nocturnal sounds of the stormy night, making Tom throw the flashlight's beam away from the sign and towards the two sisters standing together close to the cliff's edge.

The whine developed into a loud screeching scream erupting from Magdalene who lifted her delicate aquiline face high into the air and began to howl like a lone wolf crying into the night.

"Run, Tom, for feck's sake get out of here!" came Assumptia's desperate warning as Magdalene made a sudden feral lunge for him, her hands clawing the darkness like talons stopped only by Assumptia's intervention. "Don't just stand there like a complete fecking idiot, go!" Assumptia ordered as she struggled to keep a rein on her maniacally enraged sister.

Dropping the flashlight Tom turned and fled. He stopped when he reached the tower and looked back towards the cliff's edge. He could still see the beam of the flashlight he had dropped and the sign warning of the cliff edge danger but nothing or no one else.

The landscape was empty of humanity and although straining to listen intently, Tom could hear nothing above the sound of the wind and the sea. He started back towards the mini-bus but after only a few steps, he checked his journey and turned to make his way back to the cliff's edge, all the while scanning the darkness nervously and ready to flee at the slightest indication of danger.

47
Down and Out in Miami

Roxy could hear the hotel gradually stirring back into life. Those early morning sounds made by cleaners and porters as they gathered their equipment from various hidey holes or, delivered that morning's newspapers and collected trays on which the remnants of the previous evening's room service now sat forlorn and unwanted. There was some strange comfort in those quiet sounds, a constant, well organised daily routine that would continue regardless of the trials and tribulations suffered in the outside world.

It was a nice enough hotel, with its generic decor, furnishings and prints. This had been the third night she had stayed. Not the best room, the best room had been with John or Jim on the first night but it was better than the room she had shared with George the night before last.

Roxy guessed she would have to wait for the next trade delegation to hit town before she got to stay there again. That was no bad thing as she had begun to get noticed by the night staff on the reception desk and she didn't like the knowing and disapproving looks they now pointed in her direction.

The fat man beside her grunted in his sleep. He said his name was Frank but she'd noticed the name on his credit card was A J Bright. Roxy always paid close attention when a customer opened his wallet. She didn't do what she did for kicks but it was all that she now had left to sell and if she was selling, she liked to make sure the buyer had enough money to pay.

This lesson had been cruelly learnt when, with sad eyes, a bank manager had informed her that she had been the victim of a fraud and that the five million euro she had deposited was, in fact, the proceeds of a robbery in faraway Ireland and therefore, valueless to the bank and to Agnes Buff. The bank manager had said that he'd given her details to the police and that they would soon be in contact with her.

Upon receiving this news, Roxy had been quick to move from the apartment she had been renting and she now resided under the name of Roxy Buff at a cheap motel on the city's outskirts.

Laying on her back staring up at the ceiling, Roxy wondered, not for the first time, why ceilings in hotel rooms seldomly contained a light. This conundrum sometimes helped Roxy place her mind somewhere else whilst her body was used to satisfy the lusts of her varied clients. On this occasion, her musings were again disturbed by a further smattering of grunts emanating from her sleeping bed partner.

Sighing, Roxy climbed out of the bed and picking up her clothes which lay scattered upon the floor, she made her way to the bathroom. Hoping to avoid any morning after deliberations with 'Frank', she dressed quickly, splashed her face with cold water and cleaned her teeth with the use of a finger smeared with toothpaste. She would shower once back in her motel room.

Leaving the bathroom, Roxy picked up the five hundred dollars sitting on the bedside table and stuffed it into her handbag. She undertook a quick survey of the room in the hope of locating Frank's unattended wallet but further grunts and moans curtailed her search and she instead, turned and left as quickly and as quietly as possible.

Roxy shared an elevator with a young and pretty Cuban cleaning woman who stared at her with open and undisguised contempt. When the elevator reached the lobby, Roxy pointed her face at the cleaner and poked out her tongue. Roxy's strut across the lobby towards the hotel's exit was accompanied by a stream of quick Spanish emanating from the cleaning woman, none of which sounded in the least bit complimentary.

Outside, the city was still just waking to yet another fine and glorious morning. Roxy made her way to the front of a small line of taxis, which sat patiently waiting outside of the hotel. She climbed into the taxi's interior and asked the driver to take her to the Shady Pines Motel.

The taxi driver, who also appeared to be of Cuban origin, chatted away throughout their journey but Roxy was paying no attention. She was bone tired and for the first time, as she gazed out from the cab's window, she thought, with some small degree of affection and regret, of the time she'd spent with the now incarcerated Horace Pasternak.

The taxi pulled into the lot of the Shady Pines Motel. As Roxy held out a twenty-dollar bill towards the driver, he asked with a lecherous smile whether she would consider some other and more physical way of settling up. Roxy screwed up her face in disgust and threw the money at the driver before leaving the cab and marching off towards her room.

At best, the room was functional but one thing that it definitely wasn't, was welcoming. The room was drab and careworn. Roxy sat on the unmade bed and pulled off her shoes, which she tossed across the room to land within the open wardrobe. She looked around sadly and sighed, "If walls could talk, I doubt if you'd have one happy story."

Roxy reached behind her and started to unzip the tight red dress she was wearing when a tapping came at the door. It couldn't be the landlord, she thought, as she'd had to pay one month's rent upfront. Roxy re-zipped her dress and padded slowly towards the door. When she opened it, Roxy involuntarily stepped back in suddenly horrified amazement.

"Hello, Missus Pasternak," said Frankie. "Bet you didn't expect to see me again." Frankie stepped inside the room and closed the door behind him.

"F—Frankie," exclaimed Roxy. "W—what a wonderful surprise. How did you find me here?"

Frankie smiled. "Oh, that wasn't too difficult, Missus Pasternak. I read in the papers a story about a woman who had been conned out of five million. She'd sold a rare and expensive piece of artwork to a private buyer who had paid her in cash but when she tried to deposit the money in a Miami bank, it was found to be the proceeds of a robbery.

"After that and guessing you'd soon be out of cash, I started calling every cheap hotel and motel in the Miami area. Said I was looking for my sister and that it was urgent because our mother was dying. Said you'd either be calling yourself Roxy or Agnes. People really can be very helpful and it didn't take me too long at all to track you down."

"Oh, Frankie, it really is good to see you," Roxy said nervously as she gathered her thoughts and moved towards him. "I really have missed you so very much." Roxy cosied up close to him and kissed him on the lips but Frankie's mouth remained closed and did not move.

Pulling back, Roxy looked up into Frankie's cold hard face. "Come on, Frankie," she said, desperation making her words tremble. "We can work this out."

"I loved you, Missus Pasternak," said Frankie as he pulled out the pistol Roxy had given him and pointed it at her head. "I loved you and you just used me and then left me for dead."

In terror, Roxy backed away from him and as she did so, she pleaded. "No, Frankie, you've got it all wrong, I just panicked that's all and I was going to come back and get you but with the money gone and everything, I—I—I just didn't know what to do for the best. I'm sorry if I hurt you, Frankie, you must know that that's the last thing I wanted."

Frankie lowered the gun.

"And Frankie," Roxy continued. "You do know that I love you, don't you."

Frankie raised the pistol and fired two quick shots into Roxy's head.

Staring down at the ruin that just a few moments before had been the woman he'd loved, Frankie placed the pistol under his chin, stared up through two tear drenched eyes and squeezed the trigger.

48
Aftermath

The three friends sat exhausted and dirty within the living room of Tom's flat. He had found them muddy and wet, sat disconsolately together on the pavement directly outside of the church gate leading to St Mary the Virgin.

Following a relieved and silent embrace, together they returned to the unmarked grave which now contained Michael's cold body and without a word exchanged, they started to fill the grave with earth. They struggled but eventually succeeded in replacing its flagstone and once finished, they stood holding hands under a greying rain-washed sky, whilst Tom slowly recited the Lord's prayer.

Then, collecting their tools and torches, they returned to the mini-bus and began a long and silent journey back home, each one of them lost in their own weary and fear worn thoughts.

Tom eventually pulled himself from the sofa and shuffled to the bathroom. He filled the bath with hot soapy water before undressing and climbing gratefully in. Tom submersed himself for several long seconds and when he surfaced, he found Isabelle standing naked beside the bath, her stained clothes mixed with his in a dirty dank pile on the bathroom's floor. He made room for her in the bath and she slowly eased her white body into the water before carefully reclining to face him. Her delicate and pretty face looked tired and pale through the steam.

"Where are they, Tommy?" she asked quietly.

Knowing Isabelle was asking about the fate of the two sisters, Tom shook his head. "I don't know for sure but I think the sea has taken them."

"How?"

Tom looked into Isabelle's questioning face and thought he saw fear there. Did she believe that he was in some way responsible for the nun's disappearance? Was she re-evaluating what she thought she knew about the man she had taken for a lover? Did she now fear that he was a killer? He was so tired.

“I think that Magdalene wanted to kill me,” he said at length. “She was crazy, mad. Something had snapped and she wanted to lash out but Assumptia stopped her. She told me to run and I did. When I looked back, they were gone, both of them had disappeared and so, I went back to take a look.”

“And?”

“And nothing, they were gone. Just gone.”

There followed several long seconds of silence as Isabelle searched Tom’s face with her eyes. Then, there came an urgent tapping at the door.

“Sorry,” came Zoe’s urgent voice from the other side of the door. “Are you guys going to be much longer? I really need a poo.”

This desperate sounding declaration of need slowly released the heavy spell that was possessing them. Tom and Isabelle’s dark mood was begrudgingly but inexorably nudged aside by stifled giggles that quickly erupted into hysterical and uncontrolled laughter, making them wiggle and clutch their sides in joyous agony.

“Oh pleasessse,” Zoe pleaded from beyond the door, her desperation worsened by the infectious hilarity that was also claiming her. “Oh no!” she suddenly exclaimed in horror, the bathroom door bursting open and Zoe leaping in to throw herself in blessed relief upon the toilet seat.

This happened amid cries of horror and disgust from the two bathers who, quickly extracted themselves in a wet bubbled frenzy from the bath and from the blast site of Zoe’s bodily evacuation.

Finding sanctuary in Tom’s bedroom, still laughing, the two sodden and steam-misted lovers embraced closely and after a few moments, they both began to cry.

*

Over the next few weeks, things slowly started to get back to normal and the three friends were no longer preoccupied with the events of the preceding weeks, nor did they look fearfully at one another each time the phone rang or there was an unexpected knock at the door.

Zoe had managed to get Isabelle restaurant and bar work at the Good Samaritan and this move and the additional time they now shared had, much to Tom’s amusement and occasional chagrin, made them even closer.

Following weeks of enforced absence under the heading of complete bedrest, Tom's doctor had at last, certified him fit to return to work following the gunshot incident in Florida. Tom now stood in front of his wardrobe mirror and straightened his tie in preparation for his reappearance at the office.

"You look very dashing and handsome, Tommy," Isabelle said silky voiced from where she lay on the bed, only partially covered by its rumpled quilt. "Do we have time for a proper," she paused as she mentally selected the right word; "send off?"

Tom smirked at his reflection. "How many 'send-offs'," he said with an affected French accent. "Does one woman need?"

After a few moments of thought, Isabelle responded. "I believe three is best."

"Well, in that case, I owe you two," he said as he turned and leaned over the bed to kiss her, only to be captured as her legs wrapped tightly around him and she pulled him unresistingly back down upon the bed.

Screwing up her pretty face in a determined pout she said, "No, I will let you owe me just one but I want the other one right now!"

Tom was late but happy when he arrived at Liverpool Street station and started to make his way through the busy pedestrian filled streets and towards Mallory's Bishopsgate office.

He took a short detour that led him through the grounds of St. Botolph's church and as he exited the gardens, his attention was taken by two bedraggled vagrants, huddled closely together beneath a heap of dirty blankets. He detected a deep Irish intonation as one of the rumpled duo held out a large grubby hand and asked if he could spare any change.

In a somewhat uncharacteristic act of generosity, Tom stopped, pulled out his wallet and selected a twenty-pound note, which he placed into the hand of the poor misfortunate. Wishing them good day and good luck, Tom continued his journey towards the office when, amid the curses of his fellow commuters, he stopped suddenly and subconsciously raised a hand to the crown of his head. Catching his breath, Tom turned and quickly retraced his steps to where the two vagrants had been stationed but the space they had occupied was now, completely empty.

*

"Good afternoon, ladies!" Harry, the manager at the Good Samaritan greeted Zoe and Isabelle as they arrived in good time to commence their lunchtime duties. "And may I say, you're looking particularly beautiful today!" he beamed, his eyes fixed admiringly upon Isabelle.

"Why thank you, Harry," Zoe muttered sarcastically as she hung her coat upon an available peg.

Harry cast an irritated look in Zoe's direction before returning his gaze to Isabelle. "And how was your morning?" he ingratiatingly enquired whilst collecting Isabelle's coat, which he passed offhandedly to Zoe.

Isabelle smiled sweetly. "Oh, you know, exhausting but ultimately satisfying."

"She's not kidding," Zoe put in glibly. "I got exhausted just listening to the bedsprings. The two of them are sex-mad, they barely come up for air."

The smile quickly fell from Harry's face as he pushed two white aprons in their direction.

"Well, you're here on time for a change and so, you'd best get on with your work. Oh, and Zoe, have you seen Michael lately; someone was in this morning looking for him."

Zoe stared at Harry in shocked silence.

"What are you gawping at?"

"No, I've not seen him for weeks," she responded nervously. "Who's asking?"

Milton Keynes UK
Ingram Content Group UK Ltd.
UKHW022026081223
434043UK00007B/390